The Eyes of the Earth

Tamara Pearson

The Eyes of the Earth

ISBN: 978-1-960326-82-9

Copyright © 2024 by Tamara Pearson

All rights reserved. No part of this book may be reproduced or transmitted in any form or by any means, electronic or mechanical, including photocopying, recording, or by any information storage and retrieval system, without permission in writing from the publisher.

Tehom Center Publishing is a 501c3 non-profit imprint of Parson's Porch Books. Tehom Center Publishing is an imprint publishing feminist and queer authors, with a commitment to elevate BIPOC writers.

I want to thank the friends who have been so kind,

so real, and so supportive.

I am grateful to the people in Mexico, Latin America, the Global

South, and the Global North who, despite obstacles and risks,

continue to fight for justice. You are the light, the hope, and the eyes

of the earth.

Myopia

People could see Clementina Cardoza Olmedo, but they didn't register that she was there. Known as La Tortuga, she was seventy-three years old, four foot ten, with two thin, white and grey plaits that descended calmly down her back. She was wearing dark grey pants with one leg folded up more than the other, and a white shirt. Her belt buckle was off-centre, and one of her draw-string backpack straps had scrunched up the top of one sleeve. She had no frills. She wasn't a show.

At this moment, she was standing completely still. Paused into statue, except for the skin of her forehead contorted into worry patterns, and her wide-open eyes oscillating from extreme left to extreme right, as though desperately seeking something.

About her, hundreds of footsteps landed with haste upon the slipperiest floor in Mexico City. The terminal was a waterhole of buses, an unsacred gasoline gathering place where people speed walked from its food court to ticket booths and departure lounges. None of the owners of those footsteps wondered why a small woman had stopped so stock-still in the central space of the terminal, or where she had come from or was going.

There was no sparkling stardust or pink mist that stopped those people from really seeing La Tortuga. Instead, their sight had been subtly trained. It had been coached to skip over the sorts of people who weren't featured on television or in the media. Over the course of their lives, apathy, stress, and selective and limited information had made their eyesight blurry. In Mexico, and much of the Americas, most news readers and actors were white, young, and upper class. And so Indigenous people found it hard to see themselves in the world. Employers couldn't see them either, it seemed, because they rarely hired them. And when La Tortuga, back in Honduras, had tried to criticise the mayor's policies at a community consultation meeting, no one had seen her speaking either. They had tuned her out, because experience taught them that other types of people analysed and decided things.

If people saw La Tortuga at all, they saw a quiet being roughly contained in clothes, who had no bearing on them. They saw dawdling and dysfunction, frailty, and an undignified wrapping up of a life. Beyond being inconspicuous, she was, for them, insignificant. And because the people in the terminal couldn't really see La Tortuga, there were two things about her that they were incapable of imagining.

The first was that she could do something heroic. The symbols and codes in their sight dictionary that they associated with heroes were muscles, youth, males, and whiteness. Their inhibited eyes confused popularity and privilege with heroism. Men in suits or capes were the role models, their costumes a modern variation of the knee-length coats and other finery of colonisers and kings.

Real heroes were quiet. They shifted worlds, battled adversity, abandoned predictability, employed resourcefulness without fanfare or applause. They were made of bony persistence, late-night stories, worn books, openness, humility, an ability to try the impossible and try again after failing, a star-draped sense of the common good, an insatiable urge to understand, and the wooden sound of critique-fed growth.

But the word 'hero' had, with time, been deprived of its real meaning, and languished. An odour of fortitude and boldness hovered about its faint memory. With a pandemic of blurred sight, so many words had lost their substance. 'Beautiful' was used for household goods, 'empowered' for someone applying deodorant. Words were bleached, apathetic, vacuous, comatose. In their place, were gaps. Little voids in the world. With sight that erased and hearing that tuned out, the world was riddled with holes. It was brittle and precarious. An unreliable place.

La Tortuga had grown up in the eastern outskirts of Tegucigalpa. The concrete house had a corrugated iron roof, no glass in the windows, and no television or radio. Her sight had been trained too, but not as much. She had spent her childhood then adulthood listening to other people and slowly growing a mind made of tiny explosions; realisations that she knitted together into profound wisdom. Most people didn't realize that she could hear the pain hovering on the edges of stories, or that she could feel the nuances of lies before they were voiced. Few people made the connection between sophisticated sensitivity and the capacity to be heroic.

The second thing the people in the bus terminal couldn't imagine was that the tiny and gentle La Tortuga would, someday soon, kill someone.

Under the domed roof of the Passenger Bus Terminal of the East, Mexico City

The Passenger Bus Terminal of the East, or the TAPO, consisted of a series of concentric rings. Buses arrived and departed from the outermost ring, then passengers followed tunnels into an inner ring, where the ticket booths and eating area were. A huge dome sat on the inner ring like a giant glass cloche. It filtered the chilly October sunlight so that it touched the taupe grey tiled floor with a diffused gentleness.

La Tortuga ceased being still and moved. She continued to desperately seek something by walking methodically. She walked around the inner circle seven times, and no one noticed. Again and again, she passed the bakery, all the Delimart stalls selling chips, packaged sandwiches, and amaranth snacks, the Subway counter, Dominoes, a hot dog stand, and the restaurants with Mexican breakfasts. There were ample signs with the logos of each bus company, but she could not find any stalls or signs with information about seeking asylum or migrant shelters.

The terminal was a pragmatic place. It didn't allow for daydreaming or sentimental smells. Instead, it was plastic seats and tables wiped down quickly, polystyrene coffee, and chilaquiles on disposable plates. Straw wrappers were scattered around the dining area as though they had been sprinkled, like inept seeds, by a giant hand. In the departure area, people stacked their bags and then stacked their children on the bags, creating little islands of families ready to go some place. Ticket sellers and Delimart cashiers wore unamused, tired and over-everything expressions. La Tortuga recognised those expressions from her barrio in Honduras, and she would see them often in Mexico. The shoe shiner who seemed to live at the entrance to the only free public women's toilets, with his comb over and peppercorn grey face, boycotted the fuss. He looked at something on his phone.

The floor was slippery smooth from the 90,000 people walking swiftly over it each day. Children skidded along it, their minds set to play mode, while the adults shouldered all the worry and awareness of life stages ending and starting. Because although the terminal was efficient and its ticket booths indifferent, within the islands of families and inside of the single person eating hurriedly at the unwiped table, moments were happening. There were restrained farewells, long greeting hugs, a new job to start, people moving homes or visiting cousins. There was apprehensiveness and anticipation hidden by the more immediate preoccupation of which pocket bus tickets were in. A continuous buzzing coated the air as people were processed through security scanners into the new episodes of their stories. Quick peeing in five-peso turnstile toilets, a dash of a look in the mirror, half-runs and funnywalks up the awkwardly-spaced tunnel stairs. Unaccountable toileting left no one trusting toilet seats.

But La Tortuga was different to many of the other arrivals. Her story episode refused to finish. She had reached the terminal after a long walk from Honduras then a bus from Puebla to Mexico City. This was the moment when things were meant to get better. But It was 10 a.m. and she hadn't eaten. She didn't know where to go. Without a bed to sleep in that night, she had not finished arriving. A bed was like a full stop to a sentence before a new one started the next day. But instead, La Tortuga was submerged in the gracelessness of no stamp or declaration or human to witness that she was here now.

People needed things to be declared. They wanted documents to witness agreements, ceremonies to mark relationships, rituals for death, confirmation by something external to them that they were citizens or adults or had graduated or had a job title. And without something like that, La Tortuga's arrival in this next, possibly last stage of her life, didn't feel real. As though, beyond not being seen, she couldn't totally confirm that she existed.

La Tortuga returned to statue mode. She planted herself to the floor again and tried to decode the chaos around her so she could work out her next step. She saw subtle magic quivering among the haste and tiredness. She distinguished between the kinds of quickness, saw the differing degrees of exhaustion and the absence or presence of excitement. People wore strong feelings on their faces and she saw that purpose gave them strength to weather the busyness. Mixed in among them, like shy sketches of people, were others that carried fear and pain with their scarce belongings. Farmers had come to the capital to fight legal battles over land, and a group of Salvadoran migrants was trying to get cheap tickets north, in order to work in the factories there. One Nahua woman sat with her three-year-old son on her lap, wrapped in a blanket. She had come from a small town into the city to take him to one of the big hospitals, but she didn't have any money left for a taxi. Her son had just now died quietly, and she didn't know yet. Near her, people finished their combo meals, wiped their faces, and headed off in a hurry. They left behind trays of plastic plates and unused serviettes.

La Tortuga's bag dug into her shoulders, as she remained still. The drawstring backpack had kicked at her lower back like a child wanting to be put down as she had walked to Mexico. It was a freebie bag, black, with a Nike logo in the centre. In it, was an empty plastic water bottle, a pillow cover, a multi-screwdriver, a pair of pliers, a toothbrush and toothpaste, a blue pen, a plastic comb, one spare pair of underpants, needle and thread, a half-used bar of soap in a plastic bag and a card wallet with Honduran ID, 125 Mexican pesos, and photos of her children and grandchildren. Nothing for hurting people.

She wanted to take the bag off and massage her shoulders, but she wouldn't let herself get comfortable until she was settled somewhere.

Her feet hurt even more. Her heels and toes were encased in a layer of water blisters, her ankles were heavy, and there was a similar weight in her lower face. It made her mouth, which was in a position somewhere between sad and blank, uncomfortable. She wanted to rub it around because it was set all wrong. She was also dehydrated, and her brain was faint and struggling to keep up with the things she had to process and decide. Her heart had a headache. It needed a break.

The outer heels of her shoes had worn to the insole, even though she had bought them just before she left. The insoles were synthetic board then. But when she started her journey, they had transformed into metal graters with blades that opened up and shredded her feet. Stopped there in the terminal, the blades were digging at her blisters and mangled skin. One popped open and she felt a short wetness. Along the journey, she had patched her feet up with band aids and sewn some of the worst gashes, but the shoes, as insistent and pernicious as poverty, undid the threads and dislodged the band aids. And when she threatened to take them off altogether, the grater holes closed for a little while, then gradually opened up again. They also closed when she slept deeply, and it was in those moments that her sores would start to heal. But in the past few weeks, she hadn't had many chances to sleep properly. She worried now that if she couldn't find a bed in the next few days, her feet would get infected or the wounds so large that she wouldn't be able to walk at all.

It seemed that walking and going places was a constant battle to not fall over. To stay upright. She had staggered from Honduras to Mexico, but she had also staggered through decades of her life. Determined to keep going despite the roadblocks and traffic spikes. Despite her husband, Enrique, telling her she wanted too much, then making her do all the housework. She had hit her thighs to keep her body awake, then carefully planned out tiptoed words when she still had to tell him something. And then it happened, and she fled the country. Somewhere around the Guatemalan border she realised she had also left Enrique and that the bed and rest she was pursuing represented more than just safety from the violence in Honduras. The rest she hoped for in Mexico would be clean of pretence, uninterrupted, owned, with ample space for dreaming and reflection.

The grater holes cut again at the blisters on her heels and more puss, blood, and serum dribbled into the shoes' edges and soaked her socks. Her jaw filled with discouraged distress. She had expected a stall for refugees or a list of shelters. There was meant to be a place with a person, where all the feet fleeing violence could queue up and ask for help. She had assumed an overwhelmed being with a ration of concern would provide some simple instructions about how to proceed.

Her assumption was reasonable. Refugees were sometimes kidnapped outside bus terminals then held for ransom until their families got loans to pay those off, or younger women migrants could be sold into the sex trade. So, for a few weeks in 2017, there had been people in purple t-shirts stationed at the TAPO and at Mexico City's airport to assist migrants and refugees. They had provided food, a toiletry bag, and information about shelters and medical assistance. It was a city initiative which coincided with an election campaign. Once the media stopped covering it, the people in purple t-shirts stopped showing up.

An unconfirmed La Tortuga concluded that she could not finish her journey chapter there in the terminal. The end to her chapter must be somewhere else.

The pageant of desperation

There were various underground tunnels going out from the bus terminal to taxi ranks, metrobuses, the street, and to two different stations. They were as wide as two car lanes, with embedded lights casting puddles of white light on the floor and with corrugated ramps on one side. La Tortuga didn't feel able to walk the four kilometres into the city centre, so she took Tunnel One to the pink train line, and would spend five pesos on a ticket. In the tunnel, she saw vendors perched precariously on the edges of ramps and staircases, their wares neatly arranged on blankets or the bare floor. They broadcast the names and prices of their products with repeated and robust cries aimed with precision at each passerby.

On the train, a few mobile vendors got on at each station. The first one yelled out a spiel for black, blue, and pink wallets. "Ten pesos!" they cried out as they walked up and down the carriage, efficiently reading each face for interest. The other vendors waited for their turn, and when the first was finished, the second shouted about their product, raising it above their head so the packed passengers could see it. A man selling plastic combs fanned out six in each hand and then fanned the passengers' faces to get their attention. A woman with a child on her hip traversed the carriage with find-a-word books. Then, a stooped man with a cane and dry eyes sang a love song from a piece of paper held up close to his eyes. He sang out of tune, but all he had to sell was his voice.

The broken city that kept on going

La Tortuga got on with it. She took her broken feet up the stairs of Pino Suárez station and entered into the broken city. Or really, it fell over her. Flooded her with the force of twenty-three million people and all their chatter and chores. The full, almost-midday light shocked her, and she was instantly engulfed by the city's traffic stress, high-pitched routine, metallic horn notes. Straight away, she took on the Mexico City face of worry and defensiveness, but with warmth just below the surface - saved for those moments when one was off the street and laughing with friends or family. She wanted to get to the Zócalo; the square-shaped heart of the city and focal point of protests and celebrations.

Mexico City topped lists. It had the largest number of museums in the Americas and its Zócalo was the second largest square in the world. It had some of the slowest traffic globally, with cars crawling at an average of fourteen kilometres per hour, and the city was sinking at two to thirty centimetres a year.

Tenochtitlán, the Aztec capital, had been built on an island in the middle of a large lake. Bigger than any European city at the time, the city's crops were planted on rectangular build-ups of soil on the water, called chinampas. The Spanish invaders then built Mexico City over the ruins of Tenochtitlán, replacing the dikes and canals with streets and roads, sinking deep wells, draining the lakes and levelling the forests so that the city sat on unstable soil. Now, Mexico City had to import nearly half its water, and as it sunk, walls sloped, and the floors of large buildings dipped in the middle. The Spanish invasion was a concrete bomb that had slow-exploded over the centuries and people now lived among the fragments, distributed so roughly over a no-longer lake.

Without rivers, and surrounded by mountains, the dry city trapped dust and smog. The concentration of pollution caused respiratory illnesses, and the air odour was a brew of matchsticks and bleach. It stuck to sweaty skin, activated allergies, and wore down immune systems. There were dust carpets on the tops of trains set into ripple patterns. Bus tailpipes farted exhaust at ten-second intervals, with extra energy when the lights turned green and the buses roar-resumed their journey over the turbulent terrain of unrepaired tarmac. The grey dust got into the drains. The city's veins. City of concrete skin and grey veins.

In the poorer parts of the city, the pollution marched through the windows that had grills but no glass. In the unvisited shanties, iron ceilings were held down by stones and glass bottles. Shared buildings frequently hosted arguments and fights because there wasn't enough water or dignity to go around.

The metro worked, shops worked. But the city and the whole country were tormented by corruption. The paths to justice, hospital care, jobs, court case outcomes, and medicine, were mangled with fees and bribes that only the wealthy could afford. Impunity of murderers and abusers forged demoralised, jagged smithereens of people who became their one and only bitter defence.

The city was a light warzone of rubble, where pigeons had learned to ignore the homeless, where mariachis drank Coca-Cola and Coca-Cola's Oxxo shops sold wheat tortillas to bored lucha libre fighters. Pedestrian bridges over highways were metal tubular cages where gun-point robberies took place. Peeling murals illustrated how old dreams crumbled with time. A man in an abandoned and wall-less building was covered with fragments of concrete, like a blanket. He may have been trying to stay warm, or trying to be buried.

And, mimicking the way problems and stress piled up, were the always-overflowing rubbish bins. Their top layers blew off into the traffic, and alternate bins developed in the nooks and crannies of the streets; in shuttered windows, traffic cones, and broken bollards. Meat shops accumulated bags of rubbish on their overhangs, the rubbish juice trickling down the wall cracks and settling in the kerbs. In one suburb, a mountain of dirt took up most of a road. Topped with a plastic washing basket and surrounded by a puddle of water, people walked around it, paying little attention because they knew no one would ever fix it. No one, they were sure, would ever fix the city. So they walked around and among and through the wreckage of the streets, of their lives, with only the occasional complaint muttered to a neighbour.

The city's sinking was taking place in its inhabitants too. Nothing was dependable, nothing improved. They could feel, like the cold slipping under their clothes, the warning from the authorities and the elites to stay broken. Make do. Consent to barely-a-life. And so every night, some took two Ibuprofen against the icy absence of social protection and care.

Others took alcohol, others consumed screen time.

But the people of Mexico City, and of all of Latin America were seeds. Seeds had dormancy in order to avoid germinating in unsuitable conditions. People had dormancy too. Their apathy was a reasonable response to hopelessness. They were holding out until the rain would come and allow them to truly open up and grow.

Others resisted in manageable ways. There was a trova singer sweating under the lights, dedicating a song to his primary school friend who died of Covid-19, and the whole bar singing with him. Night markets sold second hand clothes and people climbed Los Fuertes to watch the sun catch at the edge of the Popo volcano, then roll down its side. "Who do the clouds belong to," a girl asked, "To the volcano or to the sky?"

There were the people caught in the flood of indignity who stuck their heads above the water and insisted, against all odds, on joking and on holding those close to them. "No puedo quejar," - I can't complain - they said. Over and over, like a mantra. Determined to protect others from their sadness. People mended their cars and buildings and shoes with masking tape and Kola Loca - super glue. They carried about with them a desire to survive. "You have to stay healthy," said the hardware shop man, while handing over drill bits to a customer. "I'm seventy and I jog every morning before the sun comes up." And the retired university professor went to a collective vegetable garden on Sundays, and the nopal vendor called her daughter every night. Everyone did something to keep on going. Despite. To manage despite it all was the soundtrack to the hustle of Mexican life. A weary resilience, a tired bare minimum.

And despite it all, the second hand book stores still winked at passersby. Like old people with all the secrets, they chortled to themselves at the chain coffee shops opening up around them. Hummingbirds found their way through the treeless streets to people's patios, where they left signs among the succulents, silver tears along the barbed wire fences, and gifts of poetry among the basil flowers.

The streets breathed, coughed, and slept to the rhythm of the people. They stretched in the mornings when the pan dulce and atole were brought out on carts. The new sun was a delight and later, the falling of night was a welcome insistence that work had to be stopped for now. In complete darkness, planets slow-danced among each other. The taxis though, worked on.

Did Enrique break La Tortuga?

When they first started dating, he hugged her a lot. He held her from behind, knitting his fingers over her small stomach, smelling the top of her head and planting kisses there. He said they would grow into yucca flowers one day. As the years passed, she had to ask for hugs, and he would say he was too busy. He would go outside and sit on a crate next to the front door and yell out jovially at neighbours passing by. He took their response to his greeting as a kind of applause, which he collected until he had his fill.

The front door was his emotional barrier. He left her inside and he stood outside it, buying plain donuts from vendors and gulping down two or three before he went back in.

Sugar stuck to his shirt front and lodged in his fingernails.

Inside, Enrique argued. He scratched the cooking pot with his nails to annoy La Tortuga and when she asked him to stop, he would roar at her about not telling him what to do. He made lists. They were verbal ones of problems which he offloaded like watermelons and sacks of corn from a truck to her so that she could deal with them. He would end his rant by calling her limpiadora. Cleaner. Limpia Dora, you do it, I'm too busy.

She made lists too. She had a list of things she couldn't have, but she renamed it to Things It Was Selfish To Want, so that she could feel better about not having them. The list had six items; recognition, free time, affection, being listened to, romance, and respect.

She also had a list of the ways she was fading. It was a watch list of the strength, the glow, the joy and warmth of her thoughts. On the list was the way she had stopped sharing her questions about life with Enrique, and then eventually with others as well. Also, her delight was shrinking. It was moderated, mediocre, beige coloured. The birthday cakes she made, initially elaborate and full of flavoured cream and fruits and walnuts, were becoming single-layer dry sponge cakes, burnt on the edges. She had ideas about ways to promote their repair workshop, but he never liked them. So she kept them to herself, and then eventually she just stopped having them.

At night, Enrique used both the pillows and sweated down the back of his neck. He would act out his nightmares with punches and growls, and get up and bring back cold rice to snack on in bed. And he would climb on top of her and try to enter her without any foreplay. So she took to sleeping on the floor. She would lie there, one red ear to the concrete and her arm draped over the other side of her head. She would make a final list, that of things to be done, before she fell asleep. Enrique enjoyed barking out orders, but she was the one who knew where their payments were at, what their children were dealing with, and when Enrique's medicines were about to run out. She was the administrator of all things.

As she slept, tight clusters of goosebumps formed at the bottom of her back, where her top didn't quite meet her pants. Then, when she woke up, she left behind a dustless shape on the floor where her body had been. Though she swept the floor daily, dust would still seep into the bedroom and settle upon the floor each night.

Colour coded

The Aztecs said the two creator gods had four children; black Tezcatlipoca, blue Tezcatlipoca, white Tezcatlipoca, and red Tezcatlipoca. These four gods travelled from under the ground, up through the land, until they touched the sky, staining everything with colour as they went. In the sky, the path left by black and white Tezcatlipocas formed a white cloud snake, Iztac-Mixcoatl, or the Milky Way.

The Mayans associated colours with compass directions. East was red, for the colour of dawn, and red represented awakening and the renovation that opens one up to new ideas. West was black for resting after the sun went down, north was white like bones and death, and south was yellow for corn, harvesting, and the material side of life. In the centre were blue and green; sky and nature, the origins of life.

Colour concoctions

The Aztecs made colours from flowers, leaves, stalks, seeds, wood, roots, minerals, chalk, and smoke. They obtained sky blue and deep blue from the xiuhquilipitzahuac plant, which was similar to the indigo plant. They boiled cacao seeds and tamarind beans, and used lemon juice and worms. They got purple from the capulín fruit. Green came from sunflower stalks, and intense yellow from the cempoalxóchitl, the marigold used for Day of the Dead. Mango yellow came from the axocuilin insect, and violet from a sea snail called purpura pansa. It regenerated its ink roughly once a month. So on full moon nights, dyers would go out and collect it, applying gentle pressure to the foot of the mollusk to release the ink, then returning it to the beach rocks. The ink was white, but dabbed on to cotton, exposure to light and oxygen turned it turquoise, then violet.

With all these colours, the Aztecs painted fabric, manuscripts of pictorial history, art, and the surfaces of buildings and temples. The pyramids in Teotihuacan were painted a rich dark red, known as teotihuanaco red. It was often contrasted with malachite green. The Mayan Bonampak murals of the 9th century depicted dancers against a deep, sky-blue background and people wearing white hats, yellow, red, green, and orange clothing, playing sienna instruments.

Colour theft

This new city for La Tortuga was a raging concert of history embedded in building frames. It was old wars still going on imbued in the stressed postures of pedestrians. She walked, wide-eyed and forgetting her aching feet because there was so much happening. The Spanish invasion was right there; in the cathedral just ahead of her, that had been built over the ruins of an Aztec temple, and it was present as a hissing grey mood of the air. She could see where the colours had been forcibly disappeared, as people often were. Art had been replaced with brands and billboards. Elsewhere, flower fields had been replaced with monoculture and foreign factories, hotels and parking lots. Colours had been muzzled and deactivated. Now, grey inhabited throats and tainted the mornings. There was no longer a red beginning. Beyond the dust in the drains and the concrete city skin, she saw the human condition following prescriptive grey guidelines. Compliance grey, shrapnel grey.

But then colour was brought out on special days. Occasions for surviving. One such moment had just passed, when in August, the people of Huamantla had met at midnight and blanketed the roads of their town with coloured wood shavings poured into patterns and designs. The kilometres of temporary carpets expressed gratefulness and paid tribute to wonderful things. Down one festive alley of old restaurants, La Tortuga saw papel picado tissue paper strung over the street in rows, intricate designs cut into fifty colours. In the window of a sweet shop, she saw sugar skulls decorated with purple and green flowers, and sitting on the ground out the front, a woman in a hand-embroidered blouse sold Wixarika art; cacti and hummingbird sculptures were dressed in tiny beads in flower patterns. In a cafe, wooden chairs were painted with glittery colours, or perhaps with pieces of the moon.

La Tortuga didn't see five suited beasts shutting down a tianguis market and hauling crafts, tapestries, sunset-coloured papayas, and chayotes into the back of a police van so they could build a Burger King there. One of them put down his things, and left. At a distance of two blocks, he followed her.

Humanity parade

As La Tortuga arrived at the Zócalo, she calmed and composed her expectations. She gave them strict rules, found ways to lower them as much as possible so that the lack of help or information in the square wouldn't disappoint her this time. There would be no one there, she repeated to herself. But instead, her eradicated expectations and lowered gaze came upon a square that was full of people. The crowds obscured everything bar the four-storey Mexican flag in the middle of the square, wilting with the absence of wind. La Tortuga launched into the crowd. Around her, blurred beings stretched their necks and stood on the tips of their toes, straining to see something as the sun bit at the tops of their heads.

She asked someone what was going on. "It's the annual alebrije parade," they said, explaining that it started in the Zócalo and finished six kilometres away, at the Angel of Independence statue. For a moment, the crowd parted and little cracks opened up, allowing La Tortuga to see to the other side, where giant papier-mâché fantasy creatures were queued up. The parade was homage to an art movement that originated in the 1930s in Mexico, where unusual animals were shaped from wood or papier-mâché, then painted with vibrant colours and patterns. Prior to that, Oaxacan artists had been making small animal sculptures and woodwork since before the Spanish invasion, and Zapoteca artists and Mesoamerican cultures had used copal tree wood to make masks and musical instruments.

The parade gave La Tortuga no choice. She had to pause fleeing and survival mode. The atmosphere of anticipation infused into her, and excited, with the grates in her shoes closed for the moment, she "perdón"-ed and "permiso"-ed her way through the crowd cavities until she broke through to the front. The first thing she saw was an owl with a beard of light green thorns, carrying kisses in buckets on its back. It was three metres tall and standing on a pull trolley. The plaque on the side of the trolley said its name was Tecolotl, and it had been made by artists from the town of Malinalco.

Waiting among the alebrije floats were musicians, mariachis, acrobats, lucha libre wrestlers, and people in costumes on stilts. The floats moved forward. Parade staff held the crowds back with rope. Following the owl, came a tiger-squirrel holding a globe. That alebrije was called Joyful Breeze Journey and was made by people at Morelos University. Then, a winged giraffe with hands at the base of its neck that seemed to drive its body. The parade moved slowly. At the speed of giant papier-mâché sculptures. La Tortuga observed a cinnamon jellyfish with a long ribbon tongue. Then came a whale-tank painted with fish faces pulling exaggerated expressions of surprise right back at the crowd. Then a snake with curly leaves growing at intervals along its body, followed by a toucan with a tiny orange human skeleton sitting on its eyeball reading a book, then a pregnant seahorse with a zaffre blue scorpion tail and monarch butterflies coming out of its stomach.

Hundreds of creatures strode past La Tortuga. Greyzone loosened its grip on her and she was able to marvel. The joyful celebration injected her with soft sight. What delightful worlds must exist within each of the artists, for them to come up with such creatures.

The tail of the parade departed down Avenida 5 de Mayo, with police cars and a garbage truck following it. Onlookers were eager to leave the crowd conditions and they stretched out their legs and breathed out heavy sighs as they looked about them, deciding which way to walk. In minutes, sections of the crowd had drained down the Zócalo station steps, had trailed off toward Bellas Artes, had wandered off to the cantinas near La Catolica, and had gone back to work. La Tortuga could finally see the full expanse of the square. There were no information stalls. Still, she watched the remaining trickles of people with curiosity.

She saw a coconut lion with light and dark blue streaks in his mane. But this alebrije wasn't on a trolley, and it didn't have a plaque listing the artists who made it. And it moved. It looked about with the apprehension and confusion people often had when their plans didn't happen and they were left wondering what to do with themselves. It acted out this confusion by running a paw through its mane, over and over, as though to reassure itself there were things it did still control. It paced round and round a man who did not notice it, but looked equally confused. He got out his phone to check the time, put it back in his pocket, then brought it out and checked again. Then he ran his hands through his hair.

A few metres from him, La Tortuga saw a dog-sized rainbow beetle with curly toes, a peppery chartreuse yellow rhino horn, and a horse tail that flapped in impatience against a man selling orange juice from a cart. He preferred fleeting love, La Tortuga could tell.

But she wasn't sure what these creatures were or where they had come from. Perhaps they were manifestations of each person's essence. A copy editor stood by the Zócolo station entrance, searching her bag for her train card, and next to her, her duck-centipede alebrije rested its head on its back, eyes half closed, because the copy editor was tired and really just wanted to be home already. An octopus with a body that reflected its surroundings in highly contrasting black and white lines was with a UNAM sociology lecturer who regularly drank pulque to quieten the overwhelming clamour of their heightened empathy. A pink and sapphire egret with sugar glider eyes was with a campesino who chuckled when he harvested giant cabbages and bunches of onions, despite having backache all the time and a heavy crush on a straight man. A bird with clouds stored in its underwing that had accepted that sadness lasted for decades, was flying in circles above a radio presenter who only let his dismay hang out when the show was over.

And there was one young man whose alebrije seemed to be a small but eager flame sitting on his shoulder. It had all-white eyes that pierced the surfaces of things. The man, having studied history, economic forces, and fought in various movements and struggles, could see behind shop fronts, under the streets, and beneath skin.

One very small alebrije though, was by itself in the middle of the road, looking through the people for someone. Hey little alebrije, how could anyone forget you? La Tortuga thought at it. It caught her eye then. Like catching a fish. La Tortuga went over to it and scooped it up, then held the little thing to her chest.

Billions

Almost every person had an alebrije, though few knew it. Alebrijes were the colours and shapes of each person's unique soul; their struggles, ideas, hopes, learnings, intentions, creations, and mistakes. An alebrije was the changing body of a person's inner magic.

A few people didn't have alebrijes. They were the people who destroyed. They broke worlds. They had sold their humanity to the highest bidder, dismantling forests, undoing people, handing out fear in slick, affordable packages, stealing seeds, and shattering care systems and communities. They weren't easy to spot though, except by their empty eyes.

They were the beasts that made up the System of Monsters.

Butterfly-turtle

La Tortuga's alebrije was a butterfly-turtle. It was pebble size. Easy to lose and easy to step on. It had earwings coming out of its shell that it kept scrunched up, but which it could billow out, like fishing nets, at six times the size of its body. They were soft, delicate, turquoise and mauve sheets with pink veins and blue floral patterns that listened to everything. They soaked in people's tones, anxieties, and the little bits of unsaid important things that were woven between the lines of their daily stories. The wings heard whole communities of peoples and their agonies and victories. And then all the listening was funnelled down them and into the turtle shell.

The shell glowed warm. It had grown higher and steeper the more La Tortuga had heard and learned. Its surface was marked with tiny word engravings that moved in swirling paths around the dome. Like blood, keeping the alebrije going.

All those decades of her life, La Tortuga had thought she was living off food; off papusas, cabbage salad, and pan coffee. And she had been, but she had also been living off the things she heard and learned. Still, I was too patient, I stayed too long, she thought.

"Perhaps," the butterfly-turtle responded. Patience, it argued, could be an overtolerance that stopped one from moving forward, or the strength to resist quick-and-easy solutions that weren't going to work in the long term.

In La Tortuga's black drawstring Nike bag, she had sown a secret pocket. She had put it there before she left, cutting a slit into the internal fabric, inserting a pocket from an old pair of pants on the inside, then sewing a zipper across the opening. It wasn't impossible to find, but it made it hard for a quick thief to steal her money or her ID. The little alebrije fit in there like joey to kangaroo pouch. Like finding home, or a bed.

The purpose of walls

It was close to lunchtime now. La Tortuga still hadn't eaten anything, and her chest and throat twinged with hunger, but she ignored them. They throbbed harder, insisting, and in response she walked faster. This time, she did just one lap around the five hectares of the square. She wanted to confirm to herself that there was definitely no stall or information person, because if there was no one here or at the terminal, there would be no such help anywhere.

Her lap ended by the other side of the cathedral where a smaller square ran along its side and ended at the Templo Mayor, or Main Temple. This square was dotted with plant beds and news stands. Indigenous dancers and healers held ceremonies in the middle of it, and bicycle taxis lined the road by one corner. Families grazed on basket tacos with green and red sauce, imitating the fastest of cows in the way that they sat for just a few minutes and looked about, then quickly headed off down Moneda Avenue.

The grates in La Tortuga's shoes had reopened and were now snapping at the soles of her feet in perfect timing with the throbbing hunger. She headed through the square of human grazers and leaned on the glass fence by the entrance to the temple. She looked over its ruins, taking in the giant serpent, the skull rack, and the stumps of walls.

For the Mexicas, the Templo Mayor had been the centre of the universe and of life. It was in the middle of the four cardinal points. Its place couldn't be changed, so they had added on to it and built new buildings around the old ones, keeping the same characteristics, such as the double staircase at the main entrance. The remains of the eagle building were protected by a roof, so La Tortuga couldn't see the sculptures of eagle head warriors, the intricate red paintings, or the friezes of armed warriors.

The Spanish destroyed the Aztec's centre of universe. From its stones, they built the cathedral, right on top of where part of the temple had been. In 1573, the authorities built the current cathedral around the original one, and it evolved over the following two centuries, combining Renaissance, Baroque, and Neo-classical architecture styles.

Now it was a sixty-seven-metre high, 127,000-tonne statement of superiority. It cast its huge and silent shadow over people in the square as a display of the conquest that was untouchable and elusive. Still stomping out the sun.

La Tortuga felt a gaze on the top of her head. She looked up and saw a tall, young, white man standing on the cathedral roof, looking straight down at her and aiming his zoomed-out camera lens at her. She thought he may have been focusing on the ruins beside her, but he jerked when her gaze met his lens. Looking closer, she noticed his alebrije holding on to his back, hiding, but the top of its head poking above his shoulder, and laying its eyes on her gently. Carefully. She saw the man hesitate, trapped in a confrontation of gazes, unsure whether to feign ignorance and look away or take comfort in the distance between them and ignore her. She saw young confusion, unsubstantiated confidence, soft doubt, and a playful imagination. There was strength in the way he held himself on that sloping roof.

Harry saw the way her shadow draped through the glass fence and fell down the side of the ruins. He adjusted his zoom and angle, trying to get both the tiny person and the expansive ruins in one shot. He appreciated the way the weariness of her skin and the solemness of the ruins were seamless, and how the verticalness of her body contrasted with the horizontal layers of what was left of the Templo Mayor. He saw poetic aesthetics.

Still unseen by La Tortuga, the beast watched them both.

And for a moment more, Harry stood on the cathedral looking down at La Tortuga and the ruins. For a moment more, she stood next to the ruins and looked up at him. And then Harry disconnected his camera-gaze from hers. As he did, he heard a snap. He ignored it, and turned around to rejoin the cathedral tour group.

Harry's punctures and perforations

After the tour, Harry Devin went straight to his hostel and got into bed and curled up so that he couldn't feel or hear the hundreds of holes squeaking and creaking inside him. The holes were expressions of his ambiguity. Soul cavities. The perforations, punctures, and leaks throughout him made him squishy. When he walked, they huffed, and when he talked, his voice was breathy, like a sponge being trodden on.

And the empty spaces inside him made his nose itch, then the middle of his back, then his knee. Annoyed, he would attack each itch, saying, "Quiet Body," with a capital B because that was its name. It took him half an hour to do craps, and he would tell it, "We don't have time for this, Body."

Harry was still very young, and only starting to build out a sense of self and question his purpose. He was a rough, unfinished draft, an outline of a being. The lack of details in his character left him feeling lost. He would forget where he was going and why he was touristing. Before his trip to Mexico, he had worked a lot because he didn't know how else to fill his time, and he went out on Saturday nights because that was what people did, but his participation was lukewarm and unexcited. At home, he would start eating cereal then didn't want to anymore, so he poured it down the sink, the cornflakes wallowing near the plug for someone else to clean up.

His porousness bestowed him with a ghostly, vague presence and a doughy personality. Rain made him soggy rather than delighted. He didn't have any unshakeable convictions nor any standout strengths. He wasn't sure what he was doing or why he was being, and so he was pumice, drifting, almost helplessly.

He remembered the clear gaze of the woman standing by the Templo Mayor. A single itch travelled around his body, on a mission, and he chased it with aggressive fingers, but it was a teleporting itch that could out-dodge him. A soul hole screaming to be noticed. The single itch became bubble wrap, bursting in lines and crowds. Harry bit at the crowds; brought his wrist to his mouth and scratched it with his teeth, until the crowds quietened. Sat down.

Growing up, his family hadn't been wealthy, but money had also never been stressful. His parents had a single-storey home, two cars, he had his own bedroom, and they all went on annual camping trips. There was a mortgage that his parents couldn't pay off, so that they took out a second loan, and then a third, but Harry never found out about that and he grew up with stability and safety. There were few reasons to question the world, since it was working out fine for him.

Because he faced so few obstacles he also assumed he would do better in tests and interviews and could do well with little effort. It seemed natural to him that he deserved the best in any situation, and this mentality affected his choices. He assumed he would be sought after at parties for conversation and that people wanted to hear his stories and jokes. He took validation for granted. It was there, pleasant, comfortable, safe, and reassuring.

But something was wrong. Beyond the holes, he noticed a crookedness. He was regularly naive in everyday situations. He didn't know what to say when people were hurting, worried, or doubting themselves. He tried glittered words, but they didn't seem to work. And so, the people who enjoyed his jokes didn't turn into meaningful friendships. The big gap between his self perception and reality saw him doubting his instincts and putting off decision making. An inconsistency in life's logic drove him to learn because there was something that he needed to fix or adjust. And so he travelled, and so he consumed. He bought books and framed helpful phrases and old maps, hoping that if he collected and accumulated enough bits of world, life would be less crooked.

The air-conditioner above the room's one window exhaled. "Swish," it said, as it sent out cool air then warm air and whispered unintelligible things. Even the air-conditioner was confused. Harry reached out for the remote on the bed side table and tried to turn it off. He angled the remote up and down and held his arm out straight as though he were waving a lightsaber, but the air conditioner ignored him. "Beep," it said, and breathed even harder.

Harry hoped that Mexico would challenge him, speak to what was real and what wasn't, and put a break on any automode, any going-through-the-motions. But once he was out in the streets, he forgot about all that. Instead, he remembered in the middle of the night when he woke up from odd dreams about communal showers and screaming at all the people to leave. And he remembered at the end of the day when it all caught up to him and the holes prodded and ached and itched. But during the day he wanted to go places and take photos that people would marvel at. He tried new foods, ate salted crickets and asked for the biggest tortas so he could photograph them for social media.

His porousness affected his sight as well. As he travelled, everything he looked at was brumous and hazy. It too lacked detail. His sight wasn't sensitive, nuanced, or luminous. He felt like he was walking through a series of white lace curtains, pushing them out of his way as he tried to get closer to raw reality. But the world stayed generic and vague because he didn't know it very well. He was travelling so that he could change that, but he was finding that the tours and site visits only seemed to reinforce oversimplifications and add to the murkiness.

After an hour curled up in bed, night pulled in and illustrated the effect as its gentle darkness melted, butter like, into the room, eliminating outlines altogether and leaving just shaded shapes.

Harry thought about eating out for dinner or going to the hostel roof for beer and snacks. He uncurled and went to the bathroom to look in the mirror above the sink. At 22, his hair was already receding a little. He didn't mind that. He also kept a short, fuzzy beard because he didn't like the overly-clean look, and because shaving gave him little red bumps around his lips that he could feel, like microbones set into soft skin, tightening and tugging when he smiled or ate. Unlike his brown-blond hair, the stubble had specks of red in it.

He couldn't decide where to eat. But travelling on his own meant he couldn't let anyone down by being late. He had a habit of underestimating how long it was going to take to get ready or get somewhere, so he was always around twenty minutes late. When he arrived, he would smile at the person waiting, as though busyness and stress were the culprits.

He wasn't owned by time, he thought, though it annoyed him when others made him wait.

Still looking in the mirror, still undecided, he asked himself where he had learned his time habits. Ultimately, his itching holes and gaps were questions. If the despair of not having answers was harsh, at least the holes kept his overconfidence from growing further. He didn't realise yet that they were a gift of humility and curiosity which he needed like a survival kit for being human. And they made him go places. He would look up beliefs about time later.

Harry listened to a weekly philosophy program and it prompted these random, big questions. He watched documentaries on Friday nights and would Google more information. The veils fluttering across his path tired him and caused him anxiety, but they didn't stop him completely. Harry, like Mexico City, like Latin America, found a way to keep on going.

The migrant: Ovidio

"I get so close to giving up," Ovidio said. He grinned, then dropped the grin to the floor, and sighed.

He was in one of Mexico City's many hidden places. All over the city there were secret nooks and crannies that only a few people knew about; pocket cavities embedded into the sides of hills, daylight dungeons, and buildings without numbers or addresses. Ovidio was in a migrant shelter in Álvaro Obregón, to the west of the city. There was no building front to this shelter, just a single black door. Migrants and visitors pressed the electronic door bell, and then a remotely-activated buzz unlocked the door and they climbed two flights of enclosed and narrow concrete stairs, to arrive suddenly in the shelter. An unused fridge and a noticeboard with old news and faded poems welcomed people into the space where Central Americans, Colombians, Haitians and others slept in dorms of twelve beds. The local government had erected barbed wire over the door at the bottom of the stairs, on each side of the staircase, and around the roof and the inner garden. The space looked like an improvised high-security prison. But, after knife attacks, broken bottles thrown into the garden, name calling, and people cutting off the water or electricity, the wire wasn't meant to keep the migrants and refugees in, but rather the violence out.

Ovidio was chatting to a Guatemalan who was new to the shelter as they ate dinner. Migrants squeezed around the table in the kitchen, perched and squatted on the couches, chairs, and floor of the lounge room, and on other stairs by the kitchen, eating from plates on their laps. A few more arrived after a day of work, and panting from climbing the stairs, asked if there was any food left. Portions of rice and beans were spooned on to two reusable plastic plates and cups filled with hot milky coffee, and passed over to them.

The whole place, like many buildings in Mexico City, was built as an ad hoc and precarious stack of concrete rooms. In this neighbourhood, a giant could step on one building to the next, like stairs, and reach the top of the jumbled mountainside of housing. In the shelter, one dormitory was on top of another, while a makeshift plastic structure was on the roof of that. A small garden was squeezed into a passageway, and the toilets and washing area hung from the side over the garden. The office was on top of the doctors' room, and a social or meeting area had been created on the office roof. Resident migrants would lean a ladder against the side of the toilet and climb on to that roof and lay their wet clothes on it to catch sun and dry.

Ovidio couldn't climb though, and he couldn't help catch the now dry blankets that those who had finished eating were throwing down from the roof. He had two hernias as a result of lifting heavy building material for a company that paid refugees US$5 a day for ten hours of work. He was one of the longest residents of the shelter, having waited one and a half years for an operation and to be able to work again.

"Meanwhile, I sell chewing gum on buses," he told the Guatemalan. "I get on and tell everyone I'm a refugee from El Salvador and that I can't work. Often they donate money rather than buy the gum. But I can only do that for an hour or two, before it starts to hurt again."

Later that night, he made swans to sell. He folded hundreds of tiny pieces of paper that he then interlocked, like mini roof tiles. Then he painted the finished bird with blues and purples, glitter, and Resistol glue.

The migrant: Bryan

Bryan was young, confident, and optimistic. He gelled his short hair into a peak each morning, or wore a black Adidas hat backwards. He took selfies with his hands behind his head so that his arm muscles showed. Instead of swans, he made flowers to pass the time while he waited for a humanitarian visa. Using thread, wire, and stocking material in different colours, he made full bouquets modelled on different species from around Mexico.

During the pandemic, COMAR, the government commission for refugees, closed. To deal with even more waiting, he said, "I just freeze time. It sounds weird, but I make out as if yesterday was the first day."

One day, he drew a self-portrait. He used school pencils to depict himself in a t-shirt and orange and blue printed shorts. He had been dreaming of the beach, so he drew that in the distance, and a pair of binoculars coming out of his chest.

And when his best mate in the shelter tried to die by hanging himself in the bathroom, Bryan took care of him. They made flowers together.

Ovidio and Bryan also had grates in their shoes. But they had adapted, to an extent. Like coping with persistent extreme heat or living with the heartbreak of poverty, they lived with the grates gnawing away. They tuned out or disassociated from the pain by distracting themselves on their phones, through jokes, stories, gossip, and fights over small misunderstandings. And when they could, they sat on the dormitory roof by the solar water heater and, against the rules of the shelter, snuck alcohol into their bodies.

Bryan's feet, as well as his face and heart, grew thicker skin. One centimetre thick, then two, and then three centimetres. As hard as an outer shell. The thick, hard skin lost sensitivity and warmth. It became cold to touch, like it was dead or dying.

Six phone calls

Eleven beasts met in a white-walled room with a goal of diluting and undoing caring habits. They wrote missives that blamed all the volunteer-run migrant shelters for encouraging people to migrate. They searched for problems, and found that the biggest three of the seven shelters in Mexico City were behind on their bills. And so it was lunchtime when fifty national guards arrived at those three shelters and ordered their closure, evacuating all the migrants out on to the street. They spilled out of doors with their feet all tripping on things and their small backpacks half packed, clothes and deodorant and cans of tuna stuffed into a main pocket and socks falling into pavement puddles. Now, there were giant red 'Closed' stickers on the front doors of the shelters and enraged shelter coordinators making calls and posting on social media, urging donations so they could pay off months of water and electricity and re-open.

La Tortuga was still in the centre of the city. She was trying to find someone or somewhere that would look up migrant shelters on the Internet and give her some phone numbers and addresses. Her stomach scrunched. It was clenching and threatening to swell out in a sudden pufferfish bloat. Everywhere La Tortuga looked, she saw people with busy and distracted faces and closed-to-the-world eyes that suggested they weren't up for helping a stranger. A tour bus driver was leaning against the front of his bus and smoking. She tried to catch his glance, but he evaded hers. Just behind the tour bus, she saw a youth hostel. She couldn't afford its beds, but she could see the receptionist in there had a computer and looked bored.

He was scrolling on his phone. Without looking up, he put it to one side and cleaned his fingernails with a pen lid. Then he stared ahead and saw her standing there, only her head and neck visible above his receptionist desk. He had free city maps with advertising for local restaurants around the border, and he turned one of those over and wrote down some numbers on the back for La Tortuga. He didn't offer to let her use his phone though, and he didn't respond when she thanked him.

Outside, La Tortuga scanned the streets again, this time for pay phones. They weren't used very much anymore, so she wasn't surprised that she couldn't see any. She walked on, sticking to the larger and busier streets. Her alebrije, snug in its bag pocket, stayed alert but curled up its wings and turned down its glow. Magic had a way of dimming itself and disappearing when people were in a rush. The day was ageing and La Tortuga was running out of time, so she fast-walked, and it seemed to her that all the other people walked much too slowly and too many of them stopped in the middle of the pavement to look in shop windows or read street stall menus.

The first public phone she saw was on the corner of one of the busy streets, but there was heavy traffic nearby and she doubted she would be able to hear much. She kept going, peering down the streets she passed, stretching her neck toward the middle of the road and narrowing her eyes so they could reach as far as possible. Her arms swung vigorously, as if they too were walking extra fast.

The sun's rays curled around that stretched neck in a gesture of childish joy which only annoyed her. And then she felt the sun loosen its grip and withdraw. She calculated. Once she found a place, at least for the night, she would need time to get there, and it was unlikely any of the shelters were in the city centre. She also doubted they would accept new people after working hours.

Dusk pulled in. Finally, other people's footsteps sped up, eateries got louder and the city's pigeons suddenly had somewhere else to be. The sky announced the change with a wink of pink. Metal shutters rolled closed over shop windows and doors in a clanging sound that reverberated around the streets. And La Tortuga's shoes snapped and scraped. New grates opened up on the upper part of her shoes and stabbed downward. They made her feel tired. They made her want to stop. But now, of course, she wasn't coming across any phones.

She turned right, and told herself she would use the next phone available, no matter the noise.

Cold air fell from the sky with the speed and purposefulness of a lift carefully descending. The buildings dulled. La Tortuga refused to acknowledge the disappointment brewing in her. Her walk became a run as she tried to not let the incoming trembles topple her. There was no time to unravel now, but she was carrying around storms. They were gathering in her clenched and bloated stomach. Her arms, running with her and slicing at the air were now not just propelling her forward but also slicing up storm clouds. Stay away, disappointment. Now is not the time. Now is not the time.

Tonight, maybe.

Later, when the walking stops and the shoes can come off.

She found herself in Garibaldi Plaza, where Mariachi bands were waiting to be hired. A man was walking around with a leaning tower of gold and silver embroidered velvet sombreros. Mariachis were gathered around another man selling coffee and hot chocolate from a bike cart. A triangle garden of agave plants divided the square in two and fittingly pointed at the tequila museum on the other side. There were various benches, and beside one of them, a phone booth.

La Tortuga sat down for a few minutes to catch her breath and calm her mind. A child played soccer with himself with a plastic ball. It was the exact same purple as the jacaranda flowers on the trees lining the square, and so it looked like one of those flowers had fallen down and re-shaped itself. The boy was kicking it between the groups of Mariachis as though in a giant pinball machine.

La Tortuga deposited coins into the pay phone, and as she dialled the first number and felt around in her bag for a pen, she panicked when someone answered and she still couldn't find it. She tried the secret pocket and pulled out her Honduran ID and a pen, just in time to hear the person who answered telling her that the shelter was full and to try one of the churches. She tried three more numbers, ringing each twice, but no one answered. The fifth number did answer, and the person said, "You would need a referral from another shelter to stay here. But at the moment we are full, after the others were closed. People are sleeping in the hallway, on the floor, and there's no more floor space."

"Do you know of anywhere else I can try?"

"No, I'm so sorry."

It was during the fifth call that a kid chasing a jacaranda-coloured ball ran past her and took her Honduran ID, probably thinking the plastic ID holder contained money. Around La Tortuga, the Mariachis multiplied with the new darkness, and the restaurants and bars projected music out across the square as invisible, intersecting audio beacons announcing, here we are, come and join us.

The migrant: Marvin

Marvin and his friends made short funny videos dressed in some of the random things people had donated to the migrant shelter; a pointy hat, a glittery suit jacket, sports vests. At night when he couldn't sleep he would balance his phone on his forehead. The next morning he would wake up and it would still be there. He laughed and joked his way through life. Even when he was riding on the roof of the train up from the southern Mexican border, he had stood up and waved his hands in the air as the train passed through towns.

The migrant: Mario

Mario grew up in Honduras, but had family in the US. He mixed English and Spanish together like paint, switching between the two languages according to his mood and who he was with. He added a "ya know" to his Spanish sentences and "pendejadas" to his English.

He had been staying with family and working in the US for a few years when he was deported to Honduras. There, he started a small fleet business, but six years later, one of the drivers was shot and killed by gangs, and Mario fled to Mexico. He left two children behind.

He stayed in the shelter in Álvaro Obregón for a year, until he was able to get some work. His first pay slip was for 270 pesos (around US$14) for two weeks at a Grub Hub call centre. According to the pay slip, those two weeks were "training," but he had worked on voice calls for four hours, then chats, three at a time, for the other four hours of each shift.

Customers in the US would ring saying their drink hadn't arrived so that they could get a full refund. Those refunds were often more than his two week's pay.

Then he tried to get a maintenance job with a hotel chain but they said they'd had "bad experiences with Hondurans". Another job turned him down because he was over 35.

"Where there's life, there's struggle. I'll just have to keep looking for solutions, ya know," he said.

Ways of walking

La Tortuga trapped water in her hands and splashed it on her face. She stood by the Neptune fountain in a small city park, rubbing water over the backs of her ears and her neck. She had spent the night roaming the streets and going into shops and restaurants for warmth until they realised she wasn't going to buy anything. She wandered until nothing was open and the whole busy city had turned silent. Then she had sat at the base of a statue, her legs folded against her chest. She'd dozed, and then when the cold got too much, she had got up and swung her arms about to heat them up, then dozed some more.

When light returned and the sounds of traffic and hasty footfall restarted, she asked a traffic cop where the nearest police station was. Now, she was attempting to tidy herself up before going in. She smoothed her hair down and re-plaited it and washed the street dust off her shoes.

At the police station, a queue extended past the four plastic chairs nailed to the floor outside the general issues office, down the pickle-green hallway, to the main entrance doors. Administration air, stiff and drafty and smelling of old paper, put a curse of staleness on all who stood in it for too long. There was a cork noticeboard with just one dog-eared notice about reporting corruption to a six-digit number that was no longer in use.

From her spot at the end of the queue, La Tortuga's eyes were drawn to the shoes of the person in front of her. White was an unusual colour for hiking boots. She had seen them somewhere before. Having repaired many shoes, she could tell they had memory foam cushioning. Their soles were thick, with good traction, and there was a padded tongue, waterproof lining, and a pull top at the heel for sliding the shoes on. There were microtorches on the toes that would light the path ahead, and wings on each side of both shoes which flapped in figure eights like those of a hummingbird, so that the shoes hovered a few millimetres above the ground. This person would never feel or notice the lumpy disrepair of Mexico's roads or the gaping holes that interrupted its footpaths.

La Tortuga had always walked in uncomfortable shoes. Pain, she understood, was built into everything, and nothing worked well or did what it was supposed to. That was one of the reasons she was a fixer. There was so much to fix. But she couldn't fix her shoes. The grater holes and blades would always reappear, sharper and bigger than the last time. They taught her not to try. And she fixed her feet instead, with band aids, hot rinses, stitches, oils, and the gel from aloe vera.

The white hiking boots in front of her were mesmerizing. As the queue moved forward a few metres, she tapped their owner on the shoulder. He turned around, and straight away she recognised him as the man who had taken her photo on the cathedral roof. She saw no flash of recognition on his face.

"Hello, I like your shoes," she said in Spanish, pointing at them. Harry opened the translator app on his phone and spoke into it, "Hello, sorry, I don't speak much Spanish. Thanks, yes they are great shoes."

"Why are you here? Are you okay?" La Tortuga asked.

"My camera was stolen. I need a police report for the insurance."

"Ah, that's too bad. My ID was stolen, and I need a police report too, so I can get a new one, and then apply for a visa."

There was anxiety in Harry's brow, and she saw gentle concern wash across his face as she talked. Then a pair of wide and wrinkled eyes peered at her over his shoulder. His alebrije extended its head up towards her, then climbed on top of Harry's head. Harry wasn't yet aware of it, but what surprised La Tortuga was how similar it was to her own. It was small, though bigger than hers; the size of a guinea pig. It was mostly a tortoise. It had a brushy mauve monkey tail for swinging around, a shell with patterns outlined on it but not filled in with colour yet, and tiny balloons that formed a crest from its head down its neck. La Tortuga inferred that Harry was still creating himself, and he saw life as a party, to enjoy and celebrate.

The tortoise had large gecko feet. Its bulbous toes were covered in microscopic setae hairs, in turn split into smaller bristles. It used electromagnetic attraction to climb vertical surfaces. The only surface it couldn't stick to was Teflon. Harry was a walker; scurrying up mountains, and quickly mastering awkward surfaces like volcanic rock, snow, or sand. He walked to shops and took long strolls when he was stressed. He always carried as little as possible, so that he felt free to change his plans at the last minute, to stroll down side streets, to stay a night somewhere, to stop and gaze at a sight, and to get lost. So the tortoise shell had clasps on the side that could be clicked open like a suitcase. Inside it was just one tiny change of clothing, a tiny tent, and a ten-pocket jacket, as well as pink castles, pocketstars, storylines, and luscious landscapes. They were Harry's wandering mind, his need to paint layers of story over the plazas, parks, train stations, and streets he found himself in. But the tortoise's tummy was riddled with perforations, and sometimes the necessary things and the imaginings leaked out.

La Tortuga wanted to know more. She pointed at Harry's backpack. "Are you going hiking?"

"No, this is what I carry with me wherever I go, even back home," he said. He looked down the queue. They were almost halfway there, but there was time. He grinned at La Tortuga, "I'll show you."

In Harry's bag, there was: sunscreen, mosquito repellent, an e-reader, a filtering water bottle, a thin rain jacket rolled up in a hand-sized pocket, sunglasses in a magnetic case, wet wipes, a case of condoms, a small first aid kit, a pair of very small speakers that he could connect to his phone, an eye mask, a selfie stick, and a camera bag with a lens, lens cloth, spare battery, and USB chords.

La Tortuga was three bits impressed and two bits jealous, she calculated. Some of those things would have helped her a lot on her journey through Guatemala and Mexico. But she reigned her feelings in. We all have battles, she thought, though I can't imagine what his are.

He is young and makes a lot of mistakes, Harry's alebrije suggested to her.

But now Harry was showing her how he used Google Maps to find cheap hostels. La Tortuga quickly exchanged her bits of impressed and her bits of jealousy for five whole bits of hope. Harry took her pen and paper and noted down a list of cheap hostels, with their name, phone number, and address, but not their price.

"Practically free," he told her, unaware of how relative that was. La Tortuga now knew what she would be doing the rest of the day.

And finally, Harry was at the front of the queue. He could see the police officer sitting behind his desk with an old-style monitor; forty-five centimetres deep and dust stockpiled around its vents. He had a slouched face, and he spent five minutes scrolling through social media on his phone before signalling to Harry to enter.

Harry wanted to know more about La Tortuga. His spongey soul holes had gone quiet. As though they sensed that she had answers to his questions. He wanted to see her again and show her his plans and his photos.

La Tortuga watched Harry hurriedly pack up his bag and dash into the office. She heard the rough barking of loneliness from within her. For weeks as she had walked on her own, there had been echoes in her voice. Now, there had been the warm comfort of her words landing, roughly and through a translator app, on someone else.

The office door was left open, and she saw Harry use his phone app to say, "Good morning. My camera was stolen, and I need a police report for the insurance." The padding in Harry's shoes massaged his toes. The little wings beat fast and cooled him down.

"Good morning, where are you from? Do you like Mexico?" The police replied in reasonable English. He gave Harry an ingratiating smile and flowered nods. He offered Harry some chilli-coated nuts, from finger tips coated in red dust. Harry declined and described what had happened.

"After dinner, I sat down outside, and I put my camera down beside me. When I looked up, I saw a half-bald child staring at me, and a short man with scruffy hair turning away, as though about to run. He was also holding something under his shirt. I went to put my camera in my bag but saw that it was gone. There was a police officer standing nearby, and I yelled and pointed at the short man. They reacted quickly and took the man away, and they told me to come here and make a statement. I don't know what they did with the man, but I still haven't got my camera."

The police officer spent a few minutes entering the details into a standard report and asking Harry for his full name, passport number, and the time and place of the robbery. He printed out the statement and stamped it. Harry held up his report and waved as he glided past La Tortuga.

"My ID was stolen, and I need a report so that I can get a new one," La Tortuga told the police. The grates at the front of her shoes snickered. They bit down rapidly; machine gun bites aimed at her toenails. She stomped her feet to try to control them.

"I'll need some ID before I can help you."

"It was stolen. What should I do, where can I get a new one?"

"Not here. Next!"

He waved La Tortuga away. His hand was a broom, that with a gesture, swept her out of the room. She limped and hobbled down the pickle-green hallway.

The System of Monsters: People squashers

In the System of Monsters, that alliance of unelected and self-declared kings, there were many different kinds of beasts. There were wing pluckers, who made and enforced borders, and there were people squashers. Like all the beasts and monsters, the people squashers looked somewhat like people. They wore white shirts, suit jackets, and overly-polished shoes paired with overly-polished hair. Their official title was real estate tycoon, and they spent their time speculating on property and building empires of hotels and of commercial and residential estates. They measured their success in dollars and hectares.

The people squashers pushed everyone else Out Of The Way so they could take up all the space with their mansions, casinos, stadiums, golf courses, and luxury retail complexes.

They contrived shopping centre infestations that left some people with Nowhere To Be. Shoved to the edge of life, with flimsy roofs covering their squished and squashed bodies, with holes in their walls letting in the rain and the mosquitoes and rats, the indignity, lack of privacy, the social exclusion and the Nowhere To Think.

Around the world, walls and rooms shrank every day in the slums where one billion people lived and in the prisons where nine million people lived and in the tents, mats, and dorm rooms where one hundred million refugees lived, and in the doorways and street corners where one hundred million homeless people lived.

In Europe, there were eleven million empty homes, idling and inert, so that time could increase their financial value. The people squashers built and bet on ostentatious lethargy in the malicious form of aimless buildings that should have been homes harbouring life, but instead were budgeted to be barren. There were enough of them to house the homeless of Europe twice.

And that night, the people squashers reached up and picked a few stars each out of the sky. They dug them out with their nails, like they were thumbtacks embedded in a cork board sky. The picked and plucked stars were the currency for getting into the exclusive monsters' meeting that was fast approaching. But where those stars had been, there were now bare patches of night sky. Bald bits without twinkle. It was a desertification of the skies that caused a shadow wind to roar about the streets of the poor with far too much energy.

Where beds went 1

La Tortuga only had 125 pesos, and the hostels on Harry's list were scattered about the city. Thinking it was best not to spend money on trains or phone calls, she walked to three of the closest hostels.

Half a block away from the first, she saw its large, internally-lit sign sticking out over the street from above the doorway. The sign was lapis blue, with a white bed symbol and Hostal Viajero in Times Roman. It protruded like a blue flag waving for attention among the cluttertangle of electricity wires, internet cables, lamp posts, balconies, and other signs.

But when she got there and stood like a stiff soldier facing the door, the sign had disappeared. The cluttertangle had a gap in it. She rang the doorbell anyway, and a young man with his blond hair in a low bun, opened it. She said things: strings of words about needing a dorm bed and how much it was, and his face clouded over and he looked at her like she was speaking another language. He shook his head gravely, and she walked on to the next hostel.

The same thing happened. She got to the entrance and the sign disappeared, and the person who answered the door looked at her as though she was proposing something very strange, shook his head, and closed the door on her.

When it happened a third time, a people squasher watched her go into the juice shop next to the hostel and ask the woman cutting up watermelon if there was a hostel next door?

"Yes of course, didn't you see the sign? Why not go in there and ask them?"

"They're not answering, and the sign seems to have gone."

"Well, how strange."

"Do you know how much they charge for a bed?"

"Oh, for one of their bunks, yes, I think 250 pesos."

"I see. Do you think I can find a bed anywhere in this city for less than that?"

"I don't think I've heard of them going below 200."

"Okay, thanks so much."

***

Beds were little seed pods of rest. From thin mattresses to rugs, petate mats, to beds raised off the floor and decked in pillows, to hammocks, futons, and manji beds, they were meant to be happy spaces of daystart and dayend and soft fantasy that drifted into long sleep. They were places of cuddles and warmth, of orgasms, contemplation, movies, and rested body healing. Bed time was the hours of gentleness, of weightless darkness and sweet air that so so subtly caressed.

And because beds were the ends and starts of days, they witnessed people at their rawest. The bed in La Tortuga's home in Honduras saw many things those last few days before she fled.

The Eyes of the Earth

It saw:

-La Tortuga's multi-coloured fingers handing Enrique freshly made baleadas with red beans for a light dinner. Her fingers were red for strained muscles, dabbed with slate grey from grease, speckled with tawny brown from the dust and wood shavings, stained pumpkin from some spray paint, and there was white in her nails from the flour.

-Enrique snoozing on it while she filled all their orders and fixed all the broken television sets, bicycles, blenders and lamps waiting on the shelves of their workshop. At first, Enrique had done the repairing and she had been in charge of the receipts, buying spare parts, and organising and cleaning their workshop. But then he slept more and more and spent more time outside eating his donuts, and orders stacked up and became overdue. It turned out she was better at fixing things than him. Their workshop got a reputation in the nearby streets for quick turnaround and reliability. Neighbours would bring their broken goods and as they handed them over, they would sneak in other little problems for La Tortuga to solve. My electricity bills are always wrong, they would say casually. What should I do? Then it was a disagreement with an uncle, and eventually, their romantic problems also. La Tortuga listened, as she sat on an old three-legged wooden stool and turned the broken items around, looking at them from different angles. Fixing relaxed her. She approached it as she would a find-a-word. The answers were there, and she systematically checked all parts of the item to find them.

-Her crawling under their bed and fetching the yoghurt container where they stored their earnings and handing all the coins and notes through the window to a gang member passing by for the weekly and obligatory war tax. He called her *limpiadora* too and went off without a word.

-La Tortuga a few days later returning from the morgue and lying on the floor in the same awkward position her fourteen-year-old grandson had been in on what to her looked like a body-sized metal tray on a gurney. After refusing to join the gangs they had shot him and cut his head off, cut his legs off at the knees and his arms at the shoulders, then cut lines all over his face because there was no dignity in death, in Honduras. La Tortuga tried to point both her feet left and to put both her arms on the right side of her. Lying there, she was very aware of her attached limbs, her uninterrupted flesh and her neck's strength. There was empathy in imitation.

-The following Monday when the gang member poked his head through their window, and she had to show him the empty yoghurt container because she had helped pay for her grandson's funeral. The gang member said he didn't believe her and she was hiding the money somewhere, and if she didn't find it by the following Monday she would join her grandson.

-The way La Tortuga changed over those few days. She had run into her limit. The Limit of Tolerance made her pace around and it brought on determination, of the survival kind. The kind that stopped putting Enrique first.

-La Tortuga packing her bag while Enrique was on the toilet. He would be there for fifteen minutes, giving her that much time to leave 73 years of life behind and prepare for a 43-day walk.

***

Even if La Tortuga could find a dorm bed for a 125 pesos, there was no point spending all her remaining money on one night's sleep. She paused. She didn't just halt her walking body and plant it there on a street corner in a still very unfamiliar city, but she also paused her journey and paused the day and she paused her go-from-one-step-to-the-next until the thing is done mode. She stood there, but she also sat on an old three-legged stool, and looked at her problems as though they were find-a-words. Calmly, she acknowledged that she would not be sleeping in a bed soon. She knew what she had to do.

She pressed play. And she went in search of a hardware shop – one of her favourite types of shops, with a chaos of ropes and pipes and tubing and jars of bolts and nails, sacks of cement, shelves of glue, and every spot filled with shelving or things hung from the wall and barely any space to walk. She found one and bought a 30 x 30 centimetre piece of white plastic (3 pesos), super glue (15 pesos) and wire strippers (40 pesos). Then she sat outside the shop and laid the tools in front of her, along with her multi-screwdriver and pliers. With the plastic, she made a sign that wouldn't disappear. "Can fix anything. 10-50 pesos."

She would save up and she would get to sleep in a bed somehow, though not as soon as she had hoped.

She had 67 pesos left.

Counting pesos

When Harry Devin woke up, the sunlight grazing his face imparted exactly the same amount of warmth as the bed covers provided his legs and chest with. He thought it was the Perfect Amount of Warmth. He felt soothed and serene and like staying there in the bed on his back, gazing at the shreds of pale yellow sun dancing about like projections from the window.

He was staying in the hostel that overlooked the back of the cathedral near the Zócalo, in a room on the third floor of five. At this time of the year, most of the beds in the hostel were empty. Harry had a private room with a double bed. The mattress was firm, with inner springs and a pillow-top layer. At night, the three down pillows moved around, escaping from his arms like playful baby clouds and insisting on residing on the floor, until he blindly patted around and scooped them back up, and locked at least two of them solidly under his head. Every day, two new towels and soaps appeared on the cabinet beside the television and the bed was dressed in fresh sheets.

Harry brushed the shreds of sun to the side and got up, dressed, and put on his flying shoes. In school and college, everyone in his group of friends had had similar shoes. They were the popular group that followed mainstream trends, listened to commercial music, and bought the more expensive brands of clothes. They thought they were popular because they made good choices. But school was a replica of the world, and they were little versions of their parents and the social groups with power that their parents were a part of. Harry and his friends believed freedom meant doing what they wanted. They chose the music and themes for the school dances and drank vodka as they drove through red lights with their hands out the windows, because rules were for other people. They skipped cafeteria lines, talked over people, and demanded favours without giving any.

With the low value of the Mexican peso, Harry's graduation present would buy him plenty of that sort of freedom. After having spent a week in the country, he felt settled enough today to now plan out much of the rest of his trip, and to start his main project. He wanted to beat an informal world record for the most amount earned while busking, relative to the local minimum wage, in six months. Because he had the graduation present, the money from busking would go to a charity.

He sat down at the small wooden desk and opened up his tablet. The room noticed. The air shifted. The sun dulled. From within the walls, traces of the people who had made the sheets and built the building, wired the electricity, fixed the window, and polished the floor, watched him. The bricks and slats contained within them the dry moment a builder had fallen and cracked his skull, and the raspy memories of family members who had fought for compensation and never got it. The walls and curtains contained the burning tiredness of decades of underpaid cleaners and the muted dreams of factory fabric workers.

With a hot glaze of watchfulness traversing his back, Harry labelled spreadsheet columns. He set weekly targets and daily hour minimums in order to earn 131,000 pesos in six months. He defined initial and end stages and pasted the names of the three college friends who had graduated in journalism and had jobs already, into a new spreadsheet tab. They might publish something about his final results.

As he worked, he operated on two frequencies; one that wrote lists and strategised, the other that watched himself and thought about the meaning of what he was doing. He offered up definitions of success and freedom, but his thoughts kept dripping out his holes and he couldn't remember how they started or where they were going. "No obligations," he said out loud.

"How you define freedom is symptomatic of your relationship with the world and with others," the walls chimed in, but he didn't hear them. The shadows of workers stretched out of the walls and over the sheets and pillows and emitted warnings. They moaned and hummed and curled their eyebrows into stale frowns. Their words were blown into the air.

"Saying and doing what you like," Harry thought.

"But freedom can't be destructive or inconsiderate," the old memories hissed through the mortar joints and the curtain threads. Harry felt a coldness. He looked up from the desk, but he couldn't hear or see the people who had built the room. There were bruised bed legs, blood stains under the plaster and paint of the walls, swelling and wrist pain and missed meals in the curtains, that Harry couldn't see. He got up and walked past the bed and the corner of it pinched him. He swore and blamed his own spongey awkwardness. The walls tried to get his attention again, arguing with him in raspy screams, that freedom was about interconnection and self realisation and boundless creativity and purpose. Harry paced the room and only heard squeaks and whispers, strange nudges and hints of objection. He felt just a slight concern. That, as usual, something was missing from his plans and thoughts. That he wasn't quite nailing things.

He got up and put his bag on the bed and organised the stuff he would need for the day. Travelling made him feel that he wasn't tied down to anything. Freedom might be measured by choice and going where you wanted. He was concluding the thoughts and getting ready to leave, but he was also unsure. He was asking, and wanting conversation.

"Your brand of freedom means being unrestrained by the impact of your actions. You happen to the world, but things happen to us," murmured the walls. And Harry heard them this time, because he had wanted to. His first reaction was that it was not his problem. But that did not make him feel right. The holes in him yawned. Bile stewed in his throat.

And the walls shivered. The bed sheets writhed. And the bricks shrugged knowingly.

He would have to see eventually.

✳✳✳

La Tortuga, meanwhile, was sitting in the area where the tour buses left from, just in front of Harry's hostel. She leaned her sign against the fence and waited. She had been told this spot was one of the main places where carpenters, builders, electricians and others waited to be hired.

She saw Harry come out of the hostel, and with a purposeful walk, head towards her. She was excited to see a familiar face, and she stuck her head out and waved. She was going to wish him a wonderful day. But Harry's sight was still caught among the white curtains. He felt a strange coldness again, and he stumbled as he walked past her. Slight concern seemed to have followed him out of the hostel and on to the street. It pursued him. Eyes fixed ahead, he walked within half a metre of La Tortuga's sign, then kept on going towards the metro entrance. La Tortuga was used to not being seen by strangers, but now she wondered if she disappeared to others as well, like the hotel signs had disappeared for her.

The Eyes of the Earth

The migrant: Victor

Victor was talking, even though he didn't exist.

It was late at night, in the middle of the rainy season, and the other migrants and refugees in the shelter had already gone to bed. Waterflakes tapped out patterns on the tin roofs.

It had happened during the civil war in El Salvador, when the US-backed military government tried to "drain the sea" of support for the revolutionaries. That involved killing, torturing, raping, and displacing nearly a fifth of the country's population between 1980 and 1992.

"My wife declared me dead during the civil war, and my mother, who was illiterate and didn't really understand what was going on, put her fingerprint on the document, to second the declaration. They did it to protect my children from being killed as a way to get to me. They had a burial for me and everything," Victor said.

Since fleeing El Salvador to Mexico, Victor had been unable to open a bank account, get formal work, vote, access health care, rent, or travel.

"When I tried to get a passport at the El Salvadoran embassy, they looked me up and they said, 'But you're dead, it says you died on this date.'" Victor flicked ashes from his cigarette on to the railing, and the rain responsibly washed them away.

At sixty-six, he wouldn't ever be able to retire from his informal work as a carpenter making coat stands decorated with drawings of houses and snails. He missed his children. Every now and then, this living ghost would drink excessively and spend a few nights sleeping out in the streets.

"How do you prove you're not dead," he said. It wasn't a question.

Rain hung by its fingertips from the edges of the gutters.

Unseen magic

The sun set on her work day. La Tortuga had made seventy pesos, and though it wasn't enough, it wasn't bad for her first day. She felt lighter.

Her shoes mellowed. They let her walk unfettered. They backed off, stood down. No fight tonight. She headed to the back streets of Pino Suarez, to the quieter, overcast side lanes shooting off from the bars of Regina street, and searched for a safe street nook to pass the night.

She chose one - long, but too narrow for cars. Her eyes stretched wide, taking in as much as possible, registering quickly the details of doorways, any urine puddles, nearby noise, and all other possible dangers and subtle protections. She wanted some privacy, but not so much that someone could easily rob or hurt her. Her eyes were detectors, locking on to each post and manhole and rubbish scattering and identifying its key characteristics. Her eyes registered thirteen emptied boxes of beer balanced in a twisted tower that slouched against a street lamp, chipped gutters, and drains bent out of shape and blocked by layers of rubbish. They saw plastic rain drooling in slow motion down the sides of buildings, leaving stain trails. Off in the distance, parked at the edges of the city, were giddying waste dumps, the kings of waste that sneezed rubbish and detritus over the city. This street was lined with sick plastic bottles, split coffee lids, mangled and strangled paper bags, disgorged Doritos packets, bottle-scum, used serviettes, run-over lemon pieces, comfortable rats. Effectively, a convoy of leftover casings of a consumerism addiction and a huge informal sector that survived by selling cheap food and goods.

It was a lot, and tight air clots barged down La Tortuga's throat to her chest. The excessive amount of rubbish seemed to her to be apathy taking on physical form, enacting itself in the stage of the streets. She knelt down and picked some plastic bags and polystyrene plates out of the drain so the waiting puddles could finally flow down. Her hands tingled. She squeezed and kneaded the rubbish in her hands. She massaged it tenderly. Patiently. She stroked it until the plastic relaxed and sighed and crumbled into dirt grains, and the polystyrene unravelled into earthpieces and seedballs.

She gathered some more rubbish and built it into a pile on the footpath, and then, like treating an aching body, she massaged it too.

She moulded it, packed it close together, and kneaded it into a fine dough. It sagged, buckled, then suddenly softened and browned. Seedballs sprouted into seedlings. The chestnut and russet-coloured dirt wriggled as ants and worms and tiny snails moved within it. A poinsettia shrub, also called cuetlaxóchitl, with flaming-red leaves, extended itself out of the dirt, blushing and unfolding.

La Tortuga went to work on the rest of that section of the street. For two hours, she collected the rubbish, piled it up along the inner side of the path, and turned it into Persian blue flowers, drenched-green parsley, dandelions and lavender. A strawberry plant and its runners skipped and strode the length of the block, burying their heads at intervals and sprouting more plants with white flowers and carmine-red fruit. Lettuce babies, bean pods, satin-skinned basil, and cherry tomatoes sprouted.

La Tortuga picked some of the vegetables and herbs to eat, then finished her dinner off with strawberries. She had tomato taste left on her tongue and a small-sized itching for salt. Her sore hands throbbed. She had felt slight static as she had massaged. Interference, a weakness of signal. Her tiredness made the magic hesitant and slower. And she wondered how many nights of street sleeping it took for tiredness to turn into an inability to function.

In the dark, people walking briskly home from work didn't look down and notice the new plants. And the next morning, they still didn't notice. Because the rubbish in the street had crept into their souls. Their hearts and minds were filled to the brim with junk, distractions, things to buy, fights with neighbours, phone notifications, sneaky thoughts, crumbling egos, long lasting injuries, and recurring soul pain, so that they forgot to look around. The hazy grey-orange of the polluted skyline was in fact their own curdled sight that hadn't the scope to take in the city's tiny wonders. Their restricted imaginations didn't hope to find strawberry plants among the grey and the concrete. And so in the end not a single other person saw the garden that had grown so suddenly.

All the mistakes

There were many types of mistakes. They could be graded by intentionality, consequences, level and type of responsibility, and room for learning. There were goofy mistakes with small, laughable outcomes, preventable mistakes, unexpected mistakes that nudged and woke their victims, mistakes caused by courageous risk taking, by impulsiveness, by ego, by not paying attention, and by lack of awareness.

The first mistake Harry made on his first busking day, was assuming that the bar above the Tequila museum in Plaza Garibaldi would be crowded by the time it opened, at 2 p.m. He made his second mistake in the museum shop, which he visited before busking at the bar. He bought mezcal with a tiny snake in the bottle, but then realised he didn't have any space in his bag for it and he would have to hold on to it while he did his magic tricks.

At the rooftop bar, tables and chairs were swathed in dark and light blue, mint, and watermelon-pink paint. Rainbows of papel picado hung in rows from the ceiling. Serviettes in hand-painted cups and woven palm place mats were arranged on the tables. The chairs were docked into the tables, waiting with gentle and quiet patience for people to arrive. Just three tables of the thirty or so were occupied, and serpentine clouds prompted those few people to sit closer to the bar rather than near the edge of the terrace and its views of the square below.

People huddled; drawn together by serious subjects rather than by seductive booming music played over an electric night and forcing people to scream words against straining ears. It was quiet. Time sat there on the empty chairs, musing over the empty place mats, drawing figures among the midday dust, blowing a strong sense of Not Yet about the space. Five clay bowls of blue corn tortilla chips were in a line at the bar, ready. The party was tonight, tomorrow night. Now was in between time. A moment for thoughts and food, but not for magic tricks and performative tones and energetic applause.

The Eyes of the Earth

Still, Harry approached a table with a couple. They were leaning towards each other, hands still, eyes focused on each other, and their rigid backs seemed to frown. Harry thought he could cheer them up, and he said, "Trucos!" with a stretched smile. He performed linked ring tricks using eight-inch rings bought for US$23 from Amazon. The woman detached her head from her partner's and leaned back to also put more space between herself and Harry. The man tapped his cutlery and ate soggy chips too fast. He got the hiccups, which Harry then tried hard to ignore. He held the rings at the wrong point, showing the opening, then held out his tip jar in the same hand as his mezcal bottle. The woman looked around the room, searching for polite excuses hidden among the bar shelves and the empty chairs, and her partner pulled five pesos out of his pants pocket.

At the next table, Harry did his fire from hands trick with a gadget he had bought for US$30 at a magic and games shop. One of the three young men at the table pointed at the lighter strapped under Harry's finger and laughed. So Harry moved on to his invisible thread trick with an imitation apple. "Watch this," he said in English. He hadn't rehearsed hooking the threads to his fingers or moving his other hand around the apple and avoiding the strings. He dropped the apple, and his alebrije crawled down from his shoulder and buried itself in his shirt. Harry laughed away the mistake, but the men expected more, and sent each other eye messages. Make him go away. They shook their head at him and waved him off. One gave him ten pesos out of a sense of obligation, looking down at the table as he did.

After also trying the third table, a spongey Harry, perforations squeaking, left the bar and museum and went out into the square. Mariachi were playing to two retired sisters. A small crowd stood behind them, watching.

Harry's mistakes were accumulating. Each one rounded his shoulders a little bit more. He seemed to be getting shorter, or maybe he was finding it harder to feel like taking up space. He was translating the reactions he got as rejection. He needed reassurance that his busking project was going to work. That he as a person was going to work out in Mexico. He needed to believe that the fix was in spending more time practising and rehearsing. So he tapped and elbowed his way through the circle of people and put his arm around one of the sisters and tapped his feet and nodded to the music. The sisters looked at Harry taken aback and confused but shrugged good-humouredly. Wide-eyed, they forced a half-smile at him, which grew into whole and large smiles as they laughed. Harry took it as a sign that he was finally doing something right. Encouraged, he gestured at the crowd, motioning with his hands, "over here," with big circular movements. The small crowd followed him.

But Harry didn't see the huddles of Mariachi groups noticing this person who was not a Mariachi coming into their space and trying to earn money. He didn't see how they nudged each other and pointed at him with juts of their chins, how they tilted their head to the side as though trying to comprehend a strange creature. A few shook their heads and raised open hands outwards, shaking them tautly. One of the older ones, with thick, black eyebrows set against grey-white hair, and a silver glint in his eye that suggested he was someone who always told jokes but who also felt serious, genuine warmth for all people, waited about twenty minutes, then went up to Harry and told the crowd to leave. He invited him to sit with him.

"Hey, guero. Good tricks. But you can't do that here. For a hundred years now, this square has been where people come to listen to mariachis, northern music, Son Jorocho. You could try the metro instead. But first, find the local mafia, pay your fee okay. And then, you need a costume. In Mexico, we like theatre! Tricks aren't enough, you have to make it a performance and get your audience excited," he said, switching between basic English and Spanish. But Harry mostly understood. And at that moment, he didn't make a mistake. Like most people, he had a daily mistake limit. Denial could only survive four to five mistakes in a row. So instead of arguing with the man, he stopped. He acknowledged that things had not gone as he thought, and he needed to take his haul of lessons back to his room and make adjustments.

"Gracias, amigo," he said to silver glint man. He handed him the unwanted bottle of Mezcal. The man didn't drink alcohol, but he understood, laughed, patted Harry on the back, and walked off yelling, cheerfully, "Suerte!"

At his first busk, Harry made 120 pesos.

The colours they ate

There were 64 species of corn in Mexico, but an infinite number of corn colours. There was the blue corn species, but its kernels were so dark they almost looked black, and Sinaloan corn with lighter indigo kernels. A burnt-orange chapole corn was used for popcorn, ponteduro (caramelised popcorn balls), and pinole (a pre-Spanish invasion drink made from corn flour and panela, and flavoured with cacao, canela, or anise). Conejo corn was pale white, serrano mixe was dark hibiscus red, bolita corn had plum, amethyst, and mauve kernels, and western corn was dark magenta and cerise with a smattering of yellow and dark blue. Onaveño corn was the colour of fire and yams, and tablila de ocho had kernels that were white in the centre and pink and yellow on the edges. It was used for making tlayudas, tejate, pozole soup, huachales, tejuino, and huajatole. People also liked to eat huitlacoche, a puffy blue-grey corn fungus, on their quesadillas. There were at least 600 dishes based on corn.

Indigenous Mexicans had invented corn, domesticating it over a period of ten thousand years and making it more and more delicious, nutritious, and easier to eat than its wild grass origins. And as they created their food staple, they created themselves. They lived by cornclock and its harvest rhythm. Corn gave them life, and so it was admired and respected. It was grown as part of the milpa; an agricultural system where crops like corn, zucchini, beans, chilli, tomatoes, and various quelites were planted together. The crops complemented each other in terms of nutrients, flavours, and in the soil. The milpa was a way of life, a philosophy, and a sustainable system of cultivation that guaranteed food sovereignty for various regions of Mexico.

From 1993, the US used the North American Free Trade Agreement to force its genetically modified, single-colour yellow corn on Mexico. It subsidised its corn production, while Mexico's tariffs on such agricultural imports were removed, and Mexican small corn farmers were unable to compete. Those who continued to produce corn switched over to large-scale monoculture in order to survive in the corn market, and the milpa and agroforestry systems began to die out.

Syngenta and Monsanto had genetically designed yellow corn brands Attribute and Performance Series to resist pests, and the product spread throughout Mexico. It was efficient, profitable, and uniform. Fields of tedious tones plagued the countrysides. It only took four to five years for the soil to die of boredom. Then pests and diseases built up their armies and prepared for war.

Meanwhile, 400,000 Oxxo corner stores, owned by Coca-Cola, opened up around Mexico and colonised the country with sugar drinks, chips, and instant noodle cups. Eventually, even the pharmacies sold junk food. Working twelve-hour days, six days a week, most people had little money or time, so they bought the cheap and filling products. Companies profited from slowly poisoning people with unidentified spam meat, soft drinks made of sugar and phosphoric acid, sausages diluted with water and starch, Doritos made from baked and fried GMO corn dough, and imitation margarine and milk. Bland, barelyfood was packaged in polymer layers with happy cows in fields printed on them in order to present the dust scraps, factory concoctions, and watery vulcanised leftovers as edible.

Then, at night, slow poisoner beasts and bed stealers visited people as they slept. They snatched their alebrijes and pinned them down, then shaved and peeled a few colours off of each. Just enough

The Eyes of the Earth

to dilute people's essence; erase bits of them, but not enough for them to wake up right then in agony, and notice. A bed stealer stripped away all of La Tortuga's purple. It disturbed her dreams and poked her and she tossed and turned and barely slept. The next morning, she had forgotten how to feel proud of who she was.

Bimbo bread

Mexico City was heading into winter, and the old chilly air frosted people's nostrils and scratched their throats. In the city centre, people sought out sunny spots by dodging the shadows of tall buildings and standing in the middle of the Zócalo. They became iguanas and urban spiny lizards, turning their chests to the sun and looking upwards, tilting their faces towards the sky so that their tense faces could relax for a moment.

One young man though, was not at all interested in the sun. La Tortuga watched him from her fixing spot as he abandoned dignity and scurried about between three street phones. Amused, she realised she had walked by the phones the other day when she had needed one, so now she was curious to see if any of them worked. They were next to each other in a line, but all different heights, makes, and colours. Like incoherently planted trees. The man slammed down the handset of the third phone and ran off.

Now, she observed Harry leaving his hostel again, and this time heading straight towards the tradespeople. Today, La Tortuga was joined by two plumbers, two electricians, a painter, and a general handyperson. She hoped Harry would see her this time and stop and talk.

He dashed out of the hostel with the same focus and speed as the last time, but she saw him shift gears. His focus tilted down from the distance, away from the future, and moved in closer to a few metres away from him, to his present. He needed something now. La Tortuga predicted that his clumsy sight would see him trip right over her, spot her, but at the very last second. As it happened though, he did see her. His eyes connected with hers and there was a crack sound and a warmth, but then he performed. He acted as though it hadn't happened, that in fact he'd seen the electrician next to her. He danced distracted and hurried. The street was his stage, and he took on a role where he was a confused man that could accidentally overlook someone that he kept on bumping into. All that because he needed his magic trick gadget fixed and he didn't think La Tortuga could do it. But all the acting had made him nervous and when he tried to talk to the electrician, with a quick mix of a few Spanish words, and pointing at his gadget, the tails of the words got caught on the dry corners of his mouth. The electrician shook his head. The next man along waved his finger at Harry to say, nope, can't work on that. And so finally, Harry turned to La Tortuga. One final face of feigned surprise. Oh, you, how strange to see you again, I don't suppose you can fix this?

La Tortuga wanted to say, what was all that about hey? She held back a smile. She found people who couldn't act, who struggled to pretend and lie, whose personalities were not fireworks and theme parks, even when they tried, to be endearing. She examined the gadget; the fire-from-hands trick. She turned it over a few times and quickly spotted the problem. It took fifteen minutes of fiddling, twisting, and testing, and she had fixed it. She handed it back to Harry, and he gave her a mini loaf of Bimbo white bread that he'd bought from an Oxxo.

"You're paying me with this?"

He nodded proudly.

"Thank you. If you need something fixed again, this is my job and I charge 30 pesos per half hour or 15 pesos for quick fixes like this."

She had been very thorough, and Harry knew he would need her help many more times because he was always dropping and breaking his gadgets, and he couldn't get replacements in Mexico.

"You have a regular customer," he said. His patronage was a favour, he was telling her. So he brought the words down like a gavel but with a smile. It was a countermove to her disapproval. It aimed to dissolve it with authority. But it didn't work, because he came off as a little arrogant, and her reaction seemed even more justified. The disapproval hung there, in the air between them, refusing to let them quickly resume a comfortable conversation. And Harry couldn't leave like that. He needed to be on better terms with La Tortuga first. So the two sat there, looking at anything but each other, and Harry went through subject lists in his head, trying to find some small talk that would soften and repair things by reconnecting them a little.

Nearby, a transit cop was talking to a tourist police officer. There were also municipal and federal security guards standing in a perimeter around the palace so that Harry counted four different uniforms in the Zócalo area. A pewter-grey street dog walked past Harry and La Tortuga and stared right at them but didn't bark. They watched it walk off, and La Tortuga ate a piece of the bread. Then she talked. She used Harry's app to tell him what it was like to be forced to leave her country. Having lost her pride the night before, she talked in neutral, grey tones. Facts and dates. Harry listened closely and tightened his lips, an expression he used when people talked about hardships that he had never experienced. He went wooden when La Tortuga referenced a violent death in her barrio, and mentioned only eating because she was hungry and never for fun. He searched for wise words, perfect postcards, chamomile tea phrases to soothe, carefully woven words that could form a tight jumper to warm her and fix everything. The right gadget words to compel her to feel better, and then he would too.

But he didn't find them. There was nothing useful he could add to this conversation.

Later, he realised it wasn't necessary to add insight to everything, and he could just listen. A full three minutes after she had moved on to talking about transport in Mexico City, he said, "You've had a tough life, I'm so sorry."

"Gracias amigo," La Tortuga said, smiling right at him and like that, seeing off the last traces of the hovering disapproval. In Honduras, people rarely acknowledged how hard things were. A tough life was normal and empathy for pain was given out sparingly. The latest body found by the base of the big staircase leading to their barrio was just a topic of gossip. Gossip was a street tool for trivialising intolerable violence, and regaining importance by being the bearer of new and dramatic information.

Harry looked up at the sun and sneezed.

"Salud!" said La Tortuga. Even if a person sneezed ten times in a row, she would say salud after each sneeze. Harry nodded and kept looking at the sky, as though reading long sentences written there. As though he had something important to contemplate. He didn't know how to take the conversation back to public transport, how to chat about Mexico in a way that lightened the mood.

La Tortuga let the quietness be. Constant chatter, for her, was unnecessary and even tiring. She used the time to process. She could feel in her own body, in her clenched fists, how Harry was struggling to relate, and the effort he was making. She had also absorbed the subtle dynamic of the police, and the vulnerable coldness of the plumbers and electricians. She needed to let all the feelings sink down into her turtle shell of memories so that she could make space for new thoughts.

Harry though, made himself more and more uncomfortable. Sitting on the short brick fence next to La Tortuga was making his bottom itch, and he shifted from one side to the other, then crouched instead. And then when that strained his thighs, he sat back down again. He noted how language barriers reduced a conversation to its simplest form. There was no fluff or filler, and spontaneity and joking were difficult. He was deflated and defenceless without his jokes. La Tortuga, on the other hand, noticed how Harry tried things with little fear, but gave up too quickly. His easy life had given him enthusiasm, but not perseverance. She also saw all the work he was putting into performing the conversation, while most of her own energy was going into understanding him.

The non-barking, grey, staring street dog came back and sat next to the two of them. They scratched his head and ears, and he fell asleep on Harry's shoe just as Harry was deciding it was time to get up and head off.

He backed his shoe out and stood up, while the dog slept on. The sun shone on him and cast light through his holes and perforations so that white-yellow sun sprinkles landed about him on the ground and in La Tortuga's hands. She wanted to get a needle and thread and sew some of those holes up. But she dared not. Not yet.

The cheap texture of charity

Centuries ago, European bed stealer beasts set about manufacturing poverty on a large scale.

In the Americas, they harnessed the well-developed weapons of starvation, enslavement, and cheap labour to take almost everything. They plied minerals, metals, and crops from the reluctant lands and sent them to Europe. They had seized 100 million kilos of silver by the early 1800s, worth US$165 trillion today.

Later, their great grandchildren and other bed stealers in rich countries continued to siphon wealth and resources out of the Global South. Though US$1.3 trillion moved each year from rich to poor countries in the form of corporate spending, remittances, aid, and charity, US$3.3 trillion moved from poor countries to rich ones through interest payments on debts the poor countries had paid off over and over, unrecorded capital flight, and the profits foreign companies made in the poor countries. BP extracted Nigeria's oil, Anglo American profited from South Africa's gold mines, Amerigo Resources, and BHP took copper from Chile, and on it went. Financial segregation between rich and poor countries increased at a rate of US$2 trillion a year.

Bed stealer 73, owner of BP, held a charity event; a pity party with posters decorated with the faces of unnamed, unheard Nigerian children. He gifted aromatic posies to pacify the poor, to patch over the pollution in their rivers and soil. Then he sent out press releases boasting and bragging about the scraps of profits spent.

Charity and aid were publicity stunts to cover up the world's biggest robbery.

Seen on a Mexico City train

A man who was unable to talk entered the train. His hands shook and he made a moaning hum as he held up children's puzzles for sale. He had a threadbare forehead and illegible eyes. Vacant, but with the last remains of tenderness pinching at the corners. A line of drool hung from his lip.

Two tall men in suits eyed him and nodded to each other. Catching the train was unpleasant, they said.

Pino Suarez station, and they both pushed past to get off. Puzzles spilt. Pieces were strewn among the shoes. A misunderstood man's saliva finally fell.

The migrant: Denis

Denis had five bald patches on his head that bled in their centre. He was underweight, his hands and feet hurt, and his lower back was also bleeding and swollen. A diabetic, the Mexican government had denied his refugee application because he was too sick. Soon, he would travel back to Honduras and likely be killed by the gangs that had forced him to flee.

In downtown Puebla, on the floor of a fish shop, there was a parrot that lived in a cage just double its size. Nobody talked to him. He had bald patches too.

Companions

To pass the night and numb the cold, La Tortuga made a list:

-Bruised street palms that refused to hold their fruit
-A horse that kept on tripping
-An emaciated river paying a toll to pass through the city
-A dragon hauling sugar to the warehouse
-A valley of impatient cacti speckled black by the toxic ash coming from Ternium.
- A violoncello with bullets in its belly
- A slouched mountain
- A slouched and half-bald child with shattered imaginings welling in his chest.

And as La Tortuga drifted off to sleep, she imagined she was fixing her friends.

Pillows for the cold

For a few days, the cold got even worse. It became barbed, pungent, reckless. To the south of the city, the Popocatepetl volcano was now overlain with a smart hat of snow. In the city centre, people hunched completely over. As though curling into tight walking balls would offer them more warmth. Scarves covered the lower halves of their faces, and their eyes looked out from above them with defensive squints. The trains worked out of obligation only. There were no pigeons. They must have been hiding in the city's secret and hidden corners. The parks became crisp and unapproachable, and the sky seemed smaller and went unnoticed without its usual wash of sunlight.

La Tortuga had just finished fixing a small rice cooker, and she showed the client that it was working by connecting it to an outdoor electricity socket. It had only taken her fifteen minutes, but the man appreciated the efficiency and was clearly relieved and impressed. He paid her 50 pesos - her highest payment yet - around US$2.50. Immediately, La Tortuga packed up her bundle of tools and her sign and headed to the second-hand and wholesale market to the east of the Zócalo.

The night before, she had tried to sleep in the sheltered walkway in front of the city's government buildings. She had used her pillow case to keep her head warm. Silly old limpiadora, said the shred of Enrique that still lived in her head. But he was silent when she watched a man sleeping nearby, a deep cut on his inner thigh with a banana skin covering it as an improvised bandage. A police officer peed on that man, waking him and dislodging the banana skin. La Tortuga got up and moved on again.

She slept in bursts, tugging at sleep and holding onto it for faint pieces of time, then releasing and looking around drearily for danger. At around 4 a.m. the coldness peaked, and she walked around to warm herself until 7 a.m, when the sun rose and the temperature finally became tolerable.

Real winter would start in a month, and sleeping at night would get even harder. She would have to try what she had seen some others doing, and stuff newspaper in her clothing as padding against the cold tiles and concrete. Since she couldn't carry a blanket around everywhere, she needed a long thick coat.

The man in the second-hand market who sold her the coat was her age, and quiet. Unlike other street sellers nearby, he wasn't yelling out prices or holding a product out to each person and grazing them with it as they passed. So she settled on his stall; two spread out black plastic bin bags covered in a scattering of old clothes. She wouldn't find out that he was a refugee too, that he was from El Salvador and had spent over a year living in a bunk bed in a crowded migrant shelter for men, making boats and trains from wood scraps to pass the time. If she had struck up conversation, he might have given her the direct phone number of the shelter coordinator. But she saw her coat and she wanted him to sell it to her as cheap as possible, and he asked for twenty-five pesos, and she offered twenty.

The coat was felt wool and designed to be knee length but went down to La Tortuga's ankles. It was an ugly grey, with a torn side pocket that she would sew up, and a collar that jutted out like stiff wings from the sides of her neck. Its sleeves fell ten centimetres past the ends of her fingers, and she was glad because now her hands would be okay. When she put the hood over her head and walked off, she looked like ET, with her feet visible and waddling along under all the coat.

ET-Tortuga came across a tamale cart. The dense steam rising from the metal pots of chicken, chilli, and pork tamales and chocolate atole was a beacon of gentle warmth that day, attracting people as though to an important outdoor caucus. She bought a ten-peso jalapeño and cheese tamale and went to Soledad Square to eat it, sitting on a cube of concrete that had been erected to stop cars from entering the square. The sun hit the cube from an angle, giving it a seat of sunlight.

She unwrapped the corn husks and the steam dog-kissed her chin. The corn dough was soft but held its shape. Like a palm-sized yellow pillow. The tamale gave her an image. She was warm and wrapped in corn husks like it had been. She was in a bed wrapped in sheets and blankets right up to her head.

Then as each bite travelled down her throat and heated her stomach, the image expanded.

There were three pillows on the bed; one for her head, one for her aching upper body, and one to cuddle.

There was a large window and pot plants of cacti, herbs, and flowers.

There was a bedside table with a book she was reading on it, and a woven basket for her keys.

The door to the room locked. She could go home and close it behind her and be safe and alone.

She would lie on the bed and breathe in the sunlit quietness. Like sitting down after a marathon that had lasted 73 years.

She would finally be able to assemble the summaries of life, colourful conclusions and insights that she had stored over her decades of living.

A room would give her space to think. It would let her be okay. It was like a placeholder, announcing La Tortuga had a spot where she lived, where she kept her stuff. She existed.

"One step at a time," she said out loud.

"Doable," her alebrije said in its breathy, tiny voice. It glowed pink for a moment, just like La Tortuga's cheeks, and flapped its wings.

La Tortuga had been talking to tradespeople and customers and had learned that a room in a poorer area like Iztapalapa or Pantitlán, at the top of a hill and far from bus and train stations, could cost as little as 2,000 pesos a month. It would be of bare concrete, and she would have to make sure the area didn't have an overly high crime rate. There was no point going back to similar stress to what she had experienced in Honduras. A basic room with no glass in the windows might be rented out with just one month's deposit and no reference letter or guarantor. She was only earning 80 pesos per day, but she thought that would increase with time, and in three months of sleeping on the streets, eating the bare minimum, paying four pesos a day for a toilet and a wash in a sink, she might be able to save up enough. Three months would take her to the middle of winter. She hoped one thick coat would be sufficient.

In another part of the city - where there were three-storey mansion homes and no buses, only quiet, smooth roads with people pulling into long driveways - forty men in ties and overly polished shoes and overly-polished hair lolled around a table in an upscale restaurant that had closed for their meeting.

Their moneyed smirks imitated smiles. Their glib handshakes were self-congratulatory. The people squashers increased rent prices, converted more homes into short term and vacation rentals, and bought out public buildings, parks, and nature reserves to convert them into housing developments. They harnessed their economic power and sent out sent out cold winds. The winds infiltrated the city, slammed home doors shut, and blew the poor out to the farthest edges of the city. Ice air infested the city's nerves and people spent sleepless nights worrying. The people squashers collected their spoils of the war on the poor.

The last of La Tortuga's tamale was cold. It froze in her hands. Her nose went red cold, and she covered it with her long coat sleeves.

By the end of that day she had sixty pesos saved in the secret pocket of her bag.

A cachectic world

Cachexia: The weakness and wasting away of the body due to a serious chronic illness. Symptoms included fatigue, muscle loss, loss of appetite.

Wind-up people in the market yelled over and over, "What would you like to buy!" A man's face was hacked off by national guards and left by the side of the road. The private water company sent most of the water to the car factories and mines and then it overcharged people who didn't have enough water to wash with. Hungry people licked at the subtle shadows of rust. People without jobs were pushed into the river where they drifted to the bottom, and people in yachts sailed over the top of them and drank cocktails. People sought consolation in consumerism, hoping the little prizes they brought home would soften the blow of unacknowledged hurt and an illogical world. But the pain didn't vanish away into nothing, instead it was relocated elsewhere. It manifested, like a teleported storm, as disinterest, road rage, hurtled abuse, addictions, sort-of friendships and tasks half done, as bus drivers who sped past the people anxiously waving them down, and as children dying by suicide. Soft people developed hard skin. Fatigued adults declined poetry.

The woman who could fix anything

Over the next week, La Tortuga fixed a selfie stick for 25 pesos, a small electric oven for 60 pesos, a hair trimmer for 40 pesos, a rat park with spinning wheels for 15 pesos, crooked glasses for 15 pesos, a leaking gas tank connection for 30 pesos, a hearing aid for 70 pesos, four different watches for 50 pesos each, a drone for 55 pesos, a bike for 125 pesos, a pair of jeans that didn't fit well for 20 pesos, a smashed porcelain cup for 10 pesos, a mole grinder for 30 pesos, a sick pet kestrel for 75 pesos, a two-metre long etching press for 100 pesos, and a few other items.

Over that one week, word spread that there was a woman who could fix anything charging low prices by the Zócalo. Some people brought tools she needed, and she took those out of the price and her tool bag grew. They brought their broken prized possessions wrapped in shawls on the train, or wheeled them over on trolleys or carts, or hauled them in bags on their shoulders or heads. They approached the workers waiting with their signs and they said, "I'm looking for the *señora* who can fix anything." And the workers would grudgingly nod in La Tortuga's direction. Other customers didn't trust the rumours and they saw an old woman as a risk. They were in too much of a hurry to try out their machines and gadgets on her, so they paid more to the men nearby. But others loved a good urban myth and were happy to queue up to see her. There were also people who expected someone else when they imagined the Woman Who Can Fix Anything, and walked straight past La Tortuga, looking for her left and right and up and down, their public neck exercises conveying their confusion. La Tortuga kept her head down and dodged the attention she was getting. She focused on her work and willed the queues to be shorter, as she didn't want to attract the police. They might tell her to move on or ask for the ID or visa she didn't have.

That week, La Tortuga made 749 pesos, but gave up a third on new tools. She had to spend most of the rest of her earnings on urgent things that came up. The sorts of urgent things that only seemed to happen to the poor. The soles came off her cheap shoes because of all the walking she did, and ironically, they were of too poor quality and too wrecked for her to fix them, so she bought new cheap ones. Those immediately developed grates as well. New crisp tart edges, shrill shine, they opened for winks of time and pierced her feet quickly with their tips. Grids of tiny blood balls formed. They pierced the same place again and again, ensuring her feet were always stippled with blood. Resilience and sprightliness and problem-solving skills leaked and trickled out of the grid of holes in the soles of her feet.

Her lack of proper sleep was also affecting her, and combined with not eating enough, lowering her immunity and causing ongoing respiratory infections. The medication cost 180 pesos a box. She bought one small, bottled water a day, but it would have been cheaper if she had somewhere to live and could buy a water filter instead, or the 20-litre *garrafones* of water.

Today she was also thinking about requesting asylum. She didn't know how or where to do it, but she had heard that she had just thirty days after entering the country to do so. But given that her ID had been stolen and she knew most requests were denied or held up by red tape, with seventy percent of refugees who applied giving up after six months, it seemed more useful to spend her time working and saving up for a room.

She was fixing a heavy-duty padlock with a stuck key when a middle-aged man cradling a watch with a broken metal band, approached. La Tortuga saw his angry and flushed cheeks and a tinge of hatred in the way his eyes were narrowed, and put herself on guard, while giving the man a gentle smile. Something had probably just happened to him and his watch. Perhaps someone had tried to rob him.

"Where's that accent from then?" he barked at her. "I can tell you're not from around here. Why don't you go back to the jungle," he said. The people standing around watched on with neutral, inert expressions. La Tortuga gave him a small nod of acknowledgement, and then focused back on the padlock. She fiddled with it, put it to her ear as she made slight adjustments, and tried to work out the problem. Fuming, the man snatched the padlock out of her hand and slammed it into her foot.

"Go back to your country, stupid witch," he yelled. Pain clenched her foot, turned off her eyes for a moment, but she remained quiet. She took off her new cheap shoe and her very old, frayed sock, and held her foot tightly around its middle as though to stop the hard flames from shooting up her leg. Her big toenail was smashed. She didn't want to let it turn black, so she fixed her own toe. She took her needle-nose pliers and plucked out the loose pieces of nail. One larger piece had to be peeled off. Onlookers walked away. The grates in both her shoes retreated also. Their work had been done by someone else for now. The owner of the padlock picked it up off the ground and took it to one of the other workers. La Tortuga cut a hole in her sock for the toe, then put it on, but she left her shoe off for now. She knew she would be less picky that night in choosing somewhere to sleep. A new person approached, but on seeing the shoeless foot and raw and bloody toe, changed direction.

La Tortuga now had 120 pesos in the secret pocket of her bag.

All the things a tourist can't see

When Harry got to the TAPO bus terminal he only walked around it half a time before someone noticed his confused and overwhelmed tourist face and showed him the bus company that went to Cholula. Within minutes, he had bought his bus ticket, found his departure lounge, and bought a small pizza and a slice of cake for the two-hour trip.

Cholula had first been settled by the Olmecs 2,500 years ago, though its pyramid was even older. It was taken over by the Toltecas, and in 1519 Spain's Hernán Cortés massacred six thousand Indigenous Choluteca people there, including many spiritual and political leaders,

The Eyes of the Earth

in just a few days, as he made his way to the Aztec capital. Now it was a historic and student city near Puebla, to the south of Mexico City.

Harry was looking forward to a bright and full feeling of amazement as he explored a new city. He wanted to eat a big lunch with a view of the pyramid, then do some busking in a busy tourist area. He also hoped to find an unusual souvenir that he could show to friends and family later as evidence that he had immersed himself in local culture.

When he finally stood in front of the pyramid, he felt underwhelmed. It was the biggest in the world by base size, but most of it was covered in dry grass and stubbly trees. He saw a symmetrical hill, rather than an architectural marvel. There were some stairs and altar platforms sticking out from the greenery to his right, but he didn't see the museum entrance around the side where a system of tunnels took people through the internal layers of the pyramid. A wide and steep path curved up the pyramid-hill to the top, where the Our Lady of Remedies Church sat, as though perched upon a high throne. Harry's forehead and back sweated as he walked swiftly up the path and paused, every few minutes, to look back at the increasingly beautiful view of the city below.

At the top, he sat on the brick fence that wrapped around the courtyard and the amber church and caught his breath. He untied his mind. Like it were a dog eager to play, he let it go free. One of Harry's roughly guarded secrets was that he felt happiest and unrestrained when daydreaming. He often pictured a tortoise with a bushy mauve monkey tail, and he didn't know why. Now, his un-roped mind imagined the moment the pyramid had been finished. There was a party. Tiny dragon pets and land octopuses danced with the children, while adults drank unsweetened chocolate. Flowers ran about in imitation of lizards, on their tiptoes.

And the past nudged at him. Again. It insisted on accuracy. He opened his eyes, but he couldn't hear or see it. The things that had happened before weren't noted on the walls of the Spanish church.

The Quetzalcoatl temple that used to stand there until the Spanish built their Christian one in its place, couldn't shout or wave at him. Its long-lasting party had been quashed. All around Cholula and Mexico, the Spanish had built churches over temples, declaring with brick words, that Indigenous people were the Past. Harry couldn't see that violence and domination could be counted in churches, though he had read on the bus that Cholula had one of the highest concentrations in Mexico.

On his way back down, he took photos of the quiet city and its single-storey shops and houses laid out in gentle square blocks, but he couldn't see that Cholula had been a lively cultural and religious centre for thousands of years, specialising in cotton, pottery, and jewellery production.

Now, business people were jamming more hotels, restaurants, and shopping centres into the city. Old family homes and neat rows of cornfields behind the pyramid were replaced by parking lots and upmarket cafes. Local activists had been arrested just a few years ago for trying to stop the construction of a tourist train station at the southern corner of the pyramid, on top of archaeological relics.

Back at the bottom, a woman selling edible crickets approached Harry and asked him in English how he liked the area.

"It's beautiful," he said.

"This area has a very long history…" she started to explain. But he stopped her. Excited to speak English, he told her that he was staying in Mexico City. That the bus trip had taken a little longer than he thought. He piled his words on top of hers. Unaware, he imitated the patterns of churches built on the ruins of Indigenous temples. He couldn't see how he made her exist a little less.

Harry took a photo of himself eating the chilli and garlic-flavoured crickets, then he wandered around the souvenir and street food stalls that lined the square to the side of the pyramid. In the middle of the square, there was a thirty-metre-high pole. It had a capstan and a square frame at the top, with rungs all the way up it. Harry wondered what the pole was for but was distracted by blue and white hand-painted

Talavera plates at one stall, then by an emerald-coloured restaurant behind it serving one-litre micheladas. All the stalls had fake terracotta roofs forged from spray-painted metal sheets. Quick culture simulation. History reduced to handbags, necklaces, and little plastic pyramids. Harry saw embroidered peacock table covers, but he didn't know they were made by Indigenous women in Chiapas and that most of the profits went to the middlepeople who brought them up to Puebla state. He saw key rings and dream catchers, but didn't know they were made in China, Bolivia, and Peru. He couldn't see the difference between handcrafts made in bulk in factories and those made by people trying to keep their identities alive.

As he browsed the stalls, the white lace curtains that constantly engulfed him and his sight were bothering him, and he swatted at them. Between them though, he caught glimpses of stall workers regarding him with subtle amounts of weariness. He saw how they adjusted their posture and alertness when he looked closer at an item, and the way they resumed their old position when he walked on. Hypocrisy hovered in the air, a bullying dark grey cloud, ruining things and casting out grumpy moods among the people. The cloud was fed by the business people and municipal government using Indigenous culture as a tourist draw card while the local Nahua people weren't consulted on any policies. They earned an income by selling snacks from metal buckets on the fringes of the main tourist area.

Harry walked through the dark grey clouds, feeling their presence, tasting charcoal, but not yet able to identify them. His eyes grazed the surface of the pretty trinkets, and for a moment he did notice the business forces quivering in the air, and the calculations and profits. But he couldn't yet see how culture distribution had become an unpoetic ode to the times of colonial tempers and looting, refashioned as a common transaction in the present. A horrid plastic coagulation filled people's hearts, where their stories, memories, and identities were meant to be.

Harry didn't buy anything in the end, but he did go to the emerald-walled restaurant for lunch, then he tried to busk for a while in the square. A few people stopped to watch, but at a distance that made it easy for them to walk away. Harry saw their reluctance, but he continued performing his tricks. After a couple of people gave him some money, another busker, a street performer gladiator in golden pants, approached. He was part of the mafia who managed public space in the area and collected fees from people who wanted to work there. He told Harry a permit would cost him 60 pesos a day, and when Harry didn't understand, he put his hand on his shoulder and quietly escorted him over to the side to explain.

The Harry who caught the bus back to Mexico City felt murky, and a little off. Like the world had lost three colours and two degrees of magic and he himself had lost some shine. His eyes hurt. He rubbed them and could feel the strange texture of all the little holes in them. Upon removing his hands, everything was hazy. He scolded himself for having mishoped. That was the label he stuck to a day that hadn't gone as he had imagined. As a result, he lowered his expectations for his next outing a few notches. He was discouraged and took that out on his Life Standards.

Cholula was his fourth busking session. Harry now had a total of 550 pesos from busking.

Birdmen

There were Indigenous Mexicans who could fly. But they preferred to fly upside-down, looking at the sky. Four or five would climb up a thirty-metre pole, then sit on the square frame suspended from the capstan and tie a rope around their waist. They fell backwards, their arms free, and their feet holding on to the rope, and they spun around the pole thirteen times. Sometimes a fifth person sat on top of the pole, playing a flute as the others fell and spun and flew about. Other times, one of the four would play the flute as he flew. Their circles around the pole became bigger and bigger as they neared the ground.

The thirteen circles multiplied by the four flying men became fifty-two; the number of years in a round of the Xiuhmolpilli calendar. The ritual was a thousand years old, and the meaning, details, and clothing varied from town to town, but it was mostly performed in central Mexico by the Nahuas and Totonacos. In Cuetzalan, the pole represented the tree of life, and in Papantla, the flying was a greeting to the sun. In both cases, the air-dance was a way of asking for rain. The four birdmen represented the four cardinal points, and the flute was birdsong. As the men spun around the pole they interpreted a regeneration of life that rain would bring.

But there were other reasons for flying upside-down.

- From above, as their circles got increasingly bigger, they looked like a flower opening up.

- Perhaps they were also judging the veracity of the sky and playing with possibilities.

- Or they were engraving their stories into the air, where the Spanish or other colonisers couldn't erase them. If they repeated the dance over and over, the air would have to memorise it and people could not forget who they were.

- Or they were learning that falling didn't have to be a thing of clumsiness and failure. One could fall with the greatest view of the sky.

- Certainly, they were enacting an understanding that rain fell downwards so that plants could grow upwards. They were evoking skill and strength and embodying life's processes. And revealing, for one long moment, the ingredients of magic.

A portrait of the whole world

Paintings and photos were mysterious things that reflected back to their creators how they saw.

Just before Harry left for Mexico, one of his six uncles, Sam Devin, was commissioned to paint a mural on the side of a prominent building in New York. He was told to paint a portrait of humanity.

But Sam Devin also had spongy skin and squeaky holes and curtained sight. The history he had been taught was missing whole continents. The movies and shows he saw skipped over harsh realities and disproportionately displayed US and European characters and the lives of those similar to Harry's school and college friends.

The news he heard was potholed with the giant absence of Mexican journalists, female international politics experts, Aboriginal historians, and Syrian analysts. In the course of his life, he never heard from women factory unionists from the Philippines, the grandmothers of Argentina, slam poets of Canada, Nigerian philosophers, Turkish novelists, Iran vase painters, South African water rights campaigners, Trova composers, or Zimbabwean sculptors.

Beasts in the System of Monsters called rubbish ranters set up strange standards for music and art galleries and fashion. And they appointed special censors to argue that the poor were not qualified to comment on their own poverty.

After six weeks, Sam Devin finished his painting. His portrait of humanity was a pink, grey, and white image of a man's face. Passersby became drowsy and got headaches from the lack of colour. A poet gave-up. A kindergarten teacher stopped caring. Pigeons flew into the mural and got stuck in that icky feeling produced when gloss and shine was smothered over mediocrity.

The jagged texture of one friendship

After his turbid sightseeing, Harry was still feeling a little off, and that was translating into not guessing time well. He woke up thinking the day had started, only to check and realise it was 4 a.m. His self-esteem had bruises. He wanted reassurance. And once the day really did start, he got up and sought it like one looking for misplaced keys, dashing about the hostel and starting conversations that he hoped would make him feel better. Empty handed though, he gave up and went out, only to spot La Tortuga in her usual place. He didn't know why he found it hard to just approach her and ask her how she was. Instead, he turned with his back to her and reached into his bag and broke the nose pads of his mirrored sunglasses.

La Tortuga stood on her toes to give Harry a hug greeting. He was taken aback and got his Spanish phrases mixed up, saying, "Mucho gusto." La Tortuga didn't react to the mistake, but grinned at him and told him it was nice to see him again. Such an affectionate greeting could have been enough for the quota of reassurance that Harry needed, but he pressed for more. As she worked on his sunglasses, he used his phone to say, "It's been hard here. Things aren't quite what I expected."

La Tortuga was still not getting much sleep, her toe was aching, and her shoes, at that moment were nonchalantly gnawing at her feet. But she said, "Being a new person in a new place is always hard. Don't give up, you can do it."

Now totally reassured, Harry remembered to ask her, "Como estás?"

"Estoy bien, todo bien," she replied, patting his hand, then placing the fixed sunglasses in it.

This time, he paid. And to keep him a little longer, she asked him about something that had been in the newspapers a lot lately. What did he think about the bilateral talks between the US and Mexican presidents?

"I don't know, I haven't really been following the news lately. What do you think?" He asked, following the script of standard conversations, but not expecting her to say much.

However, she talked for quite a while. About the pressure the US was putting on Mexico to tighten its southern border and to accept foreign corporate spending in its energy sector, and how Mexico was navigating the pressure, reluctant to annoy the US too much.

Harry was surprised. He watched his phone translating it all and thought she might just be repeating things she had read. She couldn't understand things like this. He looked back at her but saw instead a cardboard cutout saying vague words. He squinted and leaned in closer, but the cutout faded and he could not hear her. He nodded. Diplomatically. Worried, he checked his eyesight by looking around, at things further away. Most people had become colourless figurines, dimming in and out, barely there.

La Tortuga felt herself disappearing this time. Her bones became lighter and baby winds curled and looped about in her face, her stomach, glad to have a new space to play in. But they felt chilly for La Tortuga, who was already too cold, who had taken to wearing her giant coat during the day also. At Harry's rhythmic nodding in her direction she tried to keep talking, but the words repelled off him and came back to her all boring and lifeless, so she gathered them all up and stuffed them back inside her. She stopped talking. Harry's alebrije, perched on his shoulder, had turned its back to her and was playing games with yellow balls, laughing as it tried to juggle and catch them.

La Tortuga suddenly felt overcome by worry. Harry didn't seem to be as harmless as she had first thought. There was a latent, ugly power residing in him. Waiting to be activated.

Harry mumbled an excuse, fist pumped La Tortuga goodbye, and left. She smiled at his back, hoping like that to somehow repair the ill feelings. Their little friendship, barely getting started, was already wrought with dents and snags.

Who has more freedom?

Every year, one hundred million monarch butterflies from across southern Canada migrated 3,200 kilometres to the world's biggest and quietest gathering held in a small section of the mountains of central Mexico.

Born in Canada, a new generation of butterflies endured deadly rainstorms, predators, and tough winds as they flew eighty kilometres a day. They crossed the Great Lakes - expanses of water so large they couldn't see the end of them, then flew over the US industrial belt, through small midwestern towns, over hundreds of kilometres of scalding desert, then followed the Sierra Madre mountain range down to Mexico for 1,500 kilometres.

They spent the winter in Mexico. The forest kept the heat in and the rain away from them, and to stay extra warm the butterflies hugged the trees in trunk clusters. They became papaya-coloured ponchos dressing the trees, which seemed to stand as a still rally of wise and sturdy beings.

A warmer midday arrived, and the ponchos broke apart. Canyon confetti against a cyan sky. Dusk, and a heavy butterfly cloud settled again on the trees, re-holstering the forest in orange.

Indigenous Mexicans in the area saw the monarchs as representing or carrying the souls of the dead, since they arrived in early November, for the Day of the Dead ceremonies.

And so it was that the dead, having flown across borders, had more freedom than the living.

The concrete canopy

La Tortuga woke up with small-grief. The sinking feeling from the chat with Harry a few days ago had persisted and festered itself into a new concern that she also wasn't seeing well. As her eyes wandered the concrete underbelly of the highway above her, she reflected that she was losing her sense of the world to the daily grind of working and constantly looking for somewhere to sleep.

The last few days she had been sleeping on the paved area next to an overpass wingwall. Though it was dry season, it reassured her to have the shelter above her. There was a tap she could use to wash her face and brush her teeth, and at night few people walked past. But the lights of the cars made her feel safe enough to fully lie down and sleep, using her bag as a pillow. Her coat kept her warm, though barely.

Now, still lying down, she closed her eyes in order to see. She drew back from her own tough days and looked at the city from a distance.

Beyond the ongoing circus of rubbish, each bit of it performing cartwheels as it rode the low curls of wind coming from the traffic, there was a lot of intangible waste. She could tell the tradespeople who set up near her wished they could be with their children or singing or playing football instead of waiting for hours for clients to turn up. She named all the intangible waste she had seen or perceived recently. Life missed out on by women who were scared of the streets at night. Story time gone as the funding for libraries went to arms manufacturing. Murals stuck in the dry throats of miners who wanted to paint splendid things but the only source of employment in their town was the dark belly of copper caves. Hopes, dreams, and long hugs buried under steep, khaki-brown mountains of bureaucracy and corruption. Mountains made of excuses so the insurance wouldn't be paid out and the sewage never fixed, and the homes lost to earthquakes never rebuilt. Forests were hacked down into deserts and drummers, inventors and comedians lost their creativity to daily unpaid overtime in jobs they took to pay the interest on their mortgages and for child care and to have the safety of certainty. La Tortuga saw the deserts and the unpaid overtime, and they were the same thing.

Society's lost learnings, she said. When some people died, they left behind a trail of memories and wisdom that was taken up by others. But there were so many people who died without having a way to pass on their discoveries and experiences. They were never written about or interviewed or listened to, and so died without witnesses to their blazing trail.

She built twenty conical piles out of the entrails of wasted time and wasted potential, along the path under the knot of highway roads. She caressed the heaps, and they softened, like a suffering man finally allowing a hug and crumpling himself into it. The way troubles, finally vented, lost all the air that was holding them up, and they weakened and wilted.

La Tortuga persuaded trees to grow out of the softness. They twisted and slow-danced out of the piles, branching up into the air and rooting down into the ground, splitting and agitating the pavement.

The street vendors who worked in the area would arrive in a few hours with their merchandise and find twenty remarkable trees. The trees had bark that had the texture of a duckling's natal down, smelled of spicy vanilla, and was egg-shell colour, speckled with magenta. Their trunks were proud columns that held old hearts within. The ends of their branches were subtle mouths spilling long white tongues that tasted the air or licked the bellies of overflying birds. A few of the trees had pine leaves and they sent their needles scaling up the highway pier columns in spirals that seemed to be trying to choke away the grey. Other trees had leaves that opened from the middle like cocktail umbrellas. Dahlia flowers grew around their base. They resembled gentle balls of fire with edible red and yellow petals.

Among these new, yet old trees, pygmy geckos surfed the leaves, and dragonflies arrived to out-race the pigeons. A black-billed streamertail hummingbird drank from the centre of the flowers, its tail ribbons curling and unfurling as it swallowed.

The last creatures to arrive were Mexico City's butterflies; Xochiquetzal and other swallowtail butterflies, Montezuma's cattleheart, and the two-barred flasher all flew in and rested on the trees, exhausted. Their populations had halved over the last few decades as the concrete city had expanded and parks disappeared. The butterflies, happy to have found an oasis, fed, then explored delicately and hastily.

La Tortuga's alebrije joined them. It flapped its ear-wings and moved from one branch to another, listening to the trees' tones and anxieties. What it heard was noted and funnelled into its shell, which grew a little taller. La Tortuga's finger tips became warm and a pleasant heat reached her eyes and lips. Every few days she was moving to new sleeping spots. So she wanted to keep a little of this for herself, to have by her while she tried to sleep, something to come back to at the end of the day. So she cut a Coke bottle in half, poked a few holes in the bottom with a blade, filled it with dirt and some water, and cut a dahlia flower at the end of the stem, then stuck that in the dirt. A Bit of Life just for her.

She gathered all her things quickly, organising her bag and wrapping her coat around it as she hurried down the road. She was late, and she hoped no one had taken her working spot. Her alebrije ran after her, sweating, colliding with street poles and legs. La Tortuga's stomach rumbled, and her biceps and wrist muscles were sore. She licked her dry lips. They tasted salty, like subtle regret. The energy she used up for the magic, combined with the lack of proper sleep, had left her at half energy. She would earn much less today.

As she crossed at the intersection, the street vendors arrived at the paved area by the overpass. They brought their ice-blocks, boxes of chewing gum, rolly-polly penguins, and hand-made plastic rope rocking chairs to sell to spontaneous buyers in cars stopped at the traffic light. Within minutes they had unfolded their tables around the new trees and hung tarps and ropes and signs from them, hung their bags up in them, stored their Coca-Cola bottles in the branch forks, nailed "10 pesos" signs into the natal-down bark. Parents set up their babies and toddlers in cardboard boxes for the day. Traffic on the highway stopped. Cars were stuck, aligned in tight-knit grids like metallic road tiles. Their smog joined with the smog of industry and coloured the air a matt granite grey. The smog was pervasive and insidious, as though acting in representation of the copper mines, the arms industry, and violent corruption. The trees with their old hearts, were nowhere to be seen.

The Eyes of the Earth

The system of monsters: Wing pluckers

There were also wing pluckers in the club of beasts and monsters. They made and monitored the borders, letting the tourists and wealthier people pass through, but blocking refugees and the migrants that were barely staying alive. They specialised in the creation of intangible waste. They sent the migrants on non-journeys with leaky boats, and pointless journeys where they deported them from the US-Mexico border after they had walked for months. They built prisons and institutionalised shoe grates. Harnessing the powers of borders, of poverty walls, of barbed wired racism, they sent out sneaky electrical currents that targeted the shoes of people who were forced to walk, and activated shoe grates. When migrants got closer to the borders, the grates opened all the way. They snarled. Their slashing sped up. They turned young feet and child feet and the music teacher's feet into mince meat.

And so the borders made a sound. They snarled too, and they emitted drawn out screams, like those of heavy vehicles in never-ending car crashes. The land at the borders hissed, all the dirt and dust and vacant air howled contempt, the shrubs were stingy and spat resentment. The border lines hated so hard that they festered, bubbled over with pus.

The wing pluckers were pleased. Great job, they told each other. Then they made phone calls and plans. Soon, they would hold a meeting to prepare their PR strategy for the upcoming exclusive monsters' summit.

Leaking hope

A globe of many gashes
Gushing
Disgorged dreams.

The migrant: Darwin

The last thing Darwin did at the migrant shelter before he left was organize a wood shavings carpet on the roof of the shelter, to help distract the migrants from missing their family over Easter. A big man with a quiet demeanour, he outlined a dove with chalk, then got the other migrants to colour the shavings celeste, cobalt blue and white.

Darwin had gotten sheet metal work in Mexico City. Then he was fired from that job, robbed, then fired again from a second job. So he moved to the north of the country where many undocumented migrants got work in the foreign-owned factories. He had work for three months, but when a machine broke, the owners blamed the Honduran, and he was fired again. The next day, his father died and he had to send what money he had back to Honduras for the funeral. For a month, he looked for more work, until finally he was hired in another factory. After two weeks, they fired him, saying he didn't have a Mexican tax number. He had wanted to stay in Mexico, but unable to pay rent, he had no choice but to cross the border into the US. It was closed to all refugees and migrants, with the Covid-19 pandemic as the excuse. He waited in Piedras Negras for days for fog, rain, or strong winds to come so that he could cross when there were no border security drones flying about. When he finally attempted to cross the border, he was kidnapped. He was kept in a dark room and beaten every few hours. The kidnappers demanded US$7,000, which his family eventually paid after getting a loan. During his first few years in the US, Darwin worked to pay off that loan, and sent any other money he could to his children.

The US$7,000 was divided among the various people involved in his kidnapping, including taxi and bus drivers who worked with the kidnappers, local police that the kidnappers paid off, the torturers, those who guarded the victims and those who managed payments. Sometimes the torturers killed the migrants even after families sent them the money, then the criminal gang requested more money, pretending the victim was still alive.

The wing pluckers snarled and watched on as thousands of migrants and refugees were kidnapped in Mexico or at the border, and none of those kidnappings were investigated. The authorities were usually complicit, so migrants never felt like they could denounce any abuses. Ransoms were sent via credit agencies, who were legally required to note large transactions, but they never did. They were making too much money from the kidnapping industry.

And so it went - the credit industry benefited from the kidnapping industry, which benefited from the borders, which were key to the profits of the arms industry, which in turn supplied organised criminals. Those criminals were just business people in the human trafficking industry, which made annual global profits of US$150 billion.

When the world was a playground

Harry had small-sorrow tickling his throat. Dents and snags now accompanied his lowered expectations. His spongy holes were enlarging rather than shrinking with time. He was confused because things were meant to work out more quickly than this. Instead, the small-sorrow began to deteriorate into a more profound disappointment. It was edging on life-sized, and Harry didn't want to deal with that.

So he left it behind for a week. He bought a plane ticket to Antigua, Guatemala for the next day, and told himself it would be time-out from serious tourism. From planning, organising, and considering the best things to do in the best way. One week of suspending reality, shedding goals and consequences, and indulging in disregard.

And because it was so last minute, he called himself spontaneous and adventurous. He toyed with the word 'brave', though buying the flight online had been easy, and he could afford the forty-minute taxi trip from the airport to Antigua. Because he was from the US, he only had to fill out a tourist visa form on the two-hour plane trip.

His plane landed at the La Aurora International Airport. He didn't have a plan, except that he was going to gorge on food and laze in a hotel bath. His alebrije's eyes glazed over and it wore a silly grin.

Antigua had been the capital of Guatemala from 1541 to 1776, when Guatemala City became the capital after a series of earthquakes. Now, the small city of 45,000 inhabitants, pastel homes and symmetrical volcanoes, was Guatemala's top tourist destination. There were tour groups huddling like penguins outside most of the main churches, and unattached tour guides hovered around the main crossings, following the un-grouped tourists with promises of the cheapest city walks. Set among the photogenic rustic structures, there were hotels, restaurants, launderettes, tour operators, discotecas, and souvenir shops charging prices that tourists could afford but Guatemalans couldn't.

Dollars, euros, and poverty had dragged starving farmers and Indigenous rural workers away from their communities and remodelled them into waiters and souvenir sellers. A child who sold popcorn outside restaurants at night eventually became a tour guide working fifteen-hour days, seven days a week.

Harry avoided the tours. He spent up on a four-star hotel suite, drank piña coladas and tequila sunrises and tried all the beers on the craft beer menus in the pubs with rooftop terraces. He frolicked and cavorted, gawked and ambled in the town-turned-theme park. He walked among the hot dog grease smell, the taste of butter and sugar, the lollipop colours infused with impatience, the sweaty shoppers walking their wallets on a long leash behind them. He ate pancake piles for breakfast, insisting on fresh milk with his coffee and reprimanding any waiters who brought powdered milk. Take-away containers and pizza boxes awaiting midday cleaners amassed by his room door.

Out in the streets, theme park mentality changed visitors into whiny children wanting every ride. The whole city a money-making stage with bold colours of paint smeared on building fronts like clownface. Stained in forced grin to attract tourists. The gushy colours of this toyland pretenced cheerful because that attracted more money. It was a fondant facade and the streets a marketing device for the tourism industry.

Harry walk-floated on his white hiking boots into a church as a funeral service was getting started, and stood by the altar taking photos. Across the road, a McDonald's had been embedded into the exteriors of a baroque building. Inside though, the plastic chairs were still slippery and the smell still clung to clothing. Harry chewed gum to counter the stirring heaviness in his chest, and left the wrappers wedged into the intricate curls of decorative lamp posts. Around him, the streets made sounds. The muffled ching of a cash register, the murmur of an ATM. He strolled about, looking for selfies. He took photos standing in front of people wearing traditional clothing, and he walked off without a nod at them. In one museum and out again, into the tobacco company and the chocolate company and another church. Merry-go-round, roller coaster, Ferris wheel of fun. Consume the town in just a few days.

On the last night, Harry drank all the beer and quetzalteca he could, then staggered through the streets looking for more Fun. But it was a quiet Monday night, and the city responded with silence to his rantings of provocation. In a small park, he saw an old man selling ten canary-yellow selfie sticks. He walked hunched over and slowly, waving his sticks at the people he saw five seconds after they passed him. His back ached, but he needed to sell the remaining sticks before he could go home. There, he would write offhanded poems in a scrapbook of the half-formed thoughts that pestered him. He never got to editing and refining them, but showed his ruminations to his wife who read them patiently, while wishing he would also notice that her own heart was overworked.

Harry was drawn to the colours of the man's woven vest. Then his drunken eyes saw pigeons singing and he laughed rhythmically. Laugh pause laugh pause, because everyone knew pigeons only existed during the day. That was hilarious. So were the hotels by the park with their lights on and silhouettes of people passing by windows. Silly silhouettes. He pointed his finger at them and wagged his finger. He looked back at the man and imagined he must be the exact same age as La Tortuga. And the same height. He laughed again. And he decided to talk to the man because now he would be able to. They would become friends and the man would like him.

Harry signalled to the man to sit next to him on the park bench, and then he told him stories in English. Also rhythmically. One story, and then another, as the man nodded politely but did not understand. Drunk Harry realised he had cracked the code to making friends. He wanted a photo with his new friend and he gave the man money for a yellow selfie stick. Enough quetzals to cover a week's earnings.

But tall, heavy, drunk Harry thought the photo would look better if he sat on the hunched man's lap. He thought that was very fun and very chummy. And the man who had money now didn't feel able to object. He laughed, nervously, but his laugh wasn't rhythmic. It was half a laugh with almost no volume. Harry leaned back so that his head would be the same size as the man's in the photo, and something happened. The man's neck was pushed backward too quickly, at the wrong angle. A click tear. A half laugh stopped. The man seemed to look at the night sky, at a half moon, and to keep on looking. Harry thought he should leave the man then, contemplating the sky so deeply like that. He ran off, almost falling this way and that, but his white shoes kept him upright.

Midnight, and the park lights turned off. Nine selfie sticks rested on a park bench, lit up by a fraction of moon. A man gone too quite failed to trigger an ambulance. Pigeons that couldn't sleep, moaned. Or maybe it was the city making that drawn-out noise. Air-conditioning from a nearby hotel was exhaled over bags of rubbish in a back street. A wife waited.

Athletes

After months of walking and sleeping outdoors, the clothes of the migrants arriving at the Mexico City shelter were torn and frayed and barely there, in a blunt mimicry of their owners' state. The shelter stored donations of secondhand clothes in a cupboard with sliding doors, jeans in one section, socks in a plastic bag, t-shirts folded. The recently arrived migrants browsed the clothing, searching for their size, changing out of old clothing immediately. One day, the shelter received a donation of forty running t-shirts. They were made of textured polyester mesh and had a Gatorade logo on the back and a jogging Snoopy on the front. Forty migrants wore them on the train on their way to the immigration office.

They looked like an amateur track team about to race. One of the refugees, who had fled to Mexico by foot and bus from Colombia, commented to the others as he looked down at the Snoopy, "Can you believe that some people run for fun?"

Hazardous

Australia's border was an ocean. In 2013, the government decided that no refugee arriving by boat would be allowed to settle in Australia. Instead, they were sent to the remote islands of Nauru and Manus. Refugees spent years in those burning-hot prison camps, far away from lawyers and the media, and sleeping in mouldy tents. The refugees said they feared they would die there, or be forgotten and become non-people.

Wing pluckers systematically patrolled the sea and cleaned it of fishing boats full of refugees. They overlooked the chemicals dumped there by the mining industry, and the waste discharged by corporations. They left behind the 9,000 pieces of plastic per square kilometre of sea.

Sides

Migrants travelling through Mexico often talked about when they were going to "*pasar al otro lado*" (pass to the other side). Like struggling Latin America was on one side of the US-Mexican border, and paradise on the other.

But the migrants who made it past the desert, the borders, and prisons, didn't find the version of life they were hoping for. They sought reasonable stress levels and pay that was high enough to let them sleep sometimes. But in the US as well, paradise was for a rich minority, and migrants ended up working 14-hour days, again.

Stamina

It was so cold that La Tortuga felt her eyes hardening. Her nose wanted to be runny but the snot was freezing and getting stuck. Her coat wasn't enough. Scared, uncomfortable, shivering, she was finding it hard to sleep again. So she wandered out into the petulant night, hoping to stumble on a solution. It wasn't long before she came across a blanket by a wall. Steeped with black dust and smelling of tarmac and unwashed body, it seemed abandoned, so she took it. She gave it a quick shake, and went to sleep, thinking she would wash it well in the morning and let it dry next to her work spot. But after an hour, she woke up to a line of itchiness around her waist. The line stung, raged, like a narky and prickly vine belted around her. She would have scratched and gone back to sleep, if a single car hadn't passed by and grazed its headlights briefly over her body. The light revealed two bed bugs running along her lower arm. She squashed them between her nails.

But now she was stuck between an intense need to sleep, and inability to. Her eyes opened wide. White round plates of horror. She realised the bed bugs would already be settling into her only change of clothing. She jumped up and flung the blanket off. Frustrated, she stomped her feet. She was on the brink of a temper. Why not lose it,

The Eyes of the Earth

there in the middle of the night when no one was watching. She curled her hands into strategic cat paws. Stretch marks glowed red on the folds of her brain. There was a pile of dead tortillas slunk by the base of the building next to her. They had stiffened into the shape they had hit the floor in. She brought her foot down on them and crunch, they became smithereens. It was all just too hard it was impossible. She slammed her foot down on the smithereens and made powder.

Her cat paws unfurled.

Somewhat vented and painfully cold again, La Tortuga paced. It was too late, she'd have to get new second-hand clothes. That would be cheaper and easier than a full wash, since there was nowhere she could access the hot water needed to kill the bugs and no way she could stand naked all day in a toilet cubicle waiting for her clothes to dry. Handle it like she had handled the walk to Mexico City, she told herself; one step at a time. Her long life had taught her not to try to achieve everything at once. And that there was no pause to the problems. Expect them, solve the most urgent one, deal with the next. She had developed a stubbornness and perseverance that were part of surviving. She called it Grit Mode. Emotions off, focused ahead like the car that had passed, its headlights strong in the darkness. She summoned Grit Mode and her alebrije acknowledged the call and dulled its colours and perked up its ear-wings, flooding their pink veins with a strict radiance. It activated selective listening and sight, where only the most necessary things were observed, then fed off its tall shell of things understood. La Tortuga would mobilise her learnings from all the horrid experiences over the course of her life, in order to find a way out of the cold.

Her toe hadn't healed yet, and she had gotten used to walking with a slight limp that avoided putting any pressure on it. So to stay warm, she limp-paced in circles, hugging her pot plant under her right arm, until the night was over. With day break, she went to the second-hand clothing market and spent half her savings on a change of clothes. There were no long coats, so she bought a weedy, cream-coloured cardigan. Then she spent the day visiting churches, as she had heard that some of them let migrants and homeless people sleep the night there, as long as they were out by early morning. But she went from church to church and from one 'no' and look of annoyance to the next. It reminded her of the disappearing hostel signs. By the day's end, she had found just one church where she was told, "just for tonight," and another with a waiting list full of names and no line left for hers. So that night, she slept on a floor again. She knew how to do that. And she thought that it was nice that this time, she wasn't the only one. The other people put down their things and got straight to sleep. Moonlight snuck into the church and cast bench leg shadow lines across the sleeping bodies.

There was a vague shoe print by her face. The unswept track of a previous sleeper perhaps, who had walked through city dirt and the last dregs of the rainy season. She settled into sleep, then snapped awake a few hours later when someone near her farted loudly. Back to sleep again. Her iced nose, melting, made her snore, and she snorted herself awake again fifteen minutes later.

By the next morning, she had decided that she couldn't lose whole days to looking for a church for the night, so she would have to spend more savings on a blanket. It would be cheapest to go to a fabric shop and buy 1.5 metres of grey polyester blanket material.

That night, La Tortuga was a warmed soul in a blanket cubby. Her limb hairs finally relaxed, her neck was snug, and the small moons that lay and rocked under each of her eyes were a carmine hue. Graceful heat doted on her in the shoddiness of that city street. She whispered good night to her pot plant, then passed into thick, sweet, sleep.

Until.

A dense, cold wind fell smack across her body. She opened one eye to see a police officer walking away with her blanket. Drowsy and freezing, she propped herself up on one arm. "Hey!" she squeaked. Her voice caught up in the knots of her breathing. "Hey!" she spoke a little louder, but not loud enough to reach the police officer. She could not chase him, could not risk trouble. To accompany her summoned grit, she called upon unmerited politeness. She stood up and followed him, and the police officer, sensing movement behind him, turned around. "Excuse me, I just need to know why you took my blanket?"

"Camping isn't permitted," he said flatly. "Neither are illegals like you. So scat, before I arrest you."

And La Tortuga scattered. With the cold air clinging to her now bare arms.

The police officer got into his van and took out his phone and deleted the last message on it. It was from a special 005 number, usually used by wing pluckers or people squashers.

La Tortuga was grateful. In just moments, she composed a full list of Well At Least He Didn'ts. At least he didn't try to extort me. At least he didn't hit me. At least he didn't call immigration. At least I got three hours of good sleep.

La Tortuga scattered all the way to the city centre where there were more lights and she thought, a bit more warmth, and where she might find a newspaper to stuff down her clothes and keep away the worst of the cold. Chance would have it, she found one at the top of a rubbish heap. She skim read it before tearing it up. A death that police wouldn't investigate, in Antigua, it noted. A cold front expected next week, bringing record-low temperatures. A new airport. A presidential candidate stabbed in Brazil. Poverty among the elderly increasing, and retirees forced back into working in restaurants and supermarkets. La Tortuga ripped the newspaper up into even strips and fed scrunched up balls down her shirt.

She didn't go to sleep straight away. Instead, she adjusted and tinkered with her goal for a room in three months. Like fixing things, she took pliers and hammers to her hopes and made them fit reality. A room of her own in six months, she calculated. No matter how hungry or cold she was, she had to put aside 25 pesos a day, which she then couldn't touch.

She now had four pesos in the secret pocket of her bag.

In the company of monsters

Sober Harry remembered but couldn't be sure. He added up the signs. A neck click and a man who stopped talking. Eyes that watched the moon without moving at all. Even as he had left, the eyes hadn't followed him. In an unacknowledged, unlit side-street of his brain, he realised it was likely. He tried saying, 'I wasn't very nice that night.' And then getting on with things.

But that omnipresent, unlit guilt stuck to the back of his head and affected his balance. It droned so consistently that it was hard to hear anything else.

So when he got back to Mexico City, instead of going back to his hostel, he chose escape for just a little longer. He found a three-star hotel to stay in, and when he couldn't sleep the first few nights there, he blamed the bed, and levelled up to a four-star hotel in the upper-class neighbourhood of La Condesa.

But even in the four-star hotel with its king bed and smart-phone-controlled lighting and heating, Harry couldn't sleep. With all his energy going into keeping regret and shame at bay, he was tired, slow to make decisions, and clumsy. He fell over everything. He fell out of bed when his short bursts of nightmare-sleep left him twisted in the sheets and his foot wouldn't come out. He tripped on the small step when leaving the shower, and stumbled across the bathroom floor. He fell when leaving the hotel elevator, and his foot twisted sideways when navigating the textures of footpaths. He got tangled in his bath towel and caught his long-sleeve shirt on a stair railing, and there always seemed to be some stone in his shoe that he couldn't find and that hurt his toes. His white shoes stopped him from spraining his foot or twisting his ankle, but they couldn't keep him upright all the time.

In La Condesa, the footpaths were tiled or pebbled, tree-lined, and wide enough for both outdoor dining and for people to walk around in groups. It seemed that the width of streets was proportionate to the wealth bands of the area. There were fountains in the middle of the roundabouts, trendy international bistros, casual taquerias, mini private art galleries, foreign fashion brand shops with backlit window displays, bars and clubs with polished wood floors and dress codes in the commercial part of the suburb, and four-storey homes with front yards and tall fences in the residential area. In most other urban areas, buildings with ten units or more had a front door that opened directly onto the street.

Along the middle of one of the main roads, there was a long park lined with trimmed bushes, and people strolled, walked their dogs, and rode their bikes there. There were stalls where people sold handmade bread or designer jewellery. Harry set up between two of the stalls. He was behind in his busking goals, so his plan was to spend three hours instead of two doing tricks. He made 650 pesos. Then he headed to his hotel and got his swimmers from his room. While he was out, the room had been cleaned, his bed with its geese feather pillows made, the hair dryer put back in its cupboard, his freestanding copper bath had been drained and cleaned, and fresh flowers had been arranged in a vase on the balcony coffee table. He took the elevator up to the roof, ordered a michelada and tostadas with guacamole, and got into the pool. But even in the pool, his feet couldn't find the floor and he scraped the back of his heel on a ladder he didn't see. He clung to the side of the pool in the deep end, not at all relaxed. There was a large Jacuzzi built into the corner of the other end of the pool, and he would have liked to have sat in that instead, but a group of men were occupying it. They were talking and laughing and patting each other on the back. Harry imagined they had just closed a business deal.

The scene gave him contradictory feelings. They made him feel like he wasn't being enterprising or cut-throat enough. He was taking his career too lightly and too slowly, if he were to be like them one day. What he wasn't able to detect, was that the men were part of the alliance of unelected and self-declared kings, the club of beasts and monsters. They were blood suckers. They sat on huge piles of inherited wealth, proud of having been given power and privilege. Harry could see their greasy hair, but he couldn't tell that they were bloated all over and had no organs. Their rib cages were packed with yellow slime-foam instead. The blood suckers gambled on low-risk investments, crypto, and the stock market to up their net worth. But their number games and wealth accumulation underwhelmed the forces of beauty, creation, and problem solving. In 2022, there were 2,668 billionaires and their combined wealth was US$12.5 trillion; fifty times the cost of eliminating global extreme poverty. But the blood suckers and other monsters made calculated choices to hoard money, telling the media that they were exceptional and unaccountable. They did not have droning guilt.

Harry attempted to imitate the carefree attitude of the men in the Jacuzzi. He tried to do laps of the pool and handstands, but his feat and calves kept cramping.

The pool water looked grey. So did the pot plants. His alebrije tried to wiggle out of grey like furiously trying to escape a jumper on the wrong way. Wrong way. But Harry didn't know that. He just felt dizzy. Confused and stuck. Brain all un-ordered.

A blood sucker noticed him. His eyes travelled over the top of Harry's head, but Harry tried to connect anyway. He nodded and pointed at his food on a plate by the pool's edge and gave a thumbs up. Look, we like the same things, he was saying. The blood sucker's eyes returned to his group, and a few minutes later he called the barperson over and ordered a seafood platter. You're not even close to our level, his eyes that refused to meet and his food order said. Your money and privilege isn't enough to have input into the decisions that affect the world.

Harry tried to heave himself out of the pool, but his arms gave way as he was half way out, and he fell back in. His big toe scraped the bottom of the pool and began to bleed. His body perforations opened up and let the water in and he became very heavy. Sunk. His whole back cramped and he hunched into a heavy body ball. A body ball that reluctantly, slowly, bobbed to the surface. Minutes had passed. The bloodsuckers and the barperson had not noticed.

A scale of translucency

The wing pluckers injected translucency into refugees. They crept into their mornings and pinned their arms down and injected them with a liquid mix of non-recognition, nonacceptance, glass, and wafts of plastic wrap. Then they aimed needles at their faces and extracted colour and much of their fiery, human essence.

And so refugees walked in painful shoes and were mostly transparent. Ghost-like, their presence was lighter and their whispers drifted off to uninhabited lands. There was a scale of invisible people, and they were high on it, preceded by humans who were starving and followed eventually by factory workers and child raisers.

Highly translucent people weren't able to open bank accounts, get ID, vote, access health care, or get formal jobs. They were off the record. Assigned to the dark alleys of life.

A refugee couple slept in a micro-tent and their legs stuck out of it and got wet. Another refugee spent the night by a grave. No one knew that the juggler at the traffic light, the house cleaner, the man guiding cars into parking spots and the woman selling dusty chewing gum on the bus were refugees. No one knew how they spent their nights. They were intangible beings, who got sick, committed suicide, and died, and no one counted them or wrote them down.

The more unacknowledged and translucent a person was, the easier it was to hurt them. No one filed a report when they were robbed or raped or forced into sex work or kidnapped or buried in an otherwise sunny field. One in eighteen migrants and refugees passing through Europe died. Child refugees in Europe disappeared, with many of them being used in forced begging rings. In the desert by the

US border with Mexico, the bones of refugees, bleached white by the sun, were found under trees.

After death

The shoes of dead people who were never buried detached themselves and took flight, high into the sky. They banded together, and from a distance were often mistaken for flocks of plovers, pigeons, or starlings.

The murmurations were the earth's grief ripples.

Who they talked to

A weary street dog with a shaggy tail and ripped lip approached La Tortuga and she sensed that her loneliness had shed its abstract state and was now looking at her with the face of a dejected animal. Being around people that other night in the church had reminded her of how much she enjoyed company and chatter. Lately, she only got to talk to customers for a few minutes, and then they were gone.

"You need people in your life who know what's going on with you," she told her dahlia pot plant. She touched the flower gently, as though patting it on the head. She liked the coolness and bouncy texture of the little petals.

"Without people knowing what is happening to me, it feels like I'm existing in a vacuum, like anything I do doesn't really matter. When I stop focusing on tasks like finding water or a place to sleep, time becomes silent and slow. I can feel bitterness edging itself in, growling low, threatening tones. If there was someone looking out for me, I think life would be warmer colours. I try to forget all that and make this work, but to be honest, little dahlia, I feel rejected by the world," she told the plant.

Harry was the only person she had talked to more than once since arriving in Mexico. She hadn't seen him in a while. Perhaps he had left Mexico City. Maybe her bluntness had put him off her.

Harry, at that moment, was getting up and going to the bathroom. Guilt clung to his neck and its bulk made him turn sideways to go through the bathroom door. He bumped his shoulder on the frame. Back on his bed, sun rays snuck through a gap in closed curtains, and grazed his arm. They mocked him with their joy and serenity. They danced lightly among his arm hairs.

"This isn't working," he told the sun rays. He flicked his finger at them repeatedly, but they weren't bugs and so they did not fly away.

"I am being cowardly." It stung to say it out loud, yet the self criticism allowed him to pity himself in a way that guilt didn't. It opened up a path forward. If he could overcome his cowardliness, he could change a loss to a victory. He could see himself as a hero, in a way. "Running away from things is weak," he told the sun rays. "I can't go back in time, but I can make things right." Others had fallen and gotten up again, as would he. The timeless cliches comforted him. Rocked him with their droned wisdom.

"How much money would I have to donate to feel better?" The sun rays couldn't tell him that. But the sun rose an inch higher and the tickle dances lifted up off his arm and transferred to the headboard. Harry saw himself handing a cheque over to poor teachers in a school and the children were running circles around him and thanking him so much. He didn't know of any schools, but he knew La Tortuga. What would blow her away and make her grateful? What if he paid for a month in his old hostel? It included a free breakfast, so she could start the day with a big meal.

He got dressed carefully and managed to gather his stuff together without tripping on anything or hurting his limbs. He ordered an Uber ride to the city centre on his phone, and as he waited, he pulled up the number of his old hostel.

La Tortuga was helping her first client for the day. An immigrant from Colombia who had lived in Mexico for a few years now, he recognised her accent and chatted away as she worked on the soles of his boots. "I've seen so many things, señora. On the way here, police pulled us off a truck we were hitching a ride on. Just those of us who weren't Mexican. They beat us until we paid them something. When I first got here, some of us set up plastic and cardboard shelters, but the police set fire to them. They are always asking you for ID, and when you tell them that only immigration can ask for it, they don't care and they threaten to arrest you. Then they want 500 pesos and give it back."

The man didn't look at her. He rested his head on his knees and stared ahead. He spoke with the neutral and matter-of-fact tone that came with a story told repeatedly until it was a string of automatic words. "You feel like prey," and for a moment his voice rose in tone then dropped as he quickly numbed fear. "You have to look over your shoulder all the time. The police also like phones, you know…" He refocused his eyes to a large squad of tourist police making its way around the square. La Tortuga felt his gaze shift and followed it.

In pairs, the police were approaching individuals and talking to them. She read their lips and expressions. "You don't look like you were born here." "You look like an illegal, do you have ID?" Some of the candy sellers by the station entrance packed their boxes of gum and Rosa marzipans into their backpacks and quietly moved into the metro and its crowds.

La Tortuga thought she should work somewhere else, with fewer police and where there were less tourists and more locals that she could establish a more regular work relationship with.

When Harry's Uber pulled up at the Zócalo, La Tortuga was gone. He walked around the area twice, and eventually asked another tradesperson about her, but he shrugged with his mouth and looked away.

The night courted bitterness

The Coppel store spread itself across half a block. It was a national chain store that allowed customers to pay off furniture, white goods, and electronics in monthly instalments. At night, its windowless second and third floors and its rows of shutters over its display windows turned it into a merchandise bunker. Five padlocks on the main shuttered door and a strong assertion of permanence in the way it took up space.

The lack of windows was intentional. Like casinos, people wandered into a Coppel shop and lost all sense of time and direction. Few remembered the time that six night shift inventory workers died in a fire because they couldn't get out.

This night though, the Coppel was cold. Looming. Cast in shadows and an ominous presence that La Tortuga had ignored when she chose to sleep at the top of the steps at its main entrance. There, she was elevated off the ground, but still lying on chilly concrete. It was still a place where shoes had landed in their hundreds, where the nightbreeze battered. If less so, because one huge wall buffeted the delirious, frenzied paths of air.

La Tortuga tried to snooze to the tune of rat slinkies tumbling among rubbish piles. Shrivelled food and curls of brown batter leftovers adorned a trail of black plastic bags that led to the road, where more garbage was roadkill smeared on the tarmac. The pervasive smell of urine alluded to the city's crusty wounds, its un-scabbed edges, and the scratches in the voices of the people skulking about like unappreciated ghosts in the darkness, looking for more shop entrances in order to evade total exposure. Other people were already parked in their sleeping places, one eye open. Resentment and impotency built up, accumulated in their lungs and grew fights and sudden creaks of violence. Three toes were stuck in a drain- fallen off from frostbite. Mouths had become asymmetrical so they could hold a cigarette always. Halfhearted street lights flashed in and out, dimmed, useless. The water trucks and their pumps rattled away at one in the morning, guzzling the night silence with their engines. Occasional midnight buses like blasts of light from another dimension, wobbled over road cavities, their windows vibrated and the chins of passengers lashed their chests. Cockroaches dangled confidently from window sills.

When the sun finally came up, it seemed too rich.

Then the Coppel's shutters were removed to reveal white-framed, floor-to-ceiling window displays. A bed draped in a duvet and more than the usual number of pillows. White mannequins sitting and standing on white platforms. It wouldn't open until 10am, so it waited, so politely, to swallow the first customers into its white, windowless halls.

La Tortuga wasn't comfortable but she didn't want to get up. She was in Promesas, a dense suburb to the north of the city centre. After the passing of NAFTA, informal housing had quickly built up there as farmers migrated in droves to the cities.

A few blocks from the Coppel there was a sprawling outdoor market. People were already unpacking carts, unwrapping tarps, joining poles together and stacking wooden boxes as they assembled their stalls along the spare spaces of the city; the wide pedestrian strip, the path under the highway, alongside the post office, and around the metro entrance until it couldn't be seen any more. On the fringes of the market where there was even less space, people arranged fruits, flowers, light bulbs, and other goods on small blankets that they sat next to on the footpath. The mafia fees were lower for spaces like these, and that was where La Tortuga hoped to set up as well.

The charcoal shop near one of the market bus stops was already busy, as people hauled off charcoal in sacks for their taco and corn cob stands. Filled to the ceiling with these sacks of charcoal, the shop was painted black, the floor was covered in black dust, the sacks were stained black, and the man standing at the front next to scales was already coated in a thick layer of black, and blending into his own shop.

The whole municipality was steeped in smog grime. It was parkless and frantic. A man by the corner of the Coppel, two shirt buttons undone, had removed his belt and was fixing it with a pair of pliers. A woman half a block down from him was slouched behind a portable table dressed in torn book cover paper, with a milk carton on it for coins. The table was at the entrance to toilet stalls, and she was folding handfuls of toilet paper to give to people in exchange for five pesos. La Tortuga needed to go. She was backed up and felt nauseous. But those toilets only had one sink at the entrance, and if she was to spend five pesos, she needed to be able to wash her face and some underwear.

She sat up, but stayed where she was. She tried to think through finding a toilet, water, and tortillas, then a spot to work in, but torpor held her down. The sun's cotton illumination was soaking the streets, being absorbed into people's bones and animating them into action. But this morning, it skipped over La Tortuga. She stayed grey tones and unenergetic. Her eyes still half closed, she patted around her, feeling for her pot plant. Her bit of life just for her. But it wasn't there. She opened her eyes fully and focused in on her shoes, on the steps around her, and saw that it was gone. She could make another, but it still felt like a rough start to this new area.

She felt Bitterness curdling within her. Latching on. Its cold claws making her sick. Her stomach felt sloppy, her head ached. Her thoughts were malicious and stuck in a rut and trying to consume her. Like she was rusting, quickly.

It is too hard, it is impossible, the world is against me, she thought, while shooting out random hate sparks at the people in the market. She found awful adjectives easily and forgot colours. But the resilience that age and resourcefulness had given her, diagnosed right then what she was going through. Bitterness, it told her, was anger merged with helplessness. It was a subtle madness that haunted at first, then lodged itself like a metal retention peg into the softest parts of the body. Heavy duty tools were needed to extract it. Usually, bitterness happened when outside circumstances were perceived as one's own failure. But, she argued, the world really was against her. Not all of it, whispered her alebrije from the pocket of her bag. She didn't hear it.

She had seen what Bitterness had done to others. She had watched her neighbour chew the inside of her lips and find comfort in shaking her head at all news and conversations. This friend had misplaced smiles and lost her spark and curiosity and become a husk of a human. Others made excuses to avoid her, as though Bitterness were a nasty cold - its monotonous sadness a catchable infection. La Tortuga had nodded, rather than disagreeing, when her friend said the world was rigged and everything was pointless. At the time, she had thought it ironic that she was being so supportive while her friend looked her in the eyes and told her no one was there for her. Now, La Tortuga conceded she had been too dismissive.

If Carla were here now, she would say, "I told you so". And then she would hug me, and it would feel nice, La Tortuga thought.

But Carla had stayed in that locked-in state, fuming, always. Caustic eyes, her mind became more and more sluggish, sunken, congealed. She had died at middle age of an illness that wasn't usually fatal. Bitterness, La Tortuga had concluded then, hurt the holder of it more than anyone else.

That's why she knew she had to keep dreaming of the room with a bed. Not because she was likely to get it soon, but because the hope warded off bitterness. And yet this morning, she could feel the old retention peg winning. Integrating itself into her character, into her Way of Being.

Fear

The market vendors were scared of a young woman who wandered daily up and down the Promesas market. She had tiger eyes and dragged her feet. Her hair had dried into a thick tangle, and soiled and black-stained clothing fell off her shoulders and hung by threads about her hips. Sometimes she roared at a passing car. The stall workers avoided looking at her and shoppers stayed out of her path. She was convinced she was invisible, or perhaps didn't exist.

So she abandoned clothing that she didn't want to wear anymore in the middle of the road. She changed into a soaking wet t-shirt she had found, as shoppers walked past her. She scratched at her breasts and stomped on fruit. Then she walked up to a bucket of water that was catching the drips from the ice of a fish stall, and washed her face in it.

Travels

On many occasions, La Tortuga had noticed how much Honduras and Mexico had in common. In both countries, public sector jobs were often given to unqualified friends or family. In the private sector, dentists, lawyers, and others paid for their qualifications and were also often incompetent. In both countries, there was a tight relationship between organised criminals and the police. Impunity rates for everything from murder to sexual violence and kidnapping and torture were at 99%, so no one ever even tried calling 911 when they urgently needed help.

But she was surprised one night when her dreams took her on long trips to Colombia then Peru. She saw women in Arequipa selling hats and second hand clothes on squares of rug along the railway track, barely leaving space for the trains to pass. She saw police chasing mobile shoe-shiners out of the parks of Barquisimeto.

And she came back from the night's travels and made an important distinction.

Loneliness type 1 was the ongoing agony of being unhugged, unprotected, unacknowledged, uncared for.

Loneliness type 2 was the unsupported perception of being out of sync with the world. Separate, isolated. The mistaken belief that one's problems were unique.

The humanity parade 2

One lunch time, La Tortuga decided to treat herself to two hot dogs for thirty pesos. Her body hints suggested it would help her feel better.

The super cheap hot dog stand was in the nearby metro station. A woman with a slight smile in a blue apron and her hair tied harshly back poked out from behind the packets of serviettes and bottles of lemonade and Coke that were lined up along the counter. She asked La Tortuga if she wanted to pay five pesos extra for a soft drink, but La Tortuga said no. It would only make her more thirsty, and drinkable water was so hard to get.

She spooned lots of diced tomatoes and onions on to her hot dogs, trying to get the most out of the meal that would have to last her until the next day. At the sauce bar, she squirted a little of each sauce from the long pumps on to parts of her hot dogs, so each bite would be different. There was mustard sauce, mayonnaise, tomato sauce, gravy, yellow cheese sauce, chipotle, pink sauce, spicy green sauce, and Botonera.

She ate slowly, watching the activity in the station tunnel as she did. With trains pulling in at the station every few minutes, there was a constant stream of people walking past her towards a connecting line. All headed in the same direction, like a rushed parade of commuters.

People entered La Tortuga's sight path, and she held them there a moment. Oblivious to their clothes, jobs, gender, or age, she saw their unique *forma de ser* - way of being. As they walked on, she followed them with her eyes and saw more and more of them; their pain, dominant emotions, their long and windy histories, then an essence. At that moment, their alebrije was revealed to her.

First, she saw a schemer. This person was constantly coming up with new plans to make everything better. Even though all previous plans had failed to bring them an income that provided them with dignity, they tried the new plan with new and bursting enthusiasm. Their almost delusional optimism was aided by short-sightedness, gullibility, and vulnerability. They were attracted to scams and quick

The Eyes of the Earth

fixes and band aid solutions. They brought in towels from El Salvador through a friend, with the intention of selling them at marked-up prices, but ended up giving most of them away to friends. La Tortuga saw the plump, sepia caterpillar alebrije sitting in their ear rim, whispering ideas. It had three eyes and lots of busy little arms. Each spiracle of its body sprayed bursts of tangerine mist.

Next, she saw Party Life. He danced down the metro tunnel to the partythoughts rocking his mind. He learned bike tricks, English and Arabic and Tango, and loved blue scarves, wearing three at a time. His alebrije was a rainbow guitar insect with excited bulging eyes that frantically tried to take the whole world in.

Another person was Stuck in Old Pain. They saw blood in the streets and they hurt every day and fell apart when faced with new pain. They were drowning in anxiety but trying to somehow keep functioning because they cared deeply about their primary school students. Walking alongside them, was an armadillo alebrije with a knotted tail and a doughy, sky-blue underbelly.

Then La Tortuga saw an eighteen-year-old who just wanted to play soccer but was crushed by the death of his mother. His long legs dribbled a ghost ball skillfully, a reassuring movement that he used even as he walked through the station. But his "hellos" were mumbled, were tissues. Holding his hand, was a night elephant with stars and comets adorning its skin, twinkling.

Then came a pain absorber. Someone who felt all of the pain that others carried and was susceptible to catching others' depression. Sometimes it was overwhelming, but she was okay because she appreciated being connected to others. Flying above her was a royal blue and cranberry pigeon alebrije that hummed and cooed gently.

La Tortuga had only eaten half of one hot dog. She took bites then chewed very slowly, not wanting to miss any of the life show going on before her. The pain absorber was talking to a friend. She was a collector of light. Having been raped repeatedly by an uncle in the dark, she accumulated fairy lights, Turkish lamps, lanterns, candles, and even torches. She wanted to be able to see always, and to be surrounded by a glowing world that looked after her. She was most excited in the mornings. An owl the size of a toddler, with four wings and tyrian purple planets for eyes, flew beside her, occasionally glancing over at the friend's pigeon alebrije and responding to its hums with sweet hoots. It didn't have a shadow. Instead, it projected a warm-white outline of light on to the woman.

She was followed by a hardened lonely person who had come too far in life, they thought, to start peeling down their walls and ask for friends. He felt destroyed, because he had lost faith in humans. He hugged a huge bag of popcorn to hide his chest, the top open so he could plunge his hand into it and eat as he walked. His alebrije was swimming in the air beside him. It was a dolphin with an exoskeleton.

Then came a person who was sceptical of everything. That was how he defended himself against the digital floods of advertising manipulation and manufactured desires. A furrow was etched into the centre of his forehead, expressing his permanent doubt. His alebrije sauntered behind him. It had a motorbike body and a tiger head and legs. The head shook back and forth, repeating, "I don't think so. I highly doubt it."

His partner was a sensual being who felt tingly and turned on when they cut their own hair in the centre of an art gallery foyer, when they were caught in a long-held gaze, or when restless people tapped their feet on the bus and caused tiny vibrations. Their alebrije was a gilded frog with blue giggles. It swung from their arms and spun around their legs.

The parade went on, and La Tortuga was hooked. Her one-and-a-half hot dogs were getting cold. Her foot was cramping. She took another bite. Enjoyed the tartness of the onion. But she kept on watching as she chewed. She was fascinated by a woman with the sun balancing on her head, who was followed by an artist who didn't have time to be one, so he left little drawings on the tables he sat at and on the bus walls he sat by. La Tortuga loved his alebrije parrot with blinking little eyes all over its body and a paintbrush tongue. Then there was a person who was okay with not fitting in, and their alebrije beluga whale rode a flying mat made of forest floor. Then an apologiser who was scared and unconfident, but also tender and caring, and had a lamb with a coat of rose petals trotting behind them. Then a person who was amazed by patterns and had a balloon axolotl with external gills that emitted laughs wrapped in bubbles floating behind her like a kite straddling the wind.

And then one person-alebrije stunned La Tortuga so much that she stood up, appalled and transfixed. It was a small boy, half bald, perhaps seven or eight years old, with a baby panda alebrije that was pink-brown. A barelyborn colour. Despite that, its eyes were ancient and guarded by five concentric wrinkle rings. But its skin was raw, soft, and furless. Its front paws had almost come off and were dangling from the short arms by a few stitches and pieces of skin. It had a swollen stomach full of soot and metal car parts. Sadness, abandon, and horror had accumulated there and were making it ache. The panda's bare skin attracted dirt and dust. This being was so broken that La Tortuga could not just let it go by without trying to help it. She carried her remaining hot dog in its paper tray and followed the boy.

How to learn about humanity

Stories were humanity manuals.

Street art, traditional handicrafts, spoken word, and old Trova songs were humanity languages, showing the way like street lamps or forest guides.

Critical readings of history, politics, and economy were boot camps.

Long relationships and social organisation were journeys.

Even architecture, calendars, and street food contained clues.

Life was a humanity school, if one looked closely.

Half bald

Miguelito Mendez Martinez, the boy with the panda alebrije, wafted, in the manner of a light smell, out of the station, and towards the market. La Tortuga was just behind him.

A few months ago, Miguelito had been with his dad in Mexico City. They were passing through on the way to the US border. His dad had bought him a surprise, which he was holding under his shirt, and was a few paces ahead of him when suddenly the police were chasing him. They knocked him to the ground and kicked and punched him and detained him. The police never noticed Miguelito standing there, shocked and sobbing, as his dad disappeared out of his life, and he was left alone in the street.

For days, he wandered about, squeaking out a "Dad?" until he didn't anymore, and he just wandered. He still cried when he was hungry though. Normally when a seven, nearly eight-year-old cried, someone came to help. So he thought perhaps when your dad disappeared, you disappeared too and that was why no one came up to him and gave him food or hugs. Within weeks, he was dirty and harrowed and even though he did not roar at passing cars, people were scared of him too. Even if they wanted to help, they didn't know how to, and they had their own problems anyway. Surely the authorities would do something. Except the authorities and the ministries and the big companies and all the towers didn't look after people either.

Anxious, confused, and insomniac, Miguelito picked at his scalp and pulled at his hair so that the right side of his head was mostly bald. He was a half-bald child who was half-deleted, who had outgrown and lost his tiny sneakers some time ago, and who now wandered the markets barefoot, waiting for a hand to pass him a bit of food, or to tap him on the shoulder and ask him to do some small task in exchange for a few pesos. In a short time, he had learnt that there was a lot of edible rubbish near markets. He had also realised that reflective surfaces scared him, and his walk started to get kinks in it from when he would raise his shoulder and twist away in order to defend his eyes from windows and mirrors. Like frequently dodging a silent but burning explosion. Even when there were no mirrors about, he trod carefully. Walked on tip toes and with regular glances around and behind him. The ground was dangerous for a person without shoes, and the world was a minefield of horror.

He was distrustful. One time, he stood in the middle of the pavement, not moving, having decided that he would stand there until he was a grandpa with glasses and a thick grey moustache and loose grey pants. Another time, he found a hole in the pavement. The lid to the electricity manhole was missing. He climbed down into it. People stepped over him and walked around the hole, and he felt a little safer.

At night, the people squashers visited Miguelito and shone their torches in his eyes and set off car alarms nearby and sent dogs to chew on his ankles. His shoe-less little toes turned pink then blue. The people squashers sent him diarrhoea, which made him run around in the dark and worsened his dehydration. Seven-year-olds needed nine to eleven hours of sleep. Without it, their development and growth slowed. But Miguelito couldn't sleep at all. He would sometimes drift off for twenty minutes, then wake up with a jerk, his mouth in screamshape but no sounds. Already, his fingernails were rusty and his elbows were creaky and his eye was infected, and there was a gaping wound he had got when he fell asleep during the day and someone selling orange juice from a shopping trolley had run over his leg. The wound wouldn't heal.

He saw himself as an ineffective monster. A pathetic, tiny, weak one that couldn't even hurt people. Rat boy. I am disgusting, he thought. Yes, you are, said the world. Your begging is so quiet that no one can hear you. And so his gaze stuck to the ground like he was holding on to the footpath with his eyeline.

La Tortuga had been following and watching the panda boy for forty-three minutes. It was time to go up to him and talk.

She cast aside thoughts of daily spending limits. There have to be exceptions, she countered. And she bought two tamales, waved one at the kid, and patted the fence space next to her.

"Hello, I'm La Tortuga."

A speck of curiosity, a trace of warmth from the child at an adult named after an animal. Then self-protection. Shadowface.

"What's your name? Do you work in the market too?"

Miguelito looked at her, stunned and quiet.

"Can I help you?"

Miguelito unwrapped his tamale and ate it.

Pigeons flew in front of buses.

A single cloud sat in the vastness of the sky.

Street vendors called out.

One bit of wind walked through the street and played with hats.

The sound of a blender blotted out little conversations.

"What do you want?" he asked when he finished.

She looked at him, and she didn't go away. That was already many many things for Miguelito.

"Where are you off to now? Can I come?"

He shrugged and walked off, and she wove in between pedestrians and hawkers in an effort to keep up.

That day, La Tortuga spent a week's savings on a tiny panda soft toy on a key ring. Miguelito wasn't aware of his alebrije, but he immediately attached the toy to his belt. And that night, he slept for a few hours, wrapping his fingers around his new small friend so that it wouldn't get cold. Finger blankets.

La Tortuga had 30 pesos in the secret pocket of her bag.

Harry's plan

Harry went back to the Zócalo seven days in a row, each day at a different time. It seemed that either La Tortuga had moved her repair spot somewhere else, or something had happened to her. He was itchy with worry, but more than that, he became obsessed. The more he went back to look for her, the more he wanted to find her. He had always wanted answers and couldn't move on while a question remained unresolved. And as he became obsessed, he found it hard to imagine other things. Helping La Tortuga seemed like the only possible option he had to feel better.

He structured his obsession into goals. He tamed it and tampered with it so that it worked for him. He would stick to his original goal of beating the busking record and raising 131,000 pesos in six months, but he was a little behind and he needed to earn more per week to make it on time. He also didn't want to wait till the end to share what he was doing with the public. He needed to regularly post photos and videos of his busking on Instagram and YouTube, and build up his following.

And, he decided he needed to find La Tortuga within three weeks. He needed these kinds of limits. An end to it, if he didn't manage to find her. An off switch to the obsession.

He shifted into tactical mode. Chess strategy mode of thinking five moves ahead. He was going to be stricter about meeting his daily hours goals, and his busking spots had to be less random now. He did two things:

- He bought a detailed map of Mexico City, and laid it out on the floor of his hotel room. He looked up the most popular or crowded markets, stations, parks, squares, museums, churches, and scenic spots, and used up all fifty orange circle stickers in a packet marking them on the map.

- He made a target of two to three places per day. At each place, he would busk, take photos and video, and look for La Tortuga.

He now had 13,540 pesos saved.

Where murder was hidden

When it matured, sugarcane looked like a soft and fluffy white broom. Each cane's tassel had thousands of tiny flowers that produced one seed each.

In the Caribbean, during the eighteenth and nineteenth centuries four million enslaved people worked among those six-metre-high downy brooms. They sent sweetness and serotonin hits and rum to Europe and in exchange, the harsh working conditions slowly killed them. Because they were dying at a higher rate than they were having children, more Africans were kidnapped to work in the fields, and a third of them died on the journey over.

Now, in the sugar cane fields of Central America, workers died of chronic kidney diseases after working long days while dehydrated, suffering heat stress and being exposed to pesticides. The raw sugar was sent to the United States.

In El Salvador and Honduras, gangs with as many members as a small country, ran the hospitals, the buses, restaurants, and bars and bought off the police force and politicians. Shopkeepers, street vendors, and mechanics paid monthly extortion fees to Barrio 18, or they were killed.

The sugar cane grass was a common place to leave the bodies.

The system of monsters: Impunity

The bloated blood suckers avoided taxes. They indulged in cocaine, hired under-age prostitutes, killed people while drink driving, set forests on fire so they could build elite ecolodges and cattle farms, committed fraud, incest and rape, and then paid lawyers and judges to get them off with light sentences or none at all.

When getting dressed, police and judges put on uniforms and suits with special brass-zippered, deep pockets for storing bribes. Then they put on satin blindfolds.

The people squashers' curly fingers passed the police and judges special wax-sealed envelopes of cash, then their infected fingers manipulated real estate photos, forced evictions, committed fraud and scams, obtained property through false representations, swindled money from homeowners, upped the rent again, sold unfinished homes, sold nonexistent homes, and erased homes, barrios, and little historic communities in order to make way for another shopping centre. They systematically scammed new home buyers, students, and renters out of hard-sweated money and vanquished decades of savings into the air like a sour magic trick. Unaffordable rents sowed fear, uncertainty, and a stressed world of Can't Barely Afford to Live Inside Walls, while the people squashers' bank accounts ballooned like that toad that ate the world.

The people squashers drew a highway through a town, and just like that the townsfolk were dispersed as a super slow explosion among the wreckage of nearby unplanned urban streets. They skipped on safety standards to save money and a Mexico City train overpass collapsed, killing 26 people. The Grenfell tower in London caught fire and 72 people died, and in Bangladesh 1,200 people died when a garment factory crumbled, and non-fireproof scaffolding saw a 28-storey apartment in Shanghai destroyed by fire along with 58 people, and malpractice in renovating the Davao City mall in the Philippines saw that catch fire and 38 people killed.

The wing pluckers openly committed indirect murder. They left razor wire in the Rio Bravo for migrants trying to cross to get caught in. People fleeing the fire of poverty knocked politely on the door to safety as flames followed them like persistent horror movie hitmen.

The wing pluckers stood at the door, and beat them back. They categorised people by skin colour, poverty level and country of origin and convinced everyone else it was reasonable to stockpile dignity for a privileged few. In Algeria, they abandoned over 13,000 migrants in the Sahara desert. They let the heat and dehydration kill them so they could pretend they hadn't done it. In Europe, they stopped boats of refugees from landing, and thousands drowned every year in the Mediterranean and the Atlantic.

One wing plucker stood over Miguelito's dad in the migration prison of Tapachula, near the Guatemala-Mexico border. Miguelito's dad said he had gotten numerous death threats in El Salvador and please please don't deport him there. He had a humanitarian visa, he needed to find his son. The wing plucker took out a pocket knife and cut the visa out of the passport. He ordered Miguelito's dad to stand up and holding him by the shoulder, pushed him into the line to get on the bus. The bus went to the airport, and a plane went to El Salvador.

Lying in a sugar cane field, Miguelito's dad noticed that the whole world smelt of burning flesh and burning trees. He wished he could tell his son that even impunity had a smell and a flavour and a sound. Impunity crackled and sizzled. It stung and buried. It tasted of stale, bitter, caramel. He wished he could send his son memories and explanations. Did you know, Miguelito, that there are strata of people who are powerless. And on the other hand, there is a club of people who pollute, invade, bomb, exploit workers, use women. He wanted to tell Miguelito a secret. And so he did. He coughed bleeding words out onto the winds and hoped they would reach him. The club harnesses the dual powers of repetition and impunity in order to define their abuses and violence as acceptable behaviour. That's how they get away with it, hijo.

Sitting statues

One late afternoon, Miguelito Mendez Martinez found La Tortuga and took her by the hand and steered her through the sagging street stalls. The sun was setting but no one was packing up yet. The mere fact that Miguelito seemed to have somewhere to go intrigued and warmed her. There was life left yet in this splintered human. He turned left and left again, and right, and she lost track. They were absorbed, swallowed up by the city's visual rhythm. A beat for each pothole and triple-padlocked door. City morse code for help, over and over. The canvas and wire grid stalls selling superfluous stuff were spaced in unmeasured ways, set down to imprecise and broken rhythms. Mannequins with cracks in their fingers and missing feet displayed cheap clothes for sale. Defeated gods they were, blushing among the petrol-stained air.

Miguelito turned around and looked urgently at La Tortuga as if to say, "Come on, hurry up." She saw one single trace of a smile in the child, and she knew he was taking her to a special space. They left the market, and still holding her hand, as though a tug boat, he took her down one quiet main road and two back streets and past three taco arabe shops and a funeral service in a garage and through a street full of auto repair workshops, until they were there. Then he sat her down, as a child arranges their soft toys. There. Sit. La Tortuga looked around and saw perhaps twelve other people.

"She's lonely," Miguelito told them.

They were in the Park of Sitting Statues. It was the size of land for a very small house. One empty, torn corner of land pausing the dense rhythm of heaped houses and shops. The statues, La Tortuga assumed, didn't see any advantage in standing for all eternity, and so instead they slouched on their bases, heads resting in hands or on tucked-up knees. The statue bases had been built in a square around the perimeter of the park, and some of them were empty; clearly those statues had gotten up and walked away. In their place, homeless people of various ages sat. They too, barely moved, and could have passed for park statues were it not for their blinking eyes, a little colour in their cheeks, and the soft ripples of clothing draped about their bodies.

Under the statue of the loafing liberator in the middle of the back wall, there were six yellow bottles of Dismex Cleaner for PVC, arranged in a neat line, like patient soldiers or Day of the Dead offerings. La Tortuga understood what was coming. She knew she would have to decide between participating and leaving.

She took stock of the people in the park. There was a young man talking about celebrities, and from the half-hearted way people listened to him, it was clear it was a recurring topic of his. He talked about what celebrities were doing, who they had married, what they said, and what they wore, as though they were his family. Because he wanted one. During the day, he made shapes out of wire and hawked them outside an ice cream shop.

An eleven-year-old girl explained to La Tortuga that she slept in the park because "people piss on you when you sleep on your own." Her teeth dominated her face. Hunger and defensiveness.

There was an Indigenous man who threw Nahuatl into most of his sentences because it felt more real to him. He couldn't stand mess or disorder. He was the one who had lined up the Dismex Cleaner and in the morning he would pick up the discarded rags or toilet paper and their sleeping cardboard and blankets.

There was a thirty-five-year-old with a story-telling dove for an alebrije, who started every day by telling himself he was a failure. This was because, in the unstaffed queue for work, he was always right at the back. He was after the recently unemployed, after the street sellers, after mothers going back to work, after children who were legally too young to work, after the alcoholics, and the Central American migrants without work visas. His stuffy shame was old, dirtied, spiky, and made his stomach curdle. It urged him to hurt others.

All of the people in the park except Miguelito were coughing and sniffing. Most had scratches or cuts that had been infected from wearing humid clothing. Instead of coughs, Miguelito had sequenced yawns.

La Tortuga didn't want to poke the people with questions. She wanted to know why they were homeless, how they were coping, and what they were doing during the day, but it wasn't yet appropriate to ask. So she listened and observed quietly. Her alebrije's earwings reached out and caught pain. They heard that soft beings felt like people-rubbish. They heard torment as a low wailing that lasted for years upon years. Never-ending grief. And they heard the silence of drowning. Because real drowning didn't happen as the movies portrayed, with screaming and flaying. A lack of air in the lungs, a lack of energy and hope, forced drowning people to be silent and still and to eventually slowly sink. La Tortuga heard all the things that weren't being said, which with this group, was everything. She saw lowered eyes and Why Bother and a lack of anger. When hopelessness reigned, anger diluted into apathy.

For now, La Tortuga was outside the outsiders. When sunlight and warmth dropped completely out of sight, everyone in the park moved into a circle. No one said a thing to La Tortuga, nor did they gesture-invite her into the circle, so she followed Miguelito, and sat just behind him. They passed around the Dismex Cleaner and inhaled, and their conversations became shards of shadowy thoughts that faded into quiet as they focused on breathing in as much poison as possible.

Everything that La Tortuga had heard was funnelled down the alebrije's ear-wings and into the turtle shell where, taking advantage of the quietness, she processed it and put it all in order.

These people were exposed beyond a lack of shelter. Their hearts were scraped and scratched daily by the wild daggers of unfriendliness. Constant hostility butted up against them, depriving them of belonging. Yet belonging was a non-negotiable term in the nonmathematical equation for being okay. So they manufactured it by forming a group that shared two things; the quick relief of poison, and societal hostility.

And for those night moments, they existed in a very tiny world that they told themselves they did run.

For the rest of the time, they had a passive relationship with the world. Life was a story they watched, unamused, as it ran past them.

Elsewhere, teachers, bus drivers, translators, park rangers, dentists, and remote seamstresses who were able to contribute one manipulated vote every six years, thanked luck and stars and gods and saints. Over hasty dinners, they spilled out testimonial creations that It Could Be Worse. They were grateful for pipette dribbles of societal decision making.

Meanwhile, in gilded and gated places, the unelected beasts in the System of Monsters made unconsulted and unconsidered Big Decisions about what to produce and where to get the raw materials from, which forests to destroy first, and what money and labour would be used for. They pressured city councils to dedicate most of their urban space to cars and parking and roads and none of their space to culture, and intervened in climate conferences, bearing the weight of secret yet revered orchestra conductors.

La Tortuga wanted at least crumbs and dribbles. She wanted to join and be part of something bigger than herself, with other people. Just for that, she wanted to inhale the drain cleaner.

A frosty wind beat at her persistently, saying in its rough language that the world did not need her. It confronted her with her loneliness. She shivered loudly, and no one turned to look at her with gifts of concerned faces. La Tortuga's alebrije argued with that nasty wind, telling her, "You are part of the world, you're part of its story, it has a narrative of pain and exclusion."

And La Tortuga thought, "Even once I have my own bed, without nightly survival to distract me, I'll probably notice the loneliness more."

The Dismex Cleaner did another round of the circle. They covered the top of the bottle with toilet paper, tipped it, and held the soaked wads up to their noses, cupping their hand. Their eyes were red, their fingers stained, their noses irritated. The effect was felt quickly, and dissipated quickly, so that the thirty-five-year-old got up and brought two more bottles over to the circle. He also brought two packets of watermelon Tang out of his bag and added the powder to the bottles to give the liquid a nicer smell. He turned around and offered a bottle to La Tortuga. Now she had to say yes or no. She shook her head, "But thank you." And like that, with such small words, she locked in her decision not to be part of the group, and not to begin a dawdled death. She had been tempted.

Miguelito didn't like the smell of the Dismex Cleaner, so normally he inhaled a few times, just to be part of the ceremony. He would try to keep his face flat and neutral rather than letting it retract into wrinkled disgust. He wanted the people in the circle to tell jokes and play games with him. But they weren't interested and avoided looking at the child. It was nice enough that they let him stay. But Miguelito did want watermelon flavour. He had turned around and seen La Tortuga shaking her head and no one getting angry, and he hadn't known he could do that.

La Tortuga moved away a bit and sat on her own. She leaned against the pedestal of a sitting statue, fiddling with her long fingernails, as the others huddled closer together. She would leave early in the morning, before they woke from their own fretful half-slumbers, in order to avoid the awkward goodbyes of people who had chosen not to be friends.

Heroism

Heroism percolated slowly. It gained momentum over decades. In La Tortuga, with each act of integrity, each hard decision and moment of generosity, neuronal changes occurred within her, and she gradually metamorphosed into someone very strong and capable. But on the outside, her eyelids were thin and falling, her legs were swollen, and her bones were losing calcium and becoming more and more brittle.

In Mexico, prior to the Spanish invasion, heroes had had a daily presence in people's lives and mindspace. Deity-heroes functioned as an omnipresent motivation. They were incredible beings that embodied what people most needed, valued, prioritised, and adored.

Water and rain

The Mexica, Toltecas, and Tlaxcaltecas deeply respected water. They knew they loved it because they missed it so quickly; feeling thirst within hours of its absence. The difficulties of the wet and dry seasons taught them that rain ruled over them. It was a crucial life force, diving headfirst into the ground with glee, then sprouting out of barren lands as new fields of flowers or corn, and eventually becoming puddles, glaciers, hectic rivers, and hot springs. Water cleansed their bodies and formed rich soups and anxious tears.

So they called rain and water life forces "Tlaloc." And in doing so, they made them worthy of moral care, understanding, and effort. Tlaloc was a hero-deity with large round eyes and heron feathers. He had fangs that were water taps and a gold standard that represented lightening. In the story of Tlaloc, the mountain peaks were water homes, and he had tiny helpers called Tlaloques. They gathered water from the warehouses that stored four types of rain, and they poured it on the earth from clay pots.

Learning

Quetzalcóatl was a feathered snake, and the god of wisdom, self-reflection, science, and learning. In a Nahuatl poem, he was knowledge growing as a flowering tree. Because learning was a life force that ensured that each person's existence was a process rather than static. It was research and study, arts, and music disseminating sight and quiet awareness on hurting people. Guiding them so that empathy was born softly, so that the world and history and the difficult art of living was gradually decoded. And like that, Quetzalcóatl gave people the powers they needed to be brave and to find true beauty.

Love

Xochiquetzal wore a cloak of quetzal feathers and a halfmoon nose piercing. She had a crown of flowers and long earrings. She was the deity-hero of love, pleasure, the arts, and flowers, so the original peoples of Mexico depicted her breastfeeding in various paintings. Her twin brother, Xochipilli, was the flower prince and the patron of gay sex. He was usually depicted as looking beyond, and of embodying poetry, creativity, love, and beauty.

Love was a warm life force. It held people, shed banality, overcame separateness and created communities. It expanded people beyond the borders of their skin into new territories, injected the days with hundreds of colours, endowed people with responsibility for others, and encouraged them to embrace uncertainty.

Consumerism

Many in the modern world worshipped a car god. It had no eyes or hands, just double round taillights, hood vents, power locks, granite trims, and an addiction to fossil fuels. In Mexico City, the old deity-heroes were stored in books and museums, incorporated into two-storey murals, or remembered in mountain ceremonies, but many people's regular rituals now consisted of visiting windowless shopping centres. Spurred on by advertising and planned obsolescence, they participated in a trance-like guzzling of earthly resources. They invoked identity by mistaking mass-produced brands for individualism.

But consumerism was a non-life force that left people feeling distracted, nauseated, and dissatisfied.

Dormancy

In the middle of the night, as ocean waves settled down into flatness and sounds sunk into a toned silence, people's life forces stirred and sparkled as they slept. Many of them went into night battles between tiredness, water shortages, and quick hits of consumerism and a craving for self expression and something more. Their alebrijes held the life forces as heartglow; a warm, throbbing light that sometimes yearned so strongly, it reached their eyes and they seemed radiant.

But in the Park of Sitting Statues, the alebrijes that were parked next to their people were disturbed and in agony. Instead of glowing, their hearts were a single ruby-red pixel. A cinder, about to go out. The life forces of the people sleeping in the park were inactive. They had the potential for music, love, learning, flow, sensitivity, science, generosity, and determination, but those forces had been disabled for so long that they were dormant. Forgotten, atrophied, barely able to be aroused. And yet, still there.

A few nights later, and back on the Coppel steps, La Tortuga's alebrije was uncomfortable. Because La Tortuga was learning and caring, in small doses each day, her alebrije was not in agony. But La Tortuga was not a fully realised person. Her metamorphosis into hero was still in process, and sometimes it was so slow, her alebrije worried it might stop and she might get stuck. La Tortuga's life forces were brewing, simmering, restless, rumbling. Her alebrije's heart was lukewarm and glowing in a muted, subtle way. The warmth was waiting. As though it needed time to recover, repair, and accumulate. As though preparing to be turned on fully. To shift into a whole new gear of living. Preparing, perhaps, for the impossible.

The alebrije slid out of La Tortuga's bag pocket and crawled into the depths of her shirt, to heat up more.

Communication forces

- Flowers communicated with bees using minute electric fields. The fields were unique to each species, varying according to flower shape and height.

- Tomato plants sent distress signals through fungal structures. Fungal threads formed networks that were many hectares in size. An infected plant shared information across the networks, and healthy plants responded by producing defensive enzymes to resist the disease.

– The honeybee told its team members where honey was by dancing. The duration of the dance told them how far away it was, and the direction of the dance told them which way the honey was.

The wonderful benefits of fixing things

Miguelito and La Tortuga were sitting on the grass under a skinny sweetgum tree in the immense Chapultepec Park. He had looked for her in the market and quietly sat down next to her, squeezing his panda toy, until she finished the job she was working on. She suggested she take the afternoon off and they go somewhere away from all the chaos.

Miguelito had never been to such a big park. Unlike the statue park, this one didn't have four corners. It seemed to go on for ever, like the sea. Like being in a whole brand-new world. The city subsided, bustle-noise receded into the past, and squirrels scooted down trees.

At 680 hectares, Chapultepec was the biggest urban park in Latin America, and the oldest. A few days were needed to see all its museums, fountains, monuments, exhibitions, gardens, and the zoo. Little Miguelito Mendez relaxed. His body unclenched. In the distance, behind La Tortuga, people who had been at an international food and product fair were walking about the park with smudged henna Arabic name tattoos on their arms and tabbouleh in polystyrene cups. Beyond the fair, a woman stood at the entrance to the free zoo, shouting out instructions over a megaphone and telling people not to bring in soft drinks.

Lurking in the air as a heavy, silent spirit, was the history of the park. Before the Spanish invasion of Mexico, Moctezuma had established botanical gardens there, and Nezahualcóyotl had built an aqueduct to supply water to Tenochtitlán. He planted the Old Tree, an ahuehuete or cypress which lived for 500 years, until 1969. Now leafless, it was still standing in the park.

And now the ruins of Miguelito sat on warm grass a few metres from the dead tree, and felt soft sun. The child ruins chatted. "Tree roots," he informed La Tortuga, "are all the trees' legs, buried in the ground. If you pull a tree out of the ground, it will run away."

"Birds," he then explained, "used to be flowers. Then one day they fell off their stalks and their petals became wings and feathers and they flew off."

La Tortuga let him run off and hide behind trees and feed the squirrels day-old tortillas, then called him over. "I want to show you some of the basics of fixing things, so you can be my assistant," she said.

She spread her tools about on the grass, and Miguelito's eyes widened. As though she had produced a huge box of toys and treasures and dumped it out in front of him. She showed him how to hold a screwdriver steady inside a nail, how to match the flat head and Phillips head with the nails they were for. She taught him about all the different glues; nail glue, super glue, silicon, and craft glue. She cut the plug of an extension cord and showed him how to strip back the plastic and twist the wires. Then she opened a new plug and wrapped the wires around the nails on the inside. "This is where the electricity travels," she said, tracing her finger over the twisted and exposed wire.

"Electricity must be very tiny," he said, awed.

As she taught him to repair things, Miguelito became a little less broken. His fingers, occupied, didn't pick at his scalp. Concentrating and learning, he would sleep better that night, and the wound on his leg would start to repair close. La Tortuga instructed him to pull apart a small garden solar lamp, then to put it back together again. She gave him some hints but wanted him to assemble it on his own. So that he could have one victory. Then other things in life would feel possible. A present of self-esteem disguised as an undone lamp.

"Is there anything that can't be fixed?" Miguelito asked.

"Everything can be fixed."

"Even people?"

"Especially people."

"How do you know if something is broken?"

"If that person or thing can't be the essence of what it is."

Miguelito slumped. Hid his face in tree shadows. La Tortuga waited.

"Lately, I haven't been child-ing very well."

"You're hurting, and that isn't your fault. You have a right to good care."

And the word Care made little Miguelito laugh nervously. A laugh of cracks and cuts. La Tortuga didn't laugh. After a while though, she said, thoughtfully, "I've never seen a broken person that I thought didn't deserve loving. But I've seen people who do the breaking; consistently, ruthlessly, purposefully - and thought that perhaps they don't."

La Tortuga knew that humans were inherent problem solvers. They relished a challenge, couldn't resist trying to find answers, found deep peace in making a thing or situation better. If there was a crooked table at a restaurant, everyone seated around it would peak under it and try to identify the shorter leg. But the non-life force that was erecting shopping centres in every spare space, was also designing electronics so they were hard to fix, with covers that couldn't be removed and essential parts that weren't easily obtained. It concocted the printer ink scam where printers were affordable for many, but the ink had to match the specific brand and model of printer and was excessively expensive. It systematised planned obsolescence and herded people into habits of buying new clothes and new phones rather than fixing them.

La Tortuga believed that repairing was a respect deed. That seeing objects as disposable was a disregard for the time and materials that went into their creation. Repairing though, cultivated memories and stories, and a mentality of endurance and care. Likewise, she preferred long relationships with people and to repair any issues, than letting people go over small problems. As though they too, were disposable. Quick use people. Consumable people.

But who was caring for her? She enjoyed the afternoon in Chapultepec Park, but it was less time spent working, less savings, and no food that night. Her feet were studded with blood holes from the shoe grates, and while that one big toe was mostly healing over, she felt that at any moment her feet would crumble into blood heaps and fall right off. Bitterness was still simmering, ten centimetres below the surface. Climbing a little closer each day to skin, to outburst. Haunting. She doubted the friendship with the boy would help. That night, as he returned to the Park of Sitting Statues, she settled in to her sleeping spot by the Coppel, and her alebrije prodded her with questions. How can you afford an assistant if you can't afford to eat, let alone save for a bed? How long can dreams be postponed until they are cancelled outright? How long can an old person go without proper sleep?

Breaking

A people squasher followed La Tortuga to her sleeping spot. It was 9 p.m. and the beasts and monsters were very busy using not-tools to not-fix. The people squasher lurking by La Tortuga had sirens, klaxons, and electricity switches. The other beasts had dynamite, guns, and media tools for mass misdirection. They didn't own screwdrivers, stethoscopes, or glue guns, and they avoided listening or dialogue. Instead, they were overcoming their obstacles by rigging elections, reclassifying land so that it could be logged, paying hired killers to murder environmental activists, bribing their way to mining permits, and fabricating studies and research outcomes. Police officers and judges followed them around with their blindfolds on. Saliva formed a crust in both corners of their lips. The beasts had spilt oil into rivers in Nigeria, and Ohio, and were spending the night finding ways to avoid cleaning it up.

The people squasher watched La Tortuga sleep. He was selling housing and commercial real estate in the busiest areas of Mexico City and the nicer the streets were, the higher the selling price. He commanded the street lights near La Tortuga and in other areas where homeless people passed the nights, to be extra bright. To flicker and flash and wake them. He erected hostile architecture. He attached metal spikes to the flat areas of urban landscaping, and he installed dividers on park benches and bollards on stair landings and in front of doors. He sent out high-pressure waves of anxiety and La Tortuga woke up every thirty minutes and worried about her savings and the increasingly cool temperatures, about her feet, and about Miguelito.

The next morning, La Tortuga had a migraine that curled all the way down her throat and made her voice hoarse and her eyes shut in fear of too much glare. Her head bobbed, resisting being alert and vertical. She stood up, but her muscles were weak and she stumbled about, making sour grunting noises. She didn't want to work. So she let herself sit, just for fifteen minutes, as she willed the migraine to dull and her brain to fire up. Her hands shook and her feet bled symmetrically into the grooves of pebbled path. Two red puddles shaped like oil spills in rivers.

Neutrality

In order to make it look like they were getting things done, the police were given quotas for the number of arrests they had to make in a day. So they targeted the poor, homeless, and migrants for drinking in the streets, robbery, or looking like wanted criminals, or they planted illegal drugs or trumped-up charges. Sometimes they would release people the next morning, other times, years would pass.

In the Park of Sitting Statues, a curled-up Miguelito watched through one eye slit as police dragged five sleepy bodies by their feet into a police van. A predawn moon revealed a line of six empty Dismex Cleaner bottles, a roll of toilet paper, newspaper cutouts of celebrities and a dose of Why Bother left behind, unscathed.

Like subdued spectators, the statues then sat back comfortably on their pedestals.

The weight of debt

As always, the day started before the sun rose. As always, the first truck pulled up at 5:30 a.m. and men unloaded pineapples. Other men whistled loudly outside a warehouse. We're here, let us in, they were saying. Every single morning, cheerful clockwork whistles. Every single morning, work time started with a ruptured dream moment because it was too early. The tortilla machines turned on at 6 a.m., then finally the sun followed them. An old woman with a curved back used rope to pull two overloaded plastic crates of potatoes along the road to her stall. The scraping noise roused La Tortuga, who did not welcome the subdued sunrise because it meant that, as always, she had run out of time to try to get to sleep.

She sat up and lied to herself. She had in fact slept last night and the one before. She just hadn't noticed it because all she did remember was trying to move into a more comfortable position exactly 35 times, and repeating "off, brain, off," to try to force it to shut down for a while. She felt exhausted. Her arm had pins and needles, her left cheek had floor tile stamped into it, and her neck was askew. There was rubbish all about her. Watching her. Lazily lounging in slump semicircle audience. Leaking drops of beer. Another self-lie came. That perhaps, under the quiet cover of a roughly lit night, people had thought the front steps of Coppel were the best place to leave their rubbish, and they hadn't seen her.

La Tortuga shook off the smithereened not-sleep, and gathered the rubbish together and moulded and squished it into a tight pile. She massaged it, ignoring how it dug into her hands and how her pins and needles weren't going away, but somehow became louder when pocked with the corners of tins and packets. She wanted a sunflower. Nothing happened, so she massaged more aggressively. Tried to thump the plastic back to life. Then she slowed down. Found tenderness. But still, no flower grew. She took the neat, fused pile of rubbish to a bin, then sat down on the Coppel steps and put her turtle alebrije on her knee. The top part of its shell was gone. Not flattened or squashed, just gone, as though blown away. She stroked its little head and worried. Worry, as an activity. As an involved process of naming and describing all the things that could get even worse.

She had 200 pesos in savings. It was taking too long to save up. And there were two reasons it could not take much longer. One, the longer it took, the worse her sleep. The less she slept, the more mistakes she made at work, and the more clients she would lose. Two, as her hope of earning enough for a bed dwindled, it would be replaced by an unwitting process of docile adjustment. She would convince herself that living on the street was the best possible outcome and she would focus on the positives of her current situation and forget any alternatives. She knew this process well, as she had gone through it with her husband. She got to the point where it became impossible to imagine things any other way, and she bound herself to the unhealthy and painful situation using hundreds of At Least phrases. He puts me down all the time, but at least I have food. He makes me do all the housework but at least I'm keeping busy. She could already feel adjustment nudging at her. This is easier. Stop fighting. Accept what is. All the cliches that had been developed to make people feel better about their acquiescence and evasion stood in a queue and tapped her on the shoulder. Tiny comfort songs. What will be will be. Make the most of what you've got. Stop trying. You don't actually need a bed.

La Tortuga was massaging her fingers and bracing herself to head over to her work spot when Miguelito's little legs dropped down beside her and he too tapped her persistently on the shoulder. The cliches moved aside, for a moment. "I've left the statue park and I'm going to stay with you now," he said.

"Oh, I'm glad," she replied, stroking his cheek, and briefly pulling him into her. Then she let him go because she did not want to make him uncomfortable. All the while thinking she was horrible for hoping he could earn his keep. She said, "Too old and too young. Neither of us should be working, but we'll make the most of what we've got." A cliche winked.

She let Miguelito prop up her sign and arrange some of her tools, while she closed her eyes. She could hear ticking. Ticking that thumped against her skull. She didn't know that it was the sleep debt countdown clock. Missed sleep added up like Global South debt did, accumulating and multiplying and crippling exponentially. A debt with increasingly harsh effects. Itchy mind. Grumpy weekends. Viscous decision making. Dragged out healing - emotional and physically. Tactless hallucinations. And lifestop.

As La Tortuga sat at the market spot, waiting for clients, Miguelito stood next to her. His back was straight. He had a thing he needed to do every day, now. A spot to belong to, a new identity as an assistant, a routine. He had a person to watch over him and buy him tortillas. "Repairs!" he yelled out. A couple heard him, and stopped in their tracks. They had a bag they needed fixing.

"Good job," La Tortuga said, as she got out a needle and thread. She sewed quickly, and Miguelito peered over her shoulder and cut the thread when she told him. But as she sewed, a new type of blade grew in each of her shoes. The fine-tooth blade of a hack saw protruded from each opening. Later, when she walked to the toilet, they moved back and forth cutting at her ankle. If they weren't stopped, they would cut through her legs, felling her, removing her feet altogether.

The sleep hierarchy

There were thousands and there were billions at the concert of the exhausted. In front of a lit up and vibrating stage, a vast and sandy plain was filled with people who were too tired to dance, who were made cranky by an endless grind, who were barely keeping up with the richness of life. They had come from all over: from double shift work and three jobs, from homeless shelters, from parenthood with no social support, from factories and mines, from 12-hour-long sales shifts and no weekends, from physical and mental health problems and unaffordable health care, from the world of women and the triple duties of emotional labour and paid work and home management, from fruit farms and hospital jobs, from night shifts, from the rough trenches where people were bombarded with unreasonable obstacles, but they never ever won.

The people at the concert of the exhausted were denied the dignity that came with down time. They missed the revelations that only burst upon the heart when one had space and quietness. They heard the music but were too tired to sing along.

They closed their eyes and hummed sporadically.

Where the magic goes

A plastic sunflower was on standby in his bag. Waiting in order to eventually become a story. Its stiff petals reached the upper bag zipper. Harry eyed the arrangement as he brushed his teeth and prepared to leave, wondering if there was a way to better pack it and protect it. But this sunflower was well glued together. It would never brown or dry up or cede to floppiness.

Because only the living got to grow old. Only non-life was unmoved by the wind.

Harry sang after he spat out the toothpaste. Bits of rock song accompanied by flecks and scraps of dance. He was able to be cheerful because of the permissibility of time. The way minutes and days could become metres and kilometres. The way time was distance. As the weeks stacked up, guilt moved into the past. Unlike the sunflower, guilt was alive, in a way, and so it could become old. It could be faded by time. The past was a different thing to the present because it was experience and memory, while the present was a descriptor of identity. And when The Past was mixed in a fire-heated cauldron with action and change, a disconnection was concocted. Because he had a plan, because he had realised things and that had shifted his character a little, because time was passing, Harry could now separate himself from that shrill guilt discomfort and move on. Or so he thought.

Guilt wasn't any ordinary memory. Its fading was a special trick. It hid but continued to cause trouble. To surprise, suddenly, its host, with a long, terrible day. But for now, it had lost tangibility, as a country's tragedies were also numbed by geographical distance, for those far away in other countries. And yet, and yet, the tragedies were still there. Still screeching, still horrid.

And so, Harry's soul cavities, his perforations, were not itching. And there were a few less, because despite it all, Harry had found determination and perseverance in his twice-daily busking routine. But his body, a squishy breathy sponge, still huffed as he danced.

The night before, Harry had fallen asleep at 10 p.m. He had slid into bed, was on the edge of sleep for two minutes, then it was morning. The edge of sleep had been a wonderful place of rain squares, warm air ribbon caresses, tree whispers, and the curly flight of a golden-orange bird. In the morning, he had stretched his shoulder blades back and labelled his mood. Less terrible. Also, eager. Because the day would entail learning, discovering, and performance. His two destinations for the day were the flower market, then the exotic meat market.

He grabbed his bag with the partially closed zipper and a still very inert and not-alive sunflower, and his fine-tuned feet and snug and winged shoes scampered down the stairs and out of the hotel, barely touching the tip of every second stair. He slipped easily through bollards newly-installed near the hotel entrance to deter homeless people. He skittered the pavement in a direct and efficient route to the metro station, then precise crowd weaving took him to the platform. On the train, he swung his bag around to the front and wrapped his arms around it so that nothing would touch the plastic sunflower.

His tortoise alebrije rode on his shoulder, still unnoticed. Since he had begun his twice-daily busking, the alebrije's purple monkey tail had grown a little longer and the outlined patterns on the lower corner of its shell had filled in with puce and turquoise. Inside the shell, the storyline characters were blinking and grabbing at things, and the landscapes were buzzing. His wandering mind was stirred awake. His sense of adventure, his habit of gazing and getting lost in what he could see and what he could imagine, was slowly being resuscitated. But the pocketstars, so ancient and evading subtlety, weren't for Harry yet. They waited with a patience beyond what most people could imagine.

There were over a thousand stalls in the flower market, and over five thousand types of flowers and plants. Harry gazed at the transparent plastic bags of flower petals, sorted by colour, the roses arranged in the shapes of crosses and hearts, the flower bunches stacked into cubes on pallets, the pickup trucks driving through the isles and overflowing with flowers, the vendors spraying their goods with water to keep them fresh, vases - huge, tiny, and in every colour, decorative bicycles made of woven branches, and the drive-by buyers yelling at the outside stall holders from their cars, holding up traffic.

He watched quietly, curiously, for a full ten minutes, then set himself up at one of the entrances, taking his one trick - the fake sunflower - out of his bag and holding it in the air. The large sunflower head hid a disproportionate receptacle that held squashable things like silk scarves, foam balls, and cigarettes.

His busking hat on the ground a metre from his feet, he yelled out, in Spanish, "Magic trick! Magic trick!" He read a translation out loud from his phone, "There are amazing flowers here at the market, but can they do this?" Then he pulled object after object out of the sunflower. A semicircle of people gathered around. They clapped and laughed each time he pulled another thing out, and put on an exaggerated expression of surprise. They chortled and accidentally spat. They leaned in and looked this funny man up and down.

At the end of the day, Harry had 18,950 pesos saved from busking.

What they did to stay stuck to the earth

Miguelito collected seven questions. It was part of the routine he and La Tortuga had established that would stop them falling off the earth.

When they finished working, La Tortuga bought their tortillas, hot and wrapped in waxy paper, which Miguelito held in his two hands out in front of him as though in a religious procession. Then after eating, he went through his questions with her.

In the morning, they did sunrise stretching. To keep their bodies glued together. You had to have physical strength, to stay stuck to earth. They stood up straight and reached their arms up as high as they could. They rotated their shoulders five times, then moved their head to their chest and back five times. They wrote *buenos* with their left foot, then *días* with their right. La Tortuga wanted to build up her ankle strength because her feet were becoming so weak and hurting so much. Miguelito always lost his balance when he added on the accent, and it made him laugh.

The routine buffered them against a feeling of imminent collapse. It was a fortress of security, and each repetition of it made Miguelito feel safer. Because he knew now, what was going to happen each day. Food was confirmed. La Tortuga's gentle glances were confirmed. He had some control. Routine was a tool that held them in place. Nailed their lives to the ground, established firmness and permanency, stopped them falling away from an unstable planet and into endless, unbearable space.

Weeks like this had passed. With someone protecting him now, Miguelito still recoiled when police walked by and shrunk when someone called out to him, but the warzone terror of the streets had diminished from an earsplitting screech to an eerie whistle. His distrust mellowed, but he held on to suspicions as one who accumulates pocket knives and pepper spray. His secret arsenal of defence. Just in case La Tortuga planned to disappear in a police van like his dad had.

He also collected learnings, stacking one upon the other. He watched La Tortuga with his right hand on her shoulder and his head centimetres from what she was fixing. He remembered the many uses of each tool, the many ways to open something, and the initial questions to ask the client. He grasped the stages La Tortuga went

The Eyes of the Earth

through with each person, starting with initial observations, then a closer examination, explaining the issue to the client, fixing, testing, and a final clean. Miguelito always did the cleaning, and it was earning them extra tips and client confidence and loyalty.

But what La Tortuga thought she was missing, was a routine for a strong mind. Hers fell down holes, particularly at night, once Miguelito was asleep. It fell into places where nothing was possible, everything was doomed, and there was no point and it was all unfair. Even during the day, she wondered if the colours of the world had faded. If the planet had gone through the wash with too much soap and too much sun. But she was convinced that helping them to stay stuck to the earth also involved pretending to be okay. Because if she showed the resentment and bitterness and hopelessness, if she cried or complained, the child would sense the ruptures and fragility of it all, and they would start to fall. Spinning, contorting, flailing, nothing left to grab on to. She followed scripts, varying them a little from client to client, so that Miguelito wouldn't catch on. When she told clients, "Que te vaya bien," she meant it, but she injected the words with extra pink and mango yellow so that they sounded joyful and full and muffled the weariness about her that could so easily stick, like muggy sweat, to the other people.

So now, she was listening to Miguelito's seven questions. To answer, she mustered together any remaining scraps of energy, until the child fell asleep. Only then could she pluck the toothpicks and ladders holding up her smile and let her mouth relax into its true shape. She sewed up the openings in her ankles then wrapped them with the tortilla paper. But the shoe grates quickly shredded the paper and then the thread. She tried taking her shoes off, but they wiggled their way back on.

What she didn't realise, was that little Miguelito only pretended to fall asleep. His suspicions kept him watchful, as did his concern. So he saw her, in the middle of the night, doing calculations, murmuring numbers, adjusting her plans. Her day time script, for him, was just that. A role they both had to play for the clients. But he could also see her beyond what strangers saw of her. Rather than frailty and slowness, Miguelito saw her starting the day even though she was tired. How she fought off bitterness like constantly defending herself against an army, with nothing but a paper shield and her bare hands. To him, she was a warrior who kept on fixing despite the pain in her feet. He wanted to be like her; someone who kept on going and going, trying, and fighting, every minute.

And because she was in pain, he carried her tools from sleeping spot to working spot, and he ran around the market looking for the extra things they needed for fixing, like cables or string or nails.

That night, Miguelito's seventh question had been, "If everything can be fixed, why don't you fix your shoes?"

La Tortuga stared at the bare bones of the moon.

She watched the crowds of stars.

She took Miguelito's panda toy and stroked its head.

In their routine, she had to answer all his questions. And so, in one last effort scrap, with the last bit of energy she had left that night, she pushed herself beyond bitterness, and she admitted, "Fixing them takes many people and a lot longer is all. Perhaps a lifetime, perhaps a few."

Migrant shelter 1: Little Money labyrinths

To cross the road at Observatorio station and get to the migrant shelter, one had to pass through layers of stalls. First, inside the station there were people in the middle of the stairs selling handbags, people at the bottom of the stairs selling gooey and bouncy toys, and people near the exit doors selling jelly in cups and bottled water. Then there was the tight maze of stalls crammed onto the footpath outside the station. Those sold tamales, tacos, phone covers, tortas, five-peso drinks poking out of bright plastic washing tubs of melting ice, five-peso amaranto snacks, breakfast cereals in plastic cups, and hundreds upon hundreds of earphones draped from horizontal bars like multi-coloured noodles. On the other side of the road there was a third layer of stalls. Vendors worked from early in the morning till late at night, seven days a week, yelling their product lists at the crowds. They fought hard for Little Money. Barely survive barely alive money.

So crossing the road at Observatorio - like many parts of Mexico - was an art. Crowds of people pouring out the station tuned out the smells of boiling and fried food and ignored the rubbled ground. They stepped over rocks, holes, ditches, puddles, cracks and discarded plastic bottles. They accumulated along the edge of the path, among the stalls, until they could no longer fit. Then they crossed the road together, giving the cars no choice but to stop.

Migrant shelter 2: Shoes for giants

In the musty, concrete storage room of the migrant shelter in Observatorio, there were 120 pairs of new white sneakers in boxes. They had been donated by a shoe company a month ago, but so far only a few pairs had been claimed.

New shoes were one of the main things migrants and refugees travelling from Central America needed by the time they reached Mexico City. After weeks of walking in slip-ons or cheap lace-ups with cardboard insoles, their feet were blistered, and their shoes shredded.

The donated sneakers were padded, stylish, and stitched well, but none of the migrants wanted them. There was now no space in the storage room for food or hygiene products, so the shelter coordinator, desperate, asked the migrants to try them on yet again. They lined the shoes up with the heels of their feet. Overly hopeful. But the shoes were still three times the size of their feet. Extra, extra, extra large.

Perhaps the shoe company had been overly hopeful too; that giving away all the big sizes they couldn't sell counted as generosity.

Migrant shelter 3: Snapshots

A photo of the migrant shelter showed three flights of concrete stairs leading up to a series of stacked, informally constructed, narrow rooms. The whole area was barnacled in murals, razor wire, and hardy pot plants. Zooming in though, you could see:

- Victor drilling tiny holes in the corners of wooden key rings. They would be sold at an upcoming fair to raise money for the shelter.

- Steel steps leading up to the roof of the top dormitory, where a makeshift room had been built from panels of plastic for extra sleeping or storage space. On the transparent corrugated roof over the garden, washing was laid out to dry, like lizards stretched out under the sun.

- Tidy piles of stuff distributed, like discarded nests, all about the corridors and stairways. A result, perhaps, of a fear of running out. There were cookie tins of dried-out, semi-usable paints, three old saws, two four-kilogram tubs of Resistol glue, a box of scrap wood for making key rings, stacks of old speakers, metal tennis rackets, and a large collection of canvas bags.

- People in the dining room eating rice with forks because there weren't enough spoons. Others had finished eating and were queuing up to dry their tray, while one migrant, assigned to post-lunch clean-up, was dancing to music on his phone as he scrubbed giant pans.

- A family of three migrants arriving. They carried Jesus portraits that they had painted for selling. One had jumped off the roof of the cargo train before it reached Mexico state and hurt his foot, so there was a big, burning lump on the inside of his ankle. Worried about bothering people, they sat quietly in the meeting room until a volunteer gave them some cans of tuna. "I don't want to see a doctor, we have to keep going," the one with the injured foot said. Before they left, they rummaged through the piles of second-hand clothing, putting on the first items that fit.

-Twenty-year-old Hector sitting in the garden, watching them go. A few weeks ago, he had fallen off the roof of the cargo train, down between two carriages, and his right leg was dismembered. He grinned and waved a crutch at the family. In a week, he would be on his way too.

Where the Big Money went

The wing pluckers' business inventory of their war on refugees included a US$30 billion global border security market, where key players like Boeing, Airbus, and Raytheon produced surveillance aircraft, patrol aircraft, ground attack and transport helicopters, amphibious aircraft, marine vessels and submarines, laser and radar systems, cameras, wideband wireless communications, perimeter intrusion systems, unmanned vehicles, and biometric systems. Their inventory also included over US$80 billion in contracts issued between 2006 and 2018 by the US Customs and Border Protection Agency, the US Coast Guard, and Immigration and Customs Enforcement to corporations. Those contracts included technology, security, and arms firms, as well as private prison companies like CoreCivic and Geo Group. Lockheed Martin, for example, landed a contract worth US$945 million to maintain sixteen P-3 surveillance planes equipped with airborne and surface-to-radar systems.

Raytheon was building border systems that included over 500 mobile surveillance systems, fifteen sustainment centres, and training 9,000 security force members. The border systems funnelled refugees and migrants into private prisons in twenty-four countries. The more people in the prisons, the more profits were made.

Letting them just disappear

His busking was going better. Encouraged, Harry practised his tricks after dinner for hours. He repeated each trick at least twenty times, correcting slight imperfections on every go until there were none left. His hand muscles memorised the precise movements required to jerk and hide the card so that it seemed to disappear, and the position and angle to grasp a spoon and make it appear to bend. The mirror attached to the dresser told him if the illusion was working.

He rehearsed the accompanying routine as well. When Spanish words got caught around his tongue, he played them on his phone and mimicked the pronunciation until he was saying the words just like the female robot voice. He kept his talking to a minimum, employing just the necessary key phrases like; Look! Wait! Where has it gone? Do you know? And there, alone in his hotel room, he acted out asking children and adults, 'Do you know where it has gone?' 'Do you have it?' 'Are you hiding it under your hat?' Until, of course, he did find the teal sponge elephant under one child's hat or under their arm. He had tried that the other day, and the delight of the child and the subsequent higher donations had uplifted him, and he had bought a whole box of the toys so that he could continue to end his routine that way.

After hours rehearsing, Harry fell asleep each night within seconds of pulling the sheets around his shoulders. In bed, he felt cradled and protected. The quietness of the room and state of complete softness melted him into healthy rounds of deep sleep that only ended when his phone alarm woke him at 8 a.m.

But there were 113,188 disappeared people in Mexico that were trying to edge into his dreams, stomping their feet in frustration on the floor of his room and the floors of all rooms in the country, wanting to be heard. Like his cards and coins and teal elephants, they too had been disappeared with little effort. Only they didn't surprise people and turn up in the end. They were still unfound. They existed and then they didn't reply to phone messages or come home one night, and their families and friends never found out why. So they inhabited night spaces and stalked the dreams of the people who missed them. They made the dreams sepia and slow and people woke up and wondered what was the point of anything if their loved one was gone and no one cared enough to investigate. Others understood that if so many Mexicans, migrants, and women could be killed or kidnapped and no one punished, then their own lives did not really matter either. They welcomed the 113,188 disappeared people into their nights, talking to the people who couldn't be talked to, bringing them wine and asking them to explain away the troubled and sharply fragmented sleep time.

But when the disappeared knocked on Harry's dreams, he didn't let them in. Instead, he woke up feeling peaceful and coated in clarity, his mind sharp, his body eager to jump out of bed, stretch and run or walk somewhere. He did his first busk at 11 a.m., and his hands were steady, he remembered the lines he'd memorised, his eye contact was confident, and his good mood attracted more onlookers.

One day, he pulled a teal sponge elephant from the shirt collar of a very old man. The man was sitting on an overturned paint bucket next to his key cutting machine. He had been cutting keys on that street corner for decades. He had also been sitting on the paint bucket for decades and his body had settled into a crinkled state, where he could hunch over his machine and look closely at the keys and wipe them down with a rag that was stiff and black with grease. The man reminded Harry of La Tortuga even though he was ninety-three and much older. Harry very much wanted the man to look up from his work and to smile and assure him that he would find La Tortuga soon. But when Harry pulled the little toy elephant out, he broke through a secret barrier of formality that had developed. A strict separation between key cutter and clients. Rules of no contact, of wishing good day but of not really seeing the man who cut the keys. The flourished magician's gesture was such a break in the man's decades of routine, that at first he looked up in shock. And then he emitted crinkled laughs and stood up from his paint bucket and hugged Harry quickly.

Harry caught it all on video.

A bubble-wrapped bed

Seven more days had passed without La Tortuga really sleeping. She had had only four clients today, whereas previously there had often been short queues of people and rarely any time between each person. Today, she had messed up three times, and the clients had stormed off, and everyone saw it. She had cracked the solar panel of a garden light, dropped a phone SIM card, which had then managed to slip itself under a passing bike wheel and break in two, and she had cut rather than stripped the short power cord of a coffee machine. She had sent Miguelito to buy a new chord, which she then attached, but she didn't make any money from that job.

Walking back from work spot to sleeping spot, though just a few hundred metres, took her thirty-five minutes because her feet were only partially attached to her legs. The blades had gnawed forty percent of the way and it was only a matter of weeks before they finished. She would have been more comfortable leaning on Miguelito as she walked, but she had sent him off to get tortillas on purpose. She didn't want him to see how it was for her to walk now. When she arrived at their sleeping spot, she took out her alebrije for warm comfort, and saw that all of its shell of learnings was gone. The bare-backed turtle was exposed and cold. Its little head dropped on her fingers and turned sideways. Dispirited heads were always heavier.

La Tortuga entered into Clinical Despair; comprised of hopelessness and panic. The hopelessness was a belief in a predetermined unjust future. The panic presented as a frantic peripheral blindness. She looked around, physically acting out her search for solutions. She saw no possibilities though, just disturbed ants, wreckage streets, a parked bus dripping petrol onto a roadkill cat, a man pick-pocketing the crowds waiting at the zebra crossing that no cars would stop for, birds falling midflight because they couldn't be bothered flapping anymore, mountains in the distance rotting from the middle outward, and immature stink clouds obscuring the sun.

Her bag fell off her lap to the ground and poured out all things. La Tortuga picked up one thing and it fell out of her hands, and then she picked up her comb and then her screwdriver and tried to place

The Eyes of the Earth

them back in her bag and they fell out of her hands also. She tried to zip the bag and the zipper head ran over the end of her plait.

She forgot that Miguelito was buying the tortillas and would join her soon. She left her open bag at their sleeping spot and went in search of Any Old Thing that would help her sleep for once. At the back end of the Coppel where the trucks docked, she saw tonnes of boxes. There were huge ones that had once contained unassembled beds, and inside there was bubble wrap, polystyrene corners used to hold bed frames in place, foam peanuts, and enormous plastic bags that had once covered the full bed.

The moon swallowed three sleeping pills and a mouthful of cheap rum to help it pass into night time.

The darkness chased her into a bed box. La Tortuga packaged herself away in a cocoon of bubble-wrap blankets and she sealed the box shut.

She breathed in. And as she breathed out, carbon dioxide began to build up.

Miguelito arrived at the front of the Coppel, a hot bundle of tortillas forming condensation on his hands. He pressed his cheek to it, and then the other, enjoying the warmth. He wanted to eat some now, but where had La Tortuga gone? Her bag was at their spot by the Coppel stairs, its guts everywhere. It looked like she had fled an attacker. He yelled out for her. He walked all the way around the Coppel to see if she was nearby, and she wasn't. He thought that she must have left him, as predicted. That the police had packed her into the back of a van also. He got shadowfaced and looked for holes in the ground so that he could jump back to safety.

But then the bigger safety of their routine held him firm. It reminded him that his legs were strong, and his brain was strong and he was stuck to the earth and standing. He searched again, this time like he was back at their work spot. Calmly diagnosing and fixing a problem. In order to diagnose, he gathered the facts he had. He knew that La Tortuga was exhausted and that she had to walk very slowly.

He had seen her heading towards the Coppel, and her bag was still there, so if the police hadn't taken her, she couldn't be far. He headed towards the back area where all the boxes were.

Inside one of them, the air had already gone from 0.04% CO_2 to 1%. Skeletons with cheeky smiles and stringless guitars danced around it. La Tortuga's breath became shorter, her heart rate sped up, her shoulders and stomach were sweaty. She was tired and sluggish and she noticed that the stars were turning up inside her box, like glib party guests. She was close to passing out and she was glad.

Miguelito saw that one of the boxes had been pulled away from the rest and it was rounded in the middle as though curving around a body. He looked inside, and having found his Tortuga, he returned for her bag and stuff, then got in the box with her and snuggled. Relieved and forgetting hunger, he balanced the tortillas on their hips and let them warm them. Oxygen had flowed in when he opened the box flap, but now two bodies breathed out carbon dioxide. The small space and the trusted company were soothing. A few hours passed. He felt her breath slowing, like a steam train pulling to a halt. He didn't know very much about sleep yet. Maybe in one of sleep stages, people did make deep, guttural brake noises and stop breathing. He coughed. He tried to say, "Abuela?" but he couldn't talk.

"The sky is a jigsaw puzzle that rarely falls apart," he mouthed into one of her ears, and then the other. It was what she had told him about that day in the park. "If you can identify the puzzle pieces of the thing that is broken, you can work out how to fix it, how to heal it," she'd said.

And he thought, maybe these are puzzles she is giving me. First to find her, and then to work out how to let the air in, without letting in the cold.

The Eyes of the Earth

A magician in a Coppel store eludes his fans

It was midday, and Harry was in a Coppel store, trying very hard to disappear. There were no gadgets he could use to make himself invisible, and misdirection only worked to shift attention away from the hand doing the trick. There was no way to misdirect people away from your entire self, at least not without an accomplice. So he used techniques like avoiding eye contact and looking busy. He hunched himself a little to make himself smaller and less noticeable. He put his earphones in and acted absorbed in a podcast so that no one would want to disturb him.

A few days ago, his most recent magic busking video had gone viral. Like all his other videos, it had been aimed at a US audience, but because it had been filmed in front of the Monument to the Revolution, it had quickly reached Mexicans as well. He had been recognised on the train yesterday, and by the receptionist of his hotel, so now he worried that anyone who made eye contact with him in the store was going to come over and talk to him. He didn't want to talk to any strangers and have to feign interest and warmth towards them.

He was looking for a new video camera. He had been paying kids small tips to hold his camera while he performed, but having watched the viral video himself a few times, he had decided that he needed at least two camera angles. He wanted a second camera, and eventually to pay two regular camera people.

The video cameras were in glass display cases with white shelving. The white tiled floor was mirrored above by white ceiling panels. To Harry's left, customers headed up an elevator to the second floor, in order to queue at the checkouts, there and pay off their twice-monthly instalments for products they had bought. On both floors, roaming assistants tried to help customers by reading the details of products out loud from their shelf tags or packaging, because they had only been trained in processing payments and knew little about the goods sold.

Continuing to avoid eye contact, Harry put his face right up to the glass, to inspect the cameras closely. He left a circle of his breath on the glass in front of three cameras in a row, the fog circles fading quickly so that the one closest to him was now the biggest.

The Coppel shop was not the same one where La Tortuga slept. The department store had over 1,500 outlets around the country, and this one was close to Harry's hotel. His three weeks to find La Tortuga were almost up, but that seemed less important now that his videos were taking off. Thanks to the recent viral video, Harry's subscriber count was now 11,000. Companies had begun sending him emails asking for paid product endorsements or to sponsor his videos.

After the first email, he had gloated. He went up to the hotel roof bar and ordered straight shots of mezcal and didn't trip once on the way there. He chatted to people and laughed too loudly. Hard sounds of LED coloured light bulbs and greasy honey. He acted like overly eager street signage. Finally, things were working out how they were meant to. The success that should come so easily to people like him, was starting to happen.

But Harry had only stayed in gloat mode for ninety-five minutes. Then he went back down to his room, and he stepped down from the clouds to hard ground and real life, and he sought moderation. He turned off the LED bulbs flashing at the edges of his laughter and rested into a kinder state of nuanced humility. He watered down the beginnings of arrogance into something more palatable. He decided, then, to fit in an extra session of magic practice and study before dinner as well, and to wake up half an hour earlier to practice conversational Spanish using a phone app. He also wanted to watch his videos after he had edited them, and they were uploaded and note at least one thing to improve on for the next one.

He was debating between two cameras when a man with eager eyes and deep creases running from either side of his nose to his chin, spotted him. He pointed right at him, clapped his hands, then approached him. It was clear that he was a permanently jolly person, and his excited, tender grin had a strength to it, like it would survive crises and disasters.

"I know you, you're in those magic trick videos. You should go to Guadalajara too sometime. That's where my family is," he said in Spanish. Harry's face lost expression, because he didn't know how to respond. But he found a few words he could use, "Si, claro," though he couldn't muster an eagerness to match the man's. He really tried though. He smiled back and shook the man's hand.

Though he didn't enjoy the interaction, he was enjoying this appreciation he was getting. This being known and seen, even in Mexico where he had so few friends or contacts.

It was small fame. And fame was a confusing thing, because it was one of the ways of loving.

Being seen was part of what it meant to be loved, but fame was limp love. Gaseous and glassy. It lacked reciprocity, meaning, comprehension, and care. And so it was a strange force that was able to build someone up and increase income, while also fomenting distrust and deepening soul cavities, punctures, and squishiness.

Harry now had 33,900 pesos saved from busking.

Noise

The noise that filled the days consisted of: a thunderous arms industry, the shrill sound of relationships clashing and crashing with work stress and large health care bills, the raging deluge of merchandise, the blaring billboards blocking out the sky, the rich and famous parading on red carpets in screaming diamond jewellery, the chainsaw murder of old forests, the grating hum of tedious promotional videos occupying all the mindspace, the high fences protecting inequality, the hissing of police gunshots penetrating protesters, and the squawking sounds of men judging women's bodies as they hurry to work.

While other things went barely heard: the slow and colourful growth of imagination, a soul given without ceremony to causes, a movement fighting for each breath, stories being planted among the calendar days, whispered hugs of solidarity, something new understood, the blanket warmth of sunsets, eyelid kisses, stars and whales, the mourning of the unloved and the morning of night shift nurses, and the unravelling of prejudice.

After filling the day, the harsh noises tore up the night and stopped soft souls from falling completely into sleep.

The day after

I have slept a full ten hours. Though I have a strong headache, I feel infatuated with the world again. The sun stroking my eyelids. An aftertaste of hot corn-coffee with a dash of cinnamon. The wind blowing in curly shapes. Flaunting its moods. This morning it is playful.

I feel ashamed now, to have thought of giving up. I didn't want to die, I just wanted to stop. The battles come at you daily, like being slow fired at by a machine gun. One day's meal solved, but tomorrow there's another to solve. Another sleep to solve. But this half-broken boy sitting on my knee eating cold tortillas solved last night's puzzles, and if he can do that then I can keep on going too. I do think that even a fair life involves taking on harder and harder things until you have tender superpowers. All mountain heart and fire sparks (star babies). That's why I have always found it odd that the superheroes in movies are born that way. Maybe the writers and producers were born with advantages, and they think that's how deep skill works.

So today, I want to show Miguelito what is possible. That if he masters fixing and care, he too will be able to conjure life from waste and hopelessness.

***

During La Tortuga's long sleep, her partially-severed ankles started to heal. Just enough to be more than half attached, and for a red-purple scar to begin forming. For now, the grates in her shoes stood down. As though in retreat after being told off. Yet, waiting and ready also. She walked to the end of the Coppel docking area and decided that the quieter back street would be a good place to test out if her magic was working again. She put little Miguelito on a wooden box. "Sit here, *chiquillo*, watch," she said.

La Tortuga built up a pile of putrid patterns, harsh noises, and rubbish paradigms. She took modicums of the war drums and the high fences and used them to start the pile. She took iotas of formulaic movies with racist stereotypes, a smidgen of the times that corruption exhausted a soul, a smattering of people stepping on the broken bones of beings and selling out to the highest bidder so they could get ahead in the race, a snippet of the distrust oozing from the pores of people regularly betrayed by society's institutions, a morsel of the fossil fuel lobby, a handful of the overuse of plastics, snippets of massacres glorified as battles, thimblefuls of sensationalised headlines, and an eyeful of a Walmart sign the size of a bedroom that stood among the barren landscape of shops like a lighthouse, so that people could find the Walmart wherever they were but not the unmarked bus stops, and added it all to the pile.

She worked like a writer. Or a journalist, or an activist. She noticed and named the rubbish and felt it - held its foul odour in her hands. She declared it unacceptable, and she inserted her hands into the agony of ranked humans, into the normalisation of suffering and she sent out barely perceived and insufficient whispers of hope into the moody wind, where they dissipated. With the same fizzing sparks that the news of injustice had, as it quickly lost its impact. And yet the world would have been smothered by icy air if not for the insufficient whispers of people who believed, against all their experience, that decency was possible.

Massaging, noticing, naming, and converting the pile took her all day and through to late at night.

Out of the pile she grew a vine of butterflies, its double leaves sprouting at intervals along the stem then detaching when fully matured and flying off. She grew a seeing tree with slowly blinking eyes dispersed about its trunk, absorbing the world around it with curiosity and concern. And tulips that dripped a deep turquoise sap, intentionally staining the bare ground around them with a colour that contrasted with their mauve petals. And a fluffy wattle-like plant that walked a metre or so a year and left behind its footprints. And ferns engaged in a slow and long-lasting seahorse dance, embracing each other in a never-ending weave. Like that, they were so hard to break. As a fixer, La Tortuga appreciated delicate things that were hard to break. Resilience with sensitivity was one of her favourite combinations.

She also grew and made the sensation of lightness that came with an absence of injustice. The kind of lightness that contained relief, alertness, and an urge to chat with strangers and take new paths home. She grew corn as it had been grown on these lands for thousands of years, with red, purple, and orange gems of colour. Zucchini flowers too. She showed Miguelito how to make fires, and they had barbecued vegetables for dinner.

And then finally, around midnight, she made pillow plants. She potted two of them in discarded plastic bags and gave one to Miguelito to hold on to. "These are for us," she said.

It was time to sleep again, but La Tortuga was paying a price for so much conversion. Not only had they missed a full day's work, but she aged quicker that day. Her morning headache became a migraine that night that took over her whole head, face, and then her shoulders and arms. Miguelito massaged her head, applied pressure to the top of her nose and smoothed it out over her eyebrows. And she bled, like slow body tears, though she'd gone through menopause twenty years ago.

Though Miguelito was half broken, he was all-child. And children tended to feel amazement rather than disbelief. So he did not doubt that his friend, his grandmother-protector-teacher did special things that he didn't know how to do.

"Can you sing too?" he asked, because he thought that was also a magical skill.

Adhesion

"Let's name all the ways broken things can be stuck together," La Tortuga said. "I'll start. Velcro."

"Sewing," said Miguelito.

"Nails," said La Tortuga. And so the list went on. Magnets, clips, soldering, brazing, mechanical fitting, string and knots, suction…

"Holding hands," said Miguelito.

They were sleeping on layers of bed boxes, with another flattened box covering them. The tops of their heads were just visible, as hints of humans in a cardboard sandwich.

Lists were what they did now when they woke up in the middle of the night. After work, after Miguelito asked his questions, La Tortuga told stories to relax them and hopefully get them to sleep. The stories had lessons and morals, or were about Honduras, or involved leaps of the imagination that made Miguelito laugh. "What then?" he asked, over and over, until the stories of clean skies, tree houses, and spells for safety, couldn't go on anymore.

But if they woke up again, it was lists. Lists of animals, of things sold in the markets, of train stations, of categories of time. He would always fall asleep first, tapping his foot to the items in the list, and then as he sleep-breathed, his tiny foot kept on tapping at the cardboard. La Tortuga tucked his panda toy back into his fingers. Her trapezius muscle spasmed and she rolled over, and Miguelito followed her. Like he was velcroed to her.

During the day, he was likewise clinging to her. She gave him more and more small tasks. "Screw that in for me," "Glue these two pieces together," "Cut and strip this wire," she would say, as she passed him the tools and the bits. And he did so, but with one hand clutching at the knee of her pants. Then he sat back down, stuck to her side, and when she got up to look for change or buy them water, he followed her, leaving no space between himself and her left leg.

It was as though a gap between them represented the start of abandon. And La Tortuga worried about that. He is being ruled by fear, she told herself. He is just a child, she counted. Let him catch up on the amount of love a child needs. After that, teach him the puzzle of being both independent and still letting people care for him.

The next morning, when La Tortuga kissed the top of his half-bald head, she noticed new hairs growing there. He was healing, self-fixing. He knew what he needed right now, she told herself. That day she also noticed his new laughter. It was unused and just unwrapped and all shiny and fresh. He laughed like that with her caresses and stories, and beamed when she gave him tasks. His eye cleared up, and the gaping wound on his leg had finally cleaned and closed and was now a dark blue-brown 10 centimetre-long furrow. A shallow trench.

Another night, she told him a story of tiny elf soldiers who fought there. She told him how a wound could become a battleground when there was an infection, between the immune system trying to live and heal and other invaders trying to destroy. "Ah, so the immune system is winning and soon there will be peace," he concluded.

La Tortuga had 720 pesos saved in the secret pocket of her bag.

The system of monsters: Rubbish ranters

Rubbish ranters were another key segment in the alliance of self-declared kings, in the elite club of beasts and monsters. These advertising execs and media moguls wore plastic pink or titanium ties and the extra-firm gel in their sleek hair smelled of bubblegum. Their lips were made of gelatin candy and their teeth of caramel shards, and a malicious purple methane gas chuffed from their flapping mouths. Decomposing fatty acids and toxic methane, the residues of their mass production of rubbish words, seeped out of their pores.

The Eyes of the Earth

The rubbish ranters smothered the world in a toxic layer of marketing and not-news, covering doctors' offices, hospitals, gas stations, roadsides, garbage cans, bus windows, most of the Internet, parts of the sky, and scenes in movies in junk words, thereby infusing brains with concoctions of mediocrity. At a rate of 3000 ads per day per person, they buried critical thought in a mound of mental smog. They used native advertising, content mills, sponsored influencers, enormous billboards and selective news stories to tamper with information and with How Life Was Understood, and to manipulate people's wishes and weaknesses. Their lying was a complex skill, and they spent US$50 billion on big data analytics per year to understand people's buying behaviour and psychology. They used social media listening, shopping data, clickstream data, psychographic analyses, and private data collection to stimulate over-the-top levels of consumerism.

And by filling the air with distortions and manipulation, they planted distrust. People knew that advertising exaggerated the pros and left out the cons of a product, they knew the mainstream media sensationalised and omitted important news and context, and this daily practising of distrust wove itself into their personal lives and moods. But the clutter still obscured their vision of the things that really mattered, and their sight was trained to latch on to the quick videos, edited bodies, and tampered reality.

The rubbish ranters breathed out more methane and Harry felt nauseous. La Tortuga and Miguelito walked past shops and billboards and hoped for things they didn't need and forgot what they had been talking about. Spy beasts had told the rubbish ranters about La Tortuga's resistance to waste and her long day of magic, and so the rubbish ranters turned up her self-doubt by three notches and turned down her voice by two notches. They released a special social media campaign about how little old people contributed to the economy and managed to increase her invisibility - how much she was overlooked, by a further four notches. She would have fewer clients over the next week. But worst of all, they used her lowered self-worth to give her a new trait she had never had before; indecisiveness. Unboldness.

In Mexico City, they injected websites and social media with extra clutter and misinformation. People kept getting lost. They tried to have hope but then got distracted. They dreamed in fluro colours and drowned in slogans, cliches, and simplifications.

Meanwhile, as the day for the grand monsters´ meeting was fast approaching, the rubbish ranters got busy preparing PR for that too. They had a lot to do. They had to make the dangerous appear safe and build momentum and support in order to avoid protests, without revealing the real motives of the global conference of beasts. They had to paint ominous clouds in sophistication and disguise immoral intentions in token gestures, formality and procedures. They glorified gluttony and acquired the appropriate costumes and props to perform quick change tricks on the monster members and turn them all into heroes.

When Harry wasn't a hero

Harry was power walking to the Promesas market when he saw La Tortuga and a tiny child sitting on the footpath with tools and a sign against the wall. By now, he had accepted that he likely wouldn't find her, and he was so focused on his busking regime - starting at 10 a.m., filming after the first thirty minutes once a crowd had built up, and leaving by midday - that he walked past her. La Tortuga didn't see him. She was unscrewing a hand-held mixer. Miguelito though, did see the tall, blond man racing along the street, his mouth moving slightly as he went over his morning plans.

Harry had a target of one thousand YouTube views in the first five hours after publication for today's video. He planned to edit it quickly that night, so he didn't want to be delayed. It took him ten strides to stop walking and turn around and check if it was her. Damn, it was. He stood there, hesitating, and a man carrying three handmade

The Eyes of the Earth

foldable wooden tables under each arm had to walk around him. She seemed okay, he told himself.

She hadn't greeted him either, maybe she didn't want to talk to him. Maybe she didn't even remember him. He wanted to keep going. To have a reason to avoid a conversation with his weak Spanish and lack of small talk skills. But she was one of his key goals, and he imagined being able to go back to the US and telling people that he had done something good on his trip, not just filmed videos. He made his way back to her.

"You disappeared one day, and I was worried. I didn't know what had happened to you," he spoke into his phone app. La Tortuga listened to the translation and peered at his troubled face, and she felt warmed that someone had noticed.

Harry didn't know how to transition to his offer. So he stated it out right.

"I'd like to help you," he said. Then he showed her a photo of his old hostel near the Zócalo, smiled at her, and called them. Speaking in English, he gave his name, reminded them he had stayed there around six weeks ago, and said he'd like to book a bunk bed for a friend for the next two weeks, and would pay in advance with his credit card. He blushed and bit his lip as he turned to La Tortuga and asked her, this time in Spanish, "What's your name?"

"My full name?" she replied, puzzled, unsure what he wanted it for, and gesturing "long" with her hands. Harry nodded. "Clementina Cardoza Olmedo," she said, seeing no reason not to tell him. She still had no identification anyway. Harry asked her to repeat it, passing the phone to her.

When he hung up, he said, "I've paid for a bunk bed in this hostel for you for two weeks. You can go there this afternoon and tell them your name. They have great showers and a big free breakfast every morning."

La Tortuga still looked puzzled. Her face clouded over and she said, somewhat coldly, "Gracias." Harry said he would come and see her in a few days, and then he left. Her lack of gratitude confused him. It contrasted, as a cumbersome shadow, with the reactions he was getting to his videos. It cast murky monochrome doubt on those reactions. Injected fragility into his new confidence.

Miguelito grasped at La Tortuga's leg, his eyes all wide with excitement and curiosity, "What did that man give us?"

***

La Tortuga's alebrije wanted to talk to Harry, to warn him about what could happen when unrequested help was given. It eased itself out of the secret bag pocket and ran, as fast as a tiny alebrije turtle could, after him. It wove in and out of feet and leaped over what seemed like giant gaps and bumps in the footpath and shook itself out of taco serviettes that fell over it. Harry was walking slowly; a thoughtful, disturbed walk, and so the tiny alebrije was able to catch up and hang on to his shoelace.

Harry tripped repeatedly. Not because of the alebrije, nor because of the uneven footpath, or the washed out and whitened Coca-Cola bottle that rolled by him, seemingly on its own strange journey somewhere. Harry knew this unprovoked tripping was guilt rearing its head and he wondered why it was back when helping La Tortuga was meant to be the antidote. She had not responded how he expected, and he couldn't imagine why.

In the end, he only busked for forty-five minutes, and it didn't go well. He went back to his hotel, stopping to pick up a family-size eggplant and salami pizza from an Italian restaurant and a bottle of white wine from the Oxxo corner store. Sitting cross-legged on his bed, with his back against the headboard and his food by his side, he tried to feel better. But the pizza slid out of its box, and he quickly put it back again, then the blanket tangled around his arm. As he tried to tug it out, he rocked his other hand holding a plastic cup of wine, which then partially spilt onto the bed. He felt sorry for himself and like quitting it all, and so he let his arm stay tangled and ignored the wet patch and kept on eating pizza. But guilt had un-faded. Stepped out of its cupboard space in The Past and emerged as a droning headache that settled into his forehead and the back of his neck. Harry's soul perforations itched as the meaning and direction he had been deriving from making the videos tapered off.

The alebrije thought that now was a good time to show itself and try to say all the things that La Tortuga wished she could have said. It climbed up on to his stomach and jumped up and down in front of his face, which was fixated on the television on the wall facing the bed. So he didn't see it. It stomped, but he didn't feel it. It yelled out tiny messages, but he didn't hear. It delivered him little packages of concern and worry, it left notes in bubbles, and it folded up outcries and tied them to the ends of bows directed at his aching head, but he did not notice.

Its messages were; unrequested help is condescending and lacking in understanding and inquiry. Your underlying intention is about you feeling good rather than about recognising the entirety of the other person. So you create a dynamic of victim and saviour rather than identifying a broader problem that needs to be solved. You're still not seeing, Harry. Your eyes are still opaqued by those white curtains. You are blind to the exercise of power and how that is perpetuated. Wake up, Harry. Ask more questions.

***

La Tortuga watched Harry leave, startled, and also aware that she hadn't been polite or grateful enough. He had given her something and she hadn't known how to thank him for a gift she couldn't accept. For the first hour after he left, there was no doubt in her mind that she would not turn up to that hostel. She couldn't leave Miguelito. But then in the second hour, the What Ifs started. What if, after a week of real rest in a bed, her work and their income improved, and she could then pay for a bunk for him too. Then they could both rest for another week, earn more, and things may start improving. In the third hour she realised this could be the leg up she needed. And in the fourth hour she noticed that she also felt very angry. Harry hadn't asked her if she already had somewhere to live, or if she would prefer, say, a hostel that was cheaper than the one right by the Zócalo and a longer stay. And he hadn't even greeted Miguelito.

And so she had a dilemma. She had come to Mexico on her own, without Miguelito, and with one main mission; to sleep on her own, in peace. Now she had spent months sleeping on the streets, and she knew that she couldn't take it much longer. At the same time, her heart would break to leave Miguelito outside, and maybe she wouldn't be able to sleep knowing that he was out there, anyway. But, how could she resist the very thing she needed right now, with breakfast and a warm shower every day? She could sneak breakfast out to Miguelito and take advantage of the showers to wash his clothes. But she also felt humiliated by Harry's gesture. She didn't know what to do.

"It's okay," Miguelito said. And he did what adults had done to him and patted her roughly on the head. She explained the problem to him and asked him what he thought the solution was. "You could take me in with you. I would be really quiet. Fold me into your bag."

She laughed, sadly, "Ah mi querido, you'd never fit, and I'm not strong enough to carry you."

Miguelito thought he knew what she was going to choose. He sensed it in the way her eyesight line was dodging his. He sensed it because it had been a short while since life had malfunctioned. A while since The Way Things Were Supposed to Be, with life safety and parents and homes, had collapsed. He supposed it was time for his feet to unstick from earth again. His cracked and peeling being breathed out and slumped, his arms dropping beside him and his head falling onto his chest. His throat filled with lumps and he let them sit there rather than trying to swallow.

La Tortuga pulled him close to her. "I wouldn't leave you little one. We could still work together during the day. Only this way, we'd have somewhere to fill our water bottles, clean our clothes, have food for breakfast, and we could save money on food because I could cook us pasta, rice, and Maggi noodles in the hostel kitchen." She was convincing herself, but not him.

"You'd just be alone at night. But I promise I would come out first thing in the morning and wake you."

She would get him to sleep right by the hostel. But she hadn't totally made up her mind yet. Or maybe she had.

Where truth bombs were hidden

There were fortune cookies; random predictions on tiny paper in biscuit parcels. Few knew though that there were also truth bombs. They were almost like poems, also on tiny rolled-up paper, stored in tiny glass bottles. But they were carried around in the pockets of people who weren't seen or heard. And so when those people opened up the tiny glass bottles, the vivid explosions usually unsettled people who would rather not be disturbed. The truths hurt and they shattered and mangled delusions that people had built up for themselves. They messed with the staged Instagram world of Things Are As They Should Be set to glossy, upbeat colours. They were undiplomatic and unpleasant.

In the Democratic Republic of the Congo, there were 24 million cases of malaria each year, and of those, 48,000 people, mostly small children, died. A young rubber farm worker who had contracted malaria and had no access to health care, carried around the following truth bombs:

- Charity was just PR for many wealthy individuals. For companies, it was an elaborate marketing campaign with the added benefit of tax deductions.

- People involved in movements for justice on the other hand did not receive PR benefits.

- Companies used charity for its convenience. They could throw money at an issue and wash their hands of responsibility.

- Justice involved persistent hunting for the threads of history, asking the hardest questions, after-hours meetings, slow growth, and sacrifice.

- Charity intensified inequality. It endowed corporations and wealthy countries and individuals with decision-making powers over the poor, and normalised their dependency on assistance.

- Justice aimed for the eradication of the systemic violence of extreme inequality. And so it threatened the pedestals and podiums of the super wealthy.

- Charity was a privatised, unaccountable, uncoordinated and short-term effort.

- Justice was a chronic illness cured, never to return.

Three beds

The first night La Tortuga spent in the hostel, Miguelito clung onto her with his feet, hands, and mouth. He wrapped himself around her leg, grabbed at her clothes and his mouth clamped down on her wrist and he refused to let her go.

She gave him one kiss on each part of him holding on to her.

"I know it's hard," she said.

Then she waited.

She watched as his grip softened. Turned into loose knots, as the street dogs walked passed them. Ignored them. As the air turned chilly.

Miguelito's jaw slacked. "I need a few nights of real sleep, little panda," she said. He liked it when she called him that. His hands let go of her clothes. "I'll look for you first thing in the morning and we'll have chilaquiles and coffee together in fresh clean clothes." His legs unwrapped.

"Okay, but say good night to me," he negotiated.

She took him to his new spot, an abandoned sponge and plastic mat in the street behind the hostel. She put his panda toy in his hand and placed her coat over him and tucked it under his sides. She had abandoned one pillow tree, but the other she put by his head and bent it down so that he could use it. "Good night pandas, until tomorrow."

In her dorm, she put her things into the locker next to her bunk. She didn't have a padlock, so she just closed the door, hoping it was enough. Then she peeled back the white sheet and climbed into the bed. She sunk into the unfamiliar mattress, and it received her and held her with medical coldness.

She felt halfway there. Half comfort. Because she was in a bed, but it wasn't her own. The dense mattress foam consoled her aches and pains, softened them, quietened them. The pillow warmed the back of her head and neck. The blanket over the white sheet was tucked in so tightly toward the bottom of the bed that her feet were rotated and pinned down. But they were safe from her shoes, stored in her locker, for now. And so they half relaxed. Safe for now but not forever.

She slept for exactly one hour. That is, her body rested. Her worries took a short break. An interlude. Then she woke up. She listened to the open window breathing harshly as the curtain got stuck, then was released. It was asthmatic. She sensed Miguelito. He was a little more comfortable but a lot more alone. She could tell that he was awake, that he was repeating her words to himself to try to calm down enough to sleep. She saw him giving up and just lying there, waving his hand in the air in a go-ahead gesture to get time to move faster. She missed him.

The quietness and temporary safety gave her space to think. She noticed things that were missing from her days, like long adult conversations. She wanted one of those passionate disagreements that ended in her realisation. One where they started out stubborn but ended up at new truths. Opened up like that, they then moved on to confiding. And she would tell that person that she had turned off half of herself so that she could get through each day.

She woke up several more times that night.

***

Miguelito could feel the street's lumps through the mat. He was cold, but his skin on the plastic was sweating and getting itchy. Though the mat was more comfortable than cardboard, he found it hard to settle on a sleeping position. He tried his back, then his side, then his back again. He missed the greater comfort, his Tortuga, with her plait tingling his cheek and her strange breathing rhythm. She had told him to focus on the next morning rather than on now. Instead, his exposed little being interpreted every sound. He counted the distant parties. He tracked the wandering drunks. He jerked each time the taxi drivers slammed their door closed, then he watched as they sagged-stood against the passenger doors of their taxis, waiting, their breath falling upwards from their mouths in pathetic white wisps. "Here I am," said the taxis with their glowing taxi signs. "Here I am," said the light posts. "I am not here," said the street sleepers, dressed in black and eyes averted. Time did pass though, and the number of drunks got less. There were just three taxis parked outside the hostel, then just one. Only the lobby light was left on in the hostel. If everybody was asleep now, nobody could hurt him, he reasoned. Even the monsters sleep eventually.

But then he saw that the night streets were in fact crowded with weary ghosts. Memories of all the disappeared people and the too-early deaths. He saw that even under the city streets there were grey people. All the barely alive ones who didn't sleep. Who took their whole lives to slow-drown, while they watched the city above them go about shopping and dining, oblivious.

***

Harry thought he had the most comfortable bed in Mexico City. The mattress had a three-inch layer of memory foam and gel for cooling, and was covered in Egyptian cotton sheets, and the fluffiest doona. He had six pillows. He also thought he was the one of the loneliest people in the city. He didn't have a person he was looking forward to seeing soon. It seemed loneliness trumped comfortable bed, because he couldn't sleep. As that day's video loaded, he squirmed and turned in the bed, his laptop by one side and his phone in his other hand.

Then he wiggled out of bed for a last pee, taking his phone with him. Like a pet or a friend.

Back in bed, he scrolled through the different apps, hoping for a message. Something more personal than a like or a comment. He turned off the bedside lamp and in darkness, he checked his phone again. He considered messaging people he hadn't talked to in a while, then decided against it. He wasn't up for small talk. He wanted someone to look straight at him and ask him how his day had gone. He wanted authentic conversations with someone who knew the details of his life. That's what you get for travelling, he thought. It wasn't the best way to develop long-term connections. He had an urge to ask La Tortuga what she thought. And because his mind often went blank when he talked with her and he was going to check on how she was going and he really wanted to get to know her better, he saved the question in the special drawer in his mind: Can you have deep and personal connections with people you meet only briefly?

He half-closed his eyes and he was walking among wrinkled mountains. As he walked, geckos scampered away, sand scattered, green jays lifted off and flew away, trees leaned away from him, the rare and remarkable flowers of succulents withered and shrivelled, and the wind fled until he was being in nothing. He was gone, and he imagined the cleaners coming into his hotel room and finding his bed still made and wondering what had happened to him. His family and friends in the US were all very worried. And La Tortuga was being told by the receptionist of the hostel that he had just vanished, and she was upset. This sensation of being missed made his eyelids heavy, and he finally managed to sleep.

Mapping the insides of things

The hardware shop on the corner of 12th and 5th was a maze of intrigue to Miguelito. Its shelves were stocked with delights, and he couldn't contain himself. There were aisles of lights, electric tools, pipe parts, gloves and tape. There were tall hessian bags of cal, sawdust, and concrete mix. In the glass cabinet at the back, there were different sized padlocks, and behind the counter, rat poison, glues, drill bits, paintbrushes, and containers full of all sorts of mysterious things. An old couple ran the shop, and every so often, in response to a customer request, one of them would disappear through a back door into a secret cave of extra mysteries. Miguelito ran from item to item, picking it up, looking at it excitedly, then spying another thing out of the corner of his eye and running to that. And so he went, like a hyperactive bee, from aisle to aisle. La Tortuga had sent him to get flange bolts and hot glue, but he had forgotten all about that. He took different products to the counter and asked the couple what they were and how they were used. As it was early in the morning and quiet, they showed him. The woman whispered special tips to him, asking him to repeat back her words, demanding accuracy, as though passing on sacred knowledge. To Miguelito, the couple were wizards of the highest order. Almost at La Tortuga level. They knew everything.

There was a box on the lowest shelf behind the counter and Miguelito wanted to know what was in it.

"That's where we keep all the broken things," the man said.

"All of them?" Miguelito was incredulous.

The man smiled. "Well, all the things that have broken in this shop. I'm sure we have something in there for you."

Miguelito stood on his toes and lifted himself up using the top of the counter and tried to see inside the box as the man crouched down and rummaged through it. He brought a chipped and scratched dentist's mirror over to the counter.

"What does it do? Why is the mirror so small?"

"Dentists use this to look inside people's mouths, but it can be used to look inside all sorts of things. We can't use it, would you like it?"

On the way back to their spot, Miguelito jabbed the tiny mirror into everything he could. And when an object had no inside area, he tapped it on the surface, like a wand. He inserted it inside a street drain grill, wondering what was under the world during day time, and if the grey people were still there. But all he saw was ninety-year-old pipes, inactive treatment plants, far off rivers cringing at the rubbish that had been swept into the drains, and unravelled storms. He tried to tap a lizard, but it got away. Passing through the market, he stuck his mirror into bouquets of flowers and he saw a beetle king lounging on the pillowy petals. He put the mirror into a basket of dried chillies and saw farm workers erecting solar tunnel dryers. Looking closer he could see the red glow of intensified heat. He stuck the mirror in through the hole in the bottom of a garden gnome from Huasca and saw classical music and rope swings. He ran through the plaza, stopped at its clock mounted on a column, and tapped it. Inside time he saw lives organised like factory assembly lines. Timetabled tasks, hectic and precise coordination that lacked any sense of the patterns and rhythms of bodies and climate and culture.

Just before reaching a slightly worried Tortuga, he stopped by the tortilleria. He wanted to know how the tortilla machine worked, and he asked them if he could look inside. To the frustration of the six people waiting in the queue, the workers stopped the machine for a few seconds so he could poke his mirror about inside.

Miguelito told La Tortuga everything he remembered seeing. He described most parts of the roller machine as "circle thing touching a long thing." She asked him to draw a diagram.

"What's a diagram?"

"It's like a map, of the inside of things."

As he drew, La Tortuga chatted. "Did you know the earliest maps were of the stars, not of the earth?"

"Why?"

"I think they wanted to find the patterns in the sky. And if they could work out where they were in all that, they thought they could understand who they were. Also, stars help you know which direction you're heading in, if you're in a boat or travelling across big stretches of land."

"Did you use stars when you walked to Mexico?"

"No, mi niño, I used roads."

"I want to map the inside of your head," Miguelito said, and pointed his mirror at her ear. He nodded seriously to himself and started another drawing.

After helping a customer with a quick fix, La Tortuga peered at his drawing. All she saw was a series of overlapping rectangles and arrows, but Miguelito explained, "These are your parents, and this is your bed in the hostel, and these are our tools, and these are all the stories you have, all piled up on each other. You need to clean them up a bit. Tidy your stories."

Over the next few days, Miguelito used the dentist's mirror to accurately diagnose issues with a portable hard drive and two cameras. He also pointed it at the things he wanted to understand. He aimed it at the rays of sunlight squeezing through the market tarpaulins and settling upon his knees, and he saw big affection from the sky. He touched it to a series of bronze commemorative plaques on buildings, and he saw history bookmarks. He aimed it at cowardice and saw a yellowish retreat away from life and into oneself and excessive safety.

The Eyes of the Earth

He learned that most things had some kind of internal map and began to see the components and objects of life differently.

Future tense

At night, Miguelito was now accompanied by two friends. His panda toy and his dentist's mirror. That made the cold night less bare. A little less cruel. With so many friends, he was almost a family, almost an army. The dangerous and scary night things slunk away, intimidated.

Also, Miguelito felt bigger and louder. Because drawing the insides of things was a fun announcement that he was capable of something. And capability was agency, which in turn was hope and possibility. There was comfort and raw joy in a newfound skill. And so to relax, he drew diagrams and fixed and made things until sleep finally conquered him. Having watched La Tortuga repair a torch earlier that day and then having pointed his mirror at it and drawn its internal map, now he made his own. He used a green soft drink bottle, a simple on/off switch, wires, an LED light, and a battery. The next night, with his torch to help him, he made a fabric coin belt with pockets for different coins and notes to use at their repair spot. On the sixth night sleeping on his own, he made a retractable pen-screwdriver.

Each morning he showed La Tortuga. No hello, just "Look!"

La Tortuga's face warmed and her eyes widened as she took the new creation in.

"Wow, that's amazing," she said, meaning it.

And she watched him playing while they waited for clients. The little guy is really talented, she thought. I'm worried about how little sleep he's getting, but on the other hand, his inventiveness will develop his initiative. He's learning to exist. I can actually believe that he'll be okay one day.

She imagined him as an adult. She would have passed on, but he would be inventing non-fossil-fuel-dependent planes, or cures for deadly illnesses.

Miguelito came over and put one hand on the top of her head to hold it still, then with the other, held his dentist's mirror to her ear.

"You're thinking about the future."

"I am. I have a lot of hope for you."

"I want to have a hardware shop where people go to get things fixed. I especially want to fix bicycles, cameras, toys, and blenders."

"Those are very different types of things. Usually, people with shops just fix one type of thing."

"Our shop will be different though," he said matter-of-factly.

On the seventh night, Miguelito stroked two empty and tiny snail shells for four long hours, until they breathed on their own. He would have one and he would give one to La Tortuga. After they held them tightly, the shells would sync with their breathing, then they would swap. At night they would place the other's shell near them and they could touch it and know that they were okay. That had been the most important problem for him to solve.

Alive

The flat, concrete roofs of Mexico City, smeared in thick coats of burgundy waterproof paint, were only a slightly darker tone of red than the sunset. As though, for a moment, the sky and city had found their harmony, with the sky's gradient seamlessly continuing into the city, the builder thought. Waiting for the mastic to be dry to the touch, he was lying on the roof and enjoying its warmth under his back. It was a rare pause. A break in...The never-ending steep stairs of work and worry, jumping like a frantic and scattered madman from barely paying one bill to paying the rent, to buying food staples. Barely getting through each day and so if he worked less, he wouldn't make it, he wouldn't feed his son.

It was a compromised pause, because awareness of what was pending never left him and only moved into the background for a moment. His frayed mind started out with hesitant somersaults, then unravelled and noticed and listed beautiful things. Collected and stored them away for future times of scarcity. He saw the sunset expanding as it sunk downwards, its arms striving to wrap all the way around the city. Wind swiped his face with gentle and quick brush strokes of evening cold. A gecko ran out to his shadeless part of the roof and joined him under the sun. It froze in push-up position, and the builder watched it. What confidence animals had. What absence of doubt. He imagined hummingbirds etching rhymes into the colours of the sky. It was the first time in many years that he had dreamed when not asleep. He thrived, like a lighter flame, for that little moment. Then he got up and went back to work.

Breaking on purpose

There was a man with dead eyes standing over a sleeping Miguelito. The man's eyes worked. In fact they looked up and down Miguelito's small body sprawled on the mat with cold calculation. But they had lost sparkle and expression a long time ago. Miguelito's green soft drink bottle torch stood by his head and pointed at the stars, saluting its sisters. The man with dead eyes wanted his plastic mattress back. He had been detained for a while, but now he was out and someone was using his mattress. He bent down and tried to push Miguelito off it.

Silently, he nudged again. He shoved three times. But Miguelito didn't wake up and so he didn't budge. Dead eyes pushed one more time. Move, he thought.

Then he picked up a Coca-Cola can lying passively on the footpath and he twisted both of its ends in opposite directions until it ripped in the middle. La Tortuga's coat was open and Miguelito's t-shirt had wiggled up in his sleep so that now his stomach was showing. Dead eyes jabbed the biggest triangle point of the can deep into Miguelito's skin, then dragged it across his stomach in a single, twelve-centimetre gash.

Agony tore Miguelito awake, and he edged and dragged himself away from the man who believed in breaking things breaking people.

The man closed his dead eyes and went to sleep on the mat, and Miguelito saw by the light of his torch that some of his small intestines had spilled out onto the ground. Their dark red colour surprised him. He had thought they would be light pink.

Miguelito didn't know to fix broken skin. He thought the usual tools like glue or nails wouldn't work on something so soft. Also, his intestines were dirty now and he thought he shouldn't just push them back. His blood was leaking all over the red intestines and the ground and his hands, and it would run out eventually. He was spilling everywhere, and he didn't know how to stop it. He had to pick up his intestines from the ground and gravel and dust and take care of them. He did so the way the market workers scooped up lentils and beans. He emptied a plastic bag of his drawings and put his hand in it, then used it like a loose-fitting surgical glove to grab a handful of intestines, then turned the bag inside out around them.

It was 6 a.m. The sun was coming up. This time he was the one breathing like a steam train pulling to a halt. Holding his intestines close to him, he went off to find a body fixer.

The system of monsters: Pain Exploiters

The pain exploiters were perhaps the most ruthless of all in the elite club of beasts and monsters. They were executives for pharma and biotech companies, and for private hospitals and clinics. By charging high fees and payments, they allowed the wealthy to live and forbade good health to others.

In the business of pain, trading in agony, commercialising help, they dressed in black two-button suits over white shirts. There were processor chips embedded in their throats and they spoke predominantly in financial calculations. They sent out hexes and curses in the form of systemic scams, where the poor would pay for some medicine and testing but never be fully able to afford all the care they needed. The pain exploiters always had blood crud in their fingernails as they went around scraping at fresh wounds and spitting in the mouths of semiconscious patients.

Every day, the high costs of health care and lack of access to it saw 16,000 children under the age of five die of pneumonia, malaria, and diarrhoea. The pain exploiters didn't research or produce drugs that people in Sub-Saharan Africa needed because they wouldn't be able to make a large profit there. Instead, they charged fifty times the production cost of medicines and sat back to watch as people with diabetes died because insulin was too expensive, and people with cystic fibrosis lost their homes because Orkambi cost US$23,000 a month.

They spent more on marketing than on research. They tested their medications on tiny samples of people, ignored the side effects, and marketed them as perfect solutions. Then they paid off academics and journals to represent their products as effective. They created distribution monopolies and protected their patents so that no one could access the cheaper generics.

In Mexico, they set up doctors' surgeries next to pharmacies, and the doctors treated people by prescribing long lists of medications that they often didn't need and couldn't afford. Under-resourced and dysfunctional public health services forced people into the private systems, where hospitals charged six months' income for an overnight stay. The pain exploiters emulated borders around those hospitals, by surrounding them with four-metre barbed wire fences and armed private security.

Assumptions

La Tortuga ate her breakfast of toast, milky coffee, and eggs scrambled with onion and tomato sitting in a pool of salsa verde, with quick chews and without noticing the rich sweetness of the coffee. She was already thinking about how they would get by after her two weeks in the hostel were over. Her eyes looked ahead fixedly, but she saw nothing. Then her food was gone. She developed Plan A, then Plan B, and Plan C. With each plan, her worry diminished by one more notch.

She went upstairs and brushed her teeth in the women's bathroom, then went to the dorm and gathered her things together, including the plastic container for Miguelito's breakfast. She tucked her squeaking little alebrije into the secret pocket in her bag, and then held the tiny breathing snail shell for a moment, before putting it next to the alebrije. It was breathing very fast, almost hyperventilating. He must already be awake and running around, she thought.

But when she went downstairs and out to his mat, balancing the plastic container on the palm of one hand as it was hot and steamed up from freshly cooked eggs, she saw a man sleeping there. She didn't know he had dead eyes because his eyes were closed. If that man was there, where had Miguelito slept? He would come to their work stall and tell all. She was not worried yet, just curious. She did see a half Coca-Cola can near some dried blood, but on the black asphalt it looked like dried sticky coke. Or a reenactment of an oil spill.

She put the breakfast down and took out the snail shell again. It quivered in the palm of her hand and its breathing was laboured. What was he up to?

At her work spot, as the morning ripened and shifted from saffron hues to white, she looked around more. She looked out for him as though by constantly straining to see him she would help him to turn up.

She had 1150 pesos in savings.

Where beds went 2

Miguelito was body bound. All he could handle was making his body okay. He couldn't think of, or see anything else. The streets were a cartoon track of sliding scenery barely registered. As he walked, he could feel himself sinking, little by little into the ground where the nobodies and the grey ghosts were. His arm holding his intestines in a bag was already starting to tire. It said, with Morse code throbbing, "stop." And Miguelito said, we can stop when we find a person fixer to mend the big hole. The pain exploiters watched on and shook their heads in contempt. Silly, silly boy. The people fixers are out of your league.

Miguelito tried one of the clinics attached to a pharmacy. He only hoped they could tell him where the nearest hospital was and help with some bandages and painkillers in the meantime. But the doctor shook her head and stared blankly somewhere past him, annoyed and impatient. "A consultation is 50 pesos. No, I don't know where the hospitals are."

And so he walked some more, heading towards the outskirts of the centre where large hospitals were more likely to be. His baby panda alebrije dragged itself behind him, reluctant, and in prolonged shock. Over the past few weeks, its pink barely-born panda skin had sprouted tufts of fur around its body like intermittent stubble. It had black eye patches now, and its swollen stomach full of soot and metal car parts and accumulated abandon had since gone down, and now comfortably contained bamboo leaves and maps. Its paws that had been almost disconnected were now semi-attached. Initially, it was that sureness and new confidence that sustained Miguelito as he searched for help. But after the clinic, the alebrije stuck its pink tongue out, desperate for water. As Miguelito continued to search for a hospital, the alebrije's tiny black round ear dropped off and it left it behind. Nights later, a gang of street dogs would eat it along with leftover red rice and chicken bones they pulled from garbage bags.

From four blocks away, Miguelito saw the brick tower that was the General Hospital Gregorio Salas Flores, and he quickened his pace. But when he got there, the pain exploiters were waiting. The receptionist told him there were no beds available and that the hospital only treated adult emergencies. She recommended he look for a paediatric hospital. She didn't tell him that only the private ones had emergency departments. She looked past him and called, "Next!"

As he walked away, the pain exploiters dug their nails into his stomach hole, scratching at its edges and opening it up further. Miguelito held the bag of intestines harder, trying to stop the blood that was trickling in single-coloured party streamers down his hips down his legs. Drawing along the path behind him, in strewn red markings, the rough amount of time left.

At the Guerrero Medical Hospital, the closest one at twelve blocks away, all treatment was by appointment. Initial tests were affordable, but then the doctors would often try to upsell patients to get more surgery than they needed. There were no signs pointing to an emergency wing. Miguelito again went to the main entrance, but he felt like he couldn't enter the palace-like building without knocking. His hand made no sound on the brick arch that framed the doors. His alebrije went in, impatient and scared, and he saw it for the first time, for just a second. His soul was way ahead of his body, encouraging him to fight for his life. He stepped inside a little way, and a security guard approached him. He said words about no unaccompanied minors and a health insurance card and Miguelito squeaked "Help" and the man said, "Leave." Two pain exploiters gripped a shoulder each and lifted his tiny body into the air and placed him back by the fence gate. Their aluminium border. They stabbed his bag of intestines with hemostatic clamps. They had the tools to fix him but they preferred to use them to break him. They sent him exhaustion and agony and then they shoved him outside the fence.

Miguelito collided with the rough gaze of suspicious passersby. More of his blood pooled on the footpath, its rough red clock gone haywire. His alebrije wanted to curl up and sleep. Its feet slackened then vanished, and as Miguelito forced himself to walk to another hospital, it dragged itself behind him with its arms. The gaping wound on Miguelito's leg that had closed and cleaned was splitting open. His leg muscles dulled. He felt like he was meat.

The Eyes of the Earth

And the adrenaline was wearing off. His stomach screamed at him like a hysterical car alarm. By the time he arrived at the third hospital, also private, his alebrije had lost its front paws as well. It dropped down on the ground half a block from the hospital and it crumpled into itself, eyes closed and packaged away.

Miguelito made it to a door. It was a single door and he didn't know where it went, but he couldn't walk anymore. When a person in a white coat came out, he pointed at his plastic bag. They pulled a face at him, something between concern and disgust and hurried on their way. The pain exploiters surrounded Miguelito and pushed him back and forth between them. You have no ID. You need tests done first. You aren't registered with this health fund. He sat on the ground, and they continued to circle and poke and scratch at him. He felt faint and dizzy. Was it blood loss, or the monsters going around and around and around? His hand holding his intestines released them and they unravelled on the ground. His packaged away alebrije appeared and curled up in his neck. If he slept, maybe the hysterical car alarm from his stomach would quieten. Maybe the monsters would get bored and leave him.

The sky was a cloudless solid blue screen. It was very quiet.

Breaths

La Tortuga realised, reluctantly, that something was wrong. It was almost midday, and the child who had stuck to her side and gripped at her clothing had still not turned up. The snail shell had been breathing heavily all morning, and she could not tell herself he had been running around all that time. Now when she held it, the breathing was very faint.

It was her turn to solve the puzzle. She took stock of the information she had. Someone had been in Miguelito's sleeping spot. His breathing indicated he wasn't okay. Instead of coming to her for help he had gone somewhere else. She asked at the hostel reception for a list of nearby hospitals, then hailed a taxi. She would pay out of her savings.

As they headed to the first hospital, the breathing of the tiny snail shell became slower still, yet clearer and sharper, like a photo in focus. She knew at least she was getting closer to Miguelito. She ran into the hospital while the taxi waited and asked about a half-bald seven-year-old boy. No one knew anything, so it was on to the second hospital on the list. The breathing of the snail shell slowed even more. He wasn't there either.

As they headed to the third hospital, the breathing stopped.

***

La Tortuga found Miguelito lying in a bow shape by a side exit door, his four limbs pulled towards his exposed stomach. His panda alebrije was lying in the curve of his neck. It looked up at La Tortuga and shook its head.

***

She picked up the alebrije and it collapsed down into a story. A story that had stopped in the first few chapters. The harshest of interruptions. But the chapters it did have contained a crude bravery, a yearning to survive, and curiosity. La Tortuga added the story to her own alebrije's shell of learning.

***

Each word weighed a kilo. "Hay un niño muerto," she told some hospital workers, pointing. Her finger twitched with wordweight.

Now they hurried over. Now they were concerned. Because a dead body in front of a hospital didn't look good.

***

La Tortuga went back to the hostel. Walking was heavy also. And sharp rain fell, slicing aggressively at the street plants and people. She passed through a small park where an old giant cactus, worn and yellowing at its edges, had fallen over. Its raw roots fretted about in the air. She passed concrete shops with half-hearted signage and giant garbage bags and tarps tied together to make street stalls and a dead dog rotting in the gutter among fish juice and ice. She felt that she wasn't there. And also that she wanted to collapse like the cactus and moan in desperate agony and she found herself scratching at her wrists and digging her nails into her upper arm to keep the crying in because the rules said you can't cry in the street. And then a bald man with lots of ear piercings and his own sad eyes stopped her and looked right at her and said, "Is everything okay?"

Of course, she just nodded, but it was nice of him to confirm she wasn't a ghost.

***

The rain lasted for four days. In the middle of the dry season. Newborn kittens tumbled in the water that was racing through the streets as though it was going somewhere important. The stations were marked with disordered patterns of muddy shoe prints, the Zócalo was emptied, and cafes packed away their outdoor seating. The sky grumbled but never thundered.

La Tortuga couldn't work and she couldn't sleep. She hadn't wanted to expect the worst. She had wanted to have trust in the child and the day, but she should have known, she thought over and over. Sadness and indigestible regret immobilised her.

***

After the fourth day, the sun came out and the drenched streets glistened with yearning to play with the humans. They seemed rude and insensitive to La Tortuga. But her time in the hostel was also over and she had no choice but to pack up her things, swallow breakfast, and go outside.

The sun warmed her forehead like a motherly hand checking her temperature and reminded her that she was alive while the child was not. That she had first gone into the hostel with a friend and that she was leaving it without one. She squinted and averted her eyes. She had failed to fix the broken boy she had first seen walking so dejectedly through the metro.

She had 950 pesos in savings.

Almost

Harry went to the hostel by the Zócalo to see how La Tortuga was going. But as he arrived, he saw her running out of there and getting into a taxi. He stopped in the middle of the path and a family of five behind him split in half to walk around him. He thought if she could afford a taxi, she must be doing a bit better now, and thanks to him. His guilt headache lifted as a heavy fog might go on home, leaving behind it a lightness of air and vivid colours.

He turned around and headed back down into the Zócalo station, walked down the stairs, scanned his metro pass at the gates, then walked briskly past the glass displays with models of the city centre, past signs, security guards, and other exits, and straight to the Tasqueña platform. As he stepped on to the train, he realised that he had moved through the full process without hesitating or thinking. He was finally getting the hang of this enormous city, walking in it like any other local, rather than as a tourist who had just arrived. And yet one of the things he loved about travel was that nothing was automatic or familiar. Not

The Eyes of the Earth

knowing a place meant a heightened awareness of the idiosyncrasies of its transport; of the sounds as doors shut, the advertising pasted over the tops of windows, the types of people who sat by the aisle and left the window seat empty, and the cheerful good mornings given by each new alighting passenger on combis. He noticed too, the novel details of architecture; all the different doors, their unusual height, their wooden or tiled frames, the six padlocks keeping them closed. He enjoyed the unfamiliarity of menus, and even the chaotic road crossing etiquette.

He had created a routine for himself so that he would meet his goals and try new places each day. But having been in that routine for a while now, he found himself also going through the motions and with that he felt his awareness dulled and even some emptiness. He had been feeling a similar emptiness with his videos. His follower numbers were still steadily increasing, but the satisfaction he felt as he refreshed and checked the latest figure, was shortlasting and languid. It was so dull, blunt, that it was ineffective. A new milestone of followers did bring a special high that lasted seven minutes. Then it too dissipated, and in the flat, blank space of its absence, he was even more aware of the two-dimensional contour of his existence. There was something missing, something important he wasn't comprehending. The holes and perforations in his body yawned and itched. His thoughts, too, often felt porous rather than strong and firelike.

And it was in that moment, squashed and twisted on the train, that he almost understood. He came so close to realising that his loneliness wasn't about a number of followers or a number of friends. That it was a lack of strong connection to people and place. Meaninglessness and loneliness were forged, tinny and dark grey, in the same workshop. The train paused at a station. He turned sideways to let those getting off push and squeeze past him. And as he focused on them, on the man in a rumpled suit who stood on his shoe and on a woman who was applying the last of her eyeliner while she edged forward, the realisation that had been so close to spawning, vanished. Yet the smell and nature of it remained. He understood that he needed to escape the loudness of the city, the blinding clutter of social media and videos, and the monotony of routine, and get some perspective. It was time to gather his hiking gear and head to the mountains for a day.

Fires

La Tortuga's alebrije wrote on the bottom of a lonely wall;
    Almost everyone thinks their pain-agony is unique
    And that therefore no one else could understand it
    So they are alone
    Almost everyone

The Sierra Norte

Harry left at 5 a.m. the next morning. He took a long-distance bus to the Sierra Norte of nearby Puebla state, then a taxi to the Tuliman waterfall hiking trail. He stumbled out of the taxi and into the forest as though he was being awkwardly teleported into another world.

The Sierra Norte was a region of steep mountains, heavy rain, and perennial tropical forest, pines, oaks, and mesophyll forest. Trees stretched all the way up towards the sun and all the way down into the ground. Yearning sustained for decades. Below the surface, their roots wrapped around those of other trees, and they held each other down when the wind blew and when the rain soaked into the forest's deep floor. Viewed from below, the tree crowns were a water painting of leaf strokes upon a gentle blue canvas. With serious postures and a calm firmness, the trees were slow, consistent parties, confettied with fruit, flowers, and leaves of two hundred shades and shapes. Among them, life buzzed. Umber, topaz, and silver lizards appeared and disappeared from hiding spots with super-power levels of gracefulness. Insects morphed into other insects, achieving things that no magician ever could. Mint green moss shimmered and acrobatic birds in multicoloured gowns traversed the labyrinth of branches. Waterfalls demonstrated how to be determined without being destructive. The Sierra was a map of patience. And if La Tortuga had been there, she would have told Harry how a six-gram seed became a two-tonne pine tree. That the seed had wings and flew on the wind to start a life in a new place. She would have told him that real magic was slow. It wasn't a click of the fingers or wave of a wand, but instead it was a process that involved tenacity, clarity of purpose, and a lot of lifeforce.

But Harry was in a rush. Slightly nauseous, he walked hastily along the narrow hiking trail, eager to get to the waterfall before anyone else. His shoes glided him seamlessly over puddles, mud pockets, leafy litter and logs and up steep inclines. They held him firm on narrow rocks and gave him traction.

And when he saw the waterfall, when he finally stopped and sat down, the fluff of life, the clutter, the raging static of unnecessary stuff dropped away, leaving him raw and exposed. Without his videos and tricks, the constant calls from street vendors, the ten signs and adverts per square metre, the senseless online chats, the new clothes and gadgets, all the snacking, the appointments and phone calls and bills, what was left?

At first, his trained sight didn't know how to look at the forest. It got bored quickly. It wandered away, recalled movies and daydreams. But with effort, he brought it back. He had come all this way for perspective. Quietness. The subtle notes of the forest. Sunlight and shadow games among the foliage. And hundreds upon hundreds of colours. Harry pushed away the white lace curtains that always made his sight hazy, and for once, they stayed drawn.

Often, doctors asked patients about their pain on a scale of ten as a way of managing and reducing it, and measuring if they were getting better or worse. Harry wondered if there was such a scale or unit of measurement for how free one felt. He settled on breaths as a unit, because freedom was so similar to being fully alive and when he hadn't felt free, he had felt as though he couldn't breathe. Then he counted. A breath for the lack of judgement there in the forest, and another for being on the verge of seeing clearly. A breath for the ability to take time out. Another because he wasn't worried about the future. A final breath for the guilt that had gone and left him able to accept himself more.

He lay down on a flat rock by the waterfall and dozed. Squawking birds flew over him, disinterested. A giant spider wanted to get past and walked across his stomach without waking him.

Nearby, in a valley to the south and in other parts of the Sierra, hundreds of mines were shredding the mountain range for gold and silver. But despite his momentarily unclogged sight, Harry couldn't see them.

The Canadian company Almaden Minerals planned to extract 130,000 ounces of gold and eight million ounces of silver per year for 14 years from the Ixtaca mine, near Ixtacamaxtitlán. They would be earning US$335 million a year in exchange for blasting up the land to obtain the metals that were the flavourless diet of the elite club of beasts and monsters. The mines used up the water of people who had lived in the area for thousands of years. The cyanide used to break up rocks contaminated and killed their rivers. They had little say in the strange exchanging of planet life for gold. Harry couldn't see these people either. If they had tried to count their freedom, they would have struggled to go beyond one or two breaths.

Some of Harry's extended family worked for mining companies. He didn't know that he had two uncles in Canada who worked for Almaden.

The system of monsters: Land rapists

The land rapists were a legion of legal, large-scale robbers. One of them was the head of Heineken, another the head of Constellation Brands. They produced beer in Mexico right near the US border so that they could use Mexicans' water, pay people US$8 a day, avoid taxes, and sell the beer in the US. A Heineken factory in Chihuahua used the water supply of 200,000 households, so locals had to buy their water from water trucks. Thousands of other corporations did the same, turning Mexico's natural resources into car parts, arms and military tech, clothing, and more

Around rural towns in Mexico, the land rapists performed unmagic. Local companies, transnationals, and organised crime initiated destructive conversions by chopping down sections of forests and selling the wood. Then other companies came in and burnt the area for charcoal. More companies came and took the rocks and other hard materials. And then the flayed land was used as a rubbish dump. Then that was covered up, and the people squashers built housing and shopping developments over it. Local small farmers were left without land for food and income. Industrial agriculture companies went on recruiting drives, promising them 2,500 pesos a week and taking them in trucks to the north, where ten people lived in a room, were in fact paid 1,000 pesos, and got gravely ill from agrochemicals.

In Nigeria, Royal Dutch Shell took 100 million barrels of crude oil each year from Nigerians and kept the billions of dollars of revenue. It left rivers of dead floating fish and farmlands soaked in oil, and the locals drank from the river and farmed that land because they had no alternatives.

In the Democratic Republic of Congo, soldiers stood alert, rifles hanging from their shoulders, as men and women in old rags for shorts, their feet sunk in mud and sludge, hacked at dirt at the bottom of a giant pit. They passed the dirt up to the top of the pit in plastic washing buckets. The cobalt would be used for rechargeable battery electrodes.

The British mining company, Glencore, the Eurasian Natural Resources Corporation, and Canada's Barrick Gold owned many of the mines in the DRC. Though the country exported cobalt, copper, diamonds, gold, oil, tin, tantalum, tungsten and zinc, over seventy percent of its population lived in extreme poverty.

The land rapists had claws for hands, for their indelicate robbery. An excess of smugness oozed from their pores as pungent sweat, and they had two eyes that didn't work, then a third eye on the tip of their tongue that did work, so that they could see what they devoured, but not the people and land around them.

The land rapists held special and secret video calls with the pain exploiters. They met in conference rooms of upscale museums and exchanged tips and ideas over tables with flower centrepieces and ornamental plates of sashimi and miniature tarts. They brainstormed ways to take away people essence and land essence. The land rapists refined ways to level jungles and mountains and leave behind landbones. They eliminated shade and eradicated refuge from the bare burning sun. They let the land sink into fever, nausea, vomiting, and a chronic migraine. The land choked and someone named the degenerative illness 'climate change'.

Deadzones: Location

Harry wanted to know Mexico. In depth and detail, like a trusted friend. But he didn't have plans to visit the poorest areas of the country, or the towns where people siphoned off fuel, or the zones where journalists were murdered and even the roads were suicidal. And he wouldn't visit the deadzones.

The deadzones were the opposite of forests. They were portions of Mexico that were owned and managed by corporations. Also called industrial parks, there were over five hundred in Mexico. Many had been built in Tijuana, Monterrey, Tecate, Mexicali, and Saltillo after trade agreements provided US and Canadian companies with tariff incentives and the advantage of low Mexican wages.

Each deadzone was similar. They had a single entrance road, twenty to fifty giant warehouses or sheds, roads leading to each warehouse, and parking lots. The warehouses were windowless steel structures with grey cladding for walls and roofs. The various

The Eyes of the Earth

companies in each warehouse were supplied with large volumes of water and high-voltage electricity. Private security guards controlled the perimeters and kept everyone but workers and management out. Workers got irritated eyes when they entered the deadzones and their heart beats became confused because there were only grey tones beyond the fences and zero wonderfulness. There was no music, no looping wind, no children, no eagerness, no confused flies. Not even a steaming atole cart stationed by the entrance.

The companies that operated within the deadzones were not accountable to anyone. They paid little or no taxes, and human rights and environmental regulations didn't apply to them or weren't enforced. And so, mysterious and heavy gases drifted from the chimneys, sludge was discharged onto the ground or into rivers from two-metre-wide pipes that exited the deadzones like the darkened back doors of nightclubs. The rivers near deadzones were thick, black incrustations with straw-yellow edges. The wind outside the zones picked up the smell of old eggs and bleach and tangy death and carried it across the land to the residential areas.

There were no tours or souvenirs in the deadzones, nor in the poorest areas of Mexico. Because they weren't places that anyone wanted to visit or remember. There was, though, a single aluminium sign at the entrance to each deadzone, which said, in a white Arial font, 'lowering expenses, no matter what'.

Deadzones: The conversion process

It took La Tortuga half an hour to turn one small piece of rubbish into a parsley plant. It took her two hours to convert waste into two fruit trees. In the deadzones, the land rapists and people squashers took one day to clear nearby land of fifteen hectares of forest. It took them a week to drain a whole lake as though it were a bathtub and send that water to their warehouses. Behind them, an excess of dust lingered thickly where fruit and fish had been. Storms stayed away.

While La Tortuga used massage and tenderness for her conversions, the beasts used workers. They stood Mexicans and migrant workers in grids, fifty centimetres between them. They put electrical tape over their eyes and dog muzzles over their mouths. Plunger-suckers were attached to their heads and to a network of pipes above them. Then, almost silently, the plungers extracted people energy, soft time, human warmth, desire, musical dreams, barely baked love, and bits of brain and blood, and conveyed it all through the pipes to the giant metal vats of hoarded nature and potential.

The transfer of life was efficient. Exhausted workers turned the sides of mountains into lithium batteries for phones and computers that were programmed for obsolescence, designed to be rubbish in a few years. They moulded shredded trees into cardboard packaging for unnecessary products. Container trucks left the deadzones packed with beer, snack foods, cars and car parts, air conditioners, phones, televisions, and semiconductors and headed to the US.

Harry

There she was, so tiny, sat on the low brick fence like a shrub, Harry observed. It was 9 a.m. and the market was ready; stalls set up, vendors waiting patiently, but only a few customers browsed the stalls slowly. It would start to get busy at 10:30 or 11. Harry wondered if La Tortuga would be happy to see him. Frequently, when he sat down next to people he felt like a car that was pulling into a tight spot and people were standing around and judging the manoeuvre.

Because he, on the other hand, was an overly large shrub. He was so big, his knees folded up as he sat beside her, and blocked off half of his face. He wanted to say, "excuse all this," and tuck them away. He asked her how she was, and his Spanish was lumpy, the sounds all wrong. He could hear the stretched vowels and yet he couldn't stop them.

The Eyes of the Earth

"Cómo estuvo el hostel?" He had practised the phrase. But that had built up the nervous anticipation he was feeling even more. Finally, she would smile at him, give him fleeting appreciation. But yet again, her eyes looked past him. He could tell that she didn't want him to read her face or her thoughts.

She said she wasn't so good and that she had lost a friend but didn't even mention the hostel bed. He understood why it wasn't foremost in her mind, but thought it was odd she didn't even say thanks.

He felt warmth and tenderness though on hearing how she really felt. Her face was guarded, or he would have asked her what happened to her friend. A closed-door face. No knocking. But he could still respond in kind and tell her honestly how he was. Quick mentions of loneliness and being lost. Her eyes shifted to empathy; the guardedness softened. The door opened a few centimetres, and a set of young, vulnerable eyes looked out at him. He sensed that it was okay to talk a little more.

And so it was time to ask her. He struggled with the transition, but eventually spelled it out. Did she want to collaborate with his videos? He watched as pigeons scooted about among people's feet. Rat birds, he thought, with no standards. Street creatures adapted to city dust and integrated into the city's grey tones. They kicked rubbish about. Urban foliage.

And Harry explained more. "A lot of people watch my videos, and see a different side to Mexico, a more human side. Once a week, I'd like to do a video with you. I will show you my tricks and you could fix something. I'd get a translator. You could become more well known as a fixer." He saw how she looked at him as though he had suddenly changed the topic to space exploration. She probably didn't own a phone, and viral videos would be removed from her reality. He tagged on to the end of his speech, silently, in his head, all the things he wasn't saying. That most of his viewers were in the US, and not potential clients for her. That it would help his videos to include more close-up reactions from a regular personality like her, and that intimate emotion wasn't just humanising, it increased followers.

Speaking into his phone translator, he continued, "I would share the income from that episode with you. It wouldn't be much, maybe 300 pesos." He felt her face. It's raised eyebrows, sceptical eyes. He was essentially proposing a business deal to her. He should have thought through his pitch better. He would do a trick, and she could see what he meant.

Look, watch, he said in English, gesturing. Three coins in his left hand turned into one when he passed them to his right. "Did you see that?" Come on, give me approval. But her smile was forced. She said nothing.

In the quiet space that followed, he heard peep noises. They had a hollowness compared to the chatter of the forest. As though the city had fewer dimensions. The city's sounds were sharp, dirtied. It's soundtrack was lacking. He had an urge to paint. To add murals to the city's grey, to the columns holding up the highways and to the tarps wrapped partially around the fast-food stalls. A little more life. If he could, he would paint:

- A lone clown in the desert.

- A cloud on a placard stick. Or a sea of small clouds on sticks, being carried, as a statement of desire, by a hoard of pedestrians.

- An unused camera snoring with boredom.

- A clock breathing harshly.

He looked back at her, and she was still there, sitting like a shrub, but watching him. She seemed to know his mind had gone to a strange place. There was a cheeky glint in her glance, until she turned away again. She passed him a cactus. She hadn't had it before, where had it come from? He wasn't sure if it was a gift, and so he didn't know whether to thank her. She spoke into his phone, and it translated, "For the loneliness. It represents resilience. A cactus grows well, even in tough climates."

La Tortuga

La Tortuga was happy to see Harry. Despite everything, a familiar face always warmed the day. But she also felt an intense anger welling up in her gut, preparing to spill out of her as sludge and stupidity and messy crying. She held it down with a hand pressed harshly to her chest. She had to be careful with her words and her face lest they betray such rusty rage.

She believed it wasn't Harry's fault that Miguelito died. She wanted to believe that it was though, because then she would have someone she could hit. A place to lash out at. But she lined up the arguments that it wasn't his fault. She squared the edges of the arguments, made them neat. She had accepted his thoughtless gift. Neither she nor Harry knew that someone would come along in the night and hurt Miguelito. But they both knew that nights were dangerous. Hurting happened more at night time. It eluded the sun spotlight that would show with such clarity its ragged details and ugly edges. Hurting happened more to people without doors to close and lock. She crafted more arguments. More squaring. More tidying up the anger. Untidied anger was undignified. There was no point in hurting Harry back. Instead, her pragmatic self reasoned that it could help to share her grief with him. She hadn't spoken it out loud yet. Control. Her emotions had buttons and she turned down their volume. Quiet, quiet, rational, reasonable. Avoid losing dignity. Because her dignity budget was almost bankrupt. But more, she asserted - standing up in her mind, standing tall - don't hit, don't lash out at the wrong person. She knew Harry wanted thanks, but the best she could do at that moment was not yell at him, not pick up her bag and hit him around the head. Not cry.

The best she could do, right then, was be a little honest with him. "I'm not so good," she told him.

She asked him how he was, genuinely curious to hear the answer. How did Harry man work. Perhaps he could share a piece of his map with her. And she was moved that he was lost and lonely. It was strange that they could share the giant gargoyle of loneliness despite their differences. Still, she didn't think he could understand her genre of loneliness or her pain and her journey. She didn't think he could respect it. Or was that her bitterness speaking? He did seem open to listening, and so many people weren't. But he was too lacking in experience and had fought too little to be able to truly imagine (as empathy and understanding were the ability to imagine) agony, wretchedness, decades of being invisible. He would hear the words, he would try, as he did, but he wouldn't feel the heat and colours of the determination that went into living.

The pigeons were pacing. She observed their serious and sour demeanour. Survival mode did that to you. She would lend them her massaging hands for a moment. They kneaded the rubbish as they walked over it. But their dreams were plain, so they just turned it into patches of grass. Still, she liked those small clumps of weeds and tiny flowers and grass that stuck out of pavement cracks. Undervalued bits of resistance.

Harry was talking about videos. It was hard for her to pay attention because she didn't understand what he wanted, and she had bigger problems on her mind. The little hack saws were cutting at her ankles again and it was excruciating. She needed to find a place to wash that night. She thought, she wished the tortillerías would sell just one peso's worth, because she couldn't eat half a kilo on her own, and they went cold and stiff so quickly. If she had access to a kitchen, she would cut them into triangles and fry them, then top them with green sauce, onion, panela cheese, cream, and avocado. Or she would make flautas and fill them with mashed potato, beans, and cheese.

Harry was talking about sharing the income from the videos, but she didn't know how to be in a video. A regular income of a small amount of pesos once a week sounded good, but she didn't understand where that came from, or how any of it worked.

He did a coin trick, but he seemed to forget that she was a fixer, and that she could see the coin shells nested into one coin. More, she watched his face. How a small amount of arrogance seeped into it as he played with the gimmicked coins. Beliefs that one was superior to others killed off empathy and knowledge, if just for moments. But she wasn't going to spoil his trick.

She missed her little friend, his questions. Her chest was tight. Trying to crumple. But she forced it to breathe. And as the pigeons finished changing the rubbish to grass patches, she tickled the street tiles with her foot. Woke them up. They slept all day, their faces blank. But as she woke them, a single slit appeared on their surface and through it, they watched shoes walk across them, and glanced at the sky. They winked at people walking over their faces, and their winks made a peep noise.

La Tortuga wanted to give Harry something. She turned a rusty nail into a dragonfly that smelt of nutmeg and that flew around adding strange and random thoughts to people's wonderings. The dragonfly poked its tail in Harry's ear, but Harry didn't notice. La Tortuga watched Harry's face again, to see kindness return as it dropped the cockiness and played with strange images. He didn't seem to realise she had given them to him. And she wanted to give him even more. She massaged her tortilla paper into a very tiny cactus. He would learn from it if he was open to doing so. But giving it to him was also her hint that he should leave.

She told him she would think about his proposal, but for now she needed to work.

The top of a sphere

At London Heathrow Airport, outside one of the main entrances to Terminal 2, the Queen's Terminal, there was a bronze statue. It was a globe of the world set upon an elaborate column. On a particularly cloudy and windy day, a playful magpie swooped at the globe. Then she sat on it and wobbled it, and dive bombed it again. Cringing and a little scared, the globe rolled over. Now the US and Europe were at the bottom, and Africa and Latin America on the top. And as though responding to an order, as though falling into line with the map of all maps, things around the world reversed.

People from Andean coffee farms went into the big cities and took photos of the strange ways of being of the locals. They were amused by the colourful costumes, the abject and sad expressions and the skills of road repairers and construction workers. Zimbabweans, Bolivians, Guatemalans, and Haitians went on cruises around the Australian coast and on safaris through the strange landscapes of northern England. Venezuelan, Iranian, and Honduran journalists observed the presidential elections in the US, reported for the global media networks on all the abnormalities and undemocratic elements, and provided the main expert analysis of the situation. A Burkinabé tourist went missing for a day in Toronto and the media was all over it. Senegalese people went to France to teach locals how to repair their roofs and to take photos with little French children.

It took a few days for airport authorities to realise there was something wrong with the globe statue. But when they did they corrected it right away and put the US and Europe back on top.

Accumulation

Each generation had a purpose. The youth had open minds, optimism, and energy. The middle generations had more measured actions and a stronger sense of self and of place within their surroundings.

While in old age, a well-developed compassion coalesced with knowledge and experience to bring wisdom. As wisdom accumulated, a new, extensive profoundness brought peace, and hope.

But, overworked, worried, and sleep deprived, few were able to fully enjoy the benefits of each stage of life. La Tortuga had found for decades that the only sweet joy she could extract from pain moments was her lists of things learned from the experience. So she hoarded learning, as her own internal security.

But a defining attribute of wisdom was that it was something shared. When it stayed within a person, unspoken, it began to lose its strength, fester into doubt, shed its petals and feel bare and burdensome. At seventy-three, La Tortuga was made of compressed colours, of a complex awareness of how to be human. She had mastered the knack of living - meaning she had learned how to handle uncertainty, bad mornings, and the hard waters of friendships with half-drowning and semi-functional people. She could listen deeply and hear the spaces between the words and read the furrows of foreheads and interpret the anxiety behind the joking. She knew how to seek out her own errors and name them. She had slowly mastered the art of transformation; of converting worry into energy, strangers into friends, rubbish into plants. It entailed finding the essence of a thing and being aware of processes and fluidity and the way actions interacted. It was the skill of humility and perspective, and more than anything, of respect.

She had learned to see history and Honduras' political and economic horrors in the same way that she saw broken machines. There were the parts, and the whole, and these two visions allowed for a path forward. And more than anything, she had learned what questions to ask. Where does my water come from? Who made this food? Who decides what information matters? What determines what is useful?

But with Miguelito gone, La Tortuga wasn't sharing her wisdom anymore. The day after she moved back out of the hostel, she had gone to the cheap toys section of the market and bought herself an inflatable panda the size of a balloon. It was easy to carry around during the day, and her night ritual now included blowing up the panda. Resting between the layers of cardboard boxes, she hugged it close to her chest, where Miguelito's death hurt the most. But her unused hugs and kisses still fell to the floor and shrivelled like snails drying into crispy nothingness under the sun. And worse still, was this aching urge to teach that Miguelito had awoken. She carried her learnings around in her shell, and they overflowed, and they weighed her down and the wasted wisdom was gradually rotting in the recesses of her body. She could smell it. Soggy papaya. And so she felt that she had to chat more than usual to her clients. But their faces were curtained, and they were in a hurry and they didn't want to listen. They wanted their broken thing solved so they could move on to the next of the day's many tasks. Her chatting slowed the fixing down. It demanded of them attention and responses, engagement with information that they didn't have time or space for. But to her, this information was important. More than the shopping and cleaning they had planned, more than getting to bed on time. Her insights had to go somewhere. They couldn't just flounder on the floors of her body. Dancers, wanting so desperately to stand up and kick about.

She caught herself though. She saw her clients' generic and impatient replies, their stressed foreheads, and their alebrijes pulling at them, away from her.

So, at the end of her work day, alone among the bed boxes, she summoned her transformation skills. She looked at her shell of learning with Miguelito's dentist's mirror and she drew a mental diagram of the essence of her problem. And she sat up straight when she realised she needed to change the way she was working. Clients in the street wanted quick cheap fixes. Ideally, she would get a regular sales position in a hardware store where there was a need for more advice. But they only ever advertised for under thirty-fives. And the position was still more focused on ringing up totals than on explaining how things worked. But if she could have a stand in a hardware store, unwaged, her service would bring the shop clients, and customers could also stop and ask her how to use tools and which tools to use. It was a long shot. Though she and the shop would both gain from such an arrangement, there was always the issue of not really being seen, of trained sight skipping over her and only ever seeing frailty.

The next day she worked all morning, then after lunch she visited six hardware stores. The day after, she did the same, trying hardware stores that were further and further from her market and sleeping spots.

Each time, she asked for the owner, and when they came out, she recited her pitch. On the third day, the owner came out wearing a greasy apron and a disinterested face. He was disengaged. There, but not there. He had heard her before she spoke. He always said no to people who came in off the street with a speech. His two hands motioned her back out. Swept her, mid-speech, through the door. He shook his head, troubled not by her proposal, but that she'd even ask.

Another owner was quietly writing out a receipt. His letters were sliding clouds. Dented lines rather than words. He looked up at her for one and a half seconds, then looked down again to draw two quick sharp lines, before writing the total. He handed the paper to the customer and was surprised to see her still there, still talking. He didn't know what she'd said, he just shook his head. "Gracias, gracias," he said, good-naturedly, automatically. He felt no hostility towards people who needed things, just regret. He had four children and a strict day that never ever changed, aside from which products were sold. He couldn't help all the people who needed spare change or were selling marzipan from trays or tightly woven wristbands, and so he helped none.

La Tortuga tried an abarrotes store. Shelves all the way to the high ceiling were stacked with goods and marked with prices written in marker on squares of red paper. Canned olives and soy oil, tied at notches to string, hung from the ceiling. The counter was covered in multi-packs of Yakult and stacks of one-kilogram bags of sugar. A plastic bin by the register was filled with yellow chicken stock. A scoop was dug into it, waiting. The owner sat on a stool behind the register all day, barking orders to her young assistants, typing one kilogram of chia, half of cleaned sunflower seeds, quarter of cornflakes, one butter. She was an aproned mountain with creaking dyed hair whose hand reached out to take the change, to deliver a thin ticket and a few coins in return, while her body never moved. When La Tortuga walked in and tried to talk to her, she pointed at one assistant, who asked her what she wanted, and when she didn't list off products, he walked away to help someone else.

Other owners leaned forward and listened to her. More generous with their time and pity, they let her finish her pitch and nodded with concern at the end of each sentence. One, in a bigger store with a turnstile to enter and a separate booth with one-way mirrors for paying, offered her a job bagging. No wages, just the tips. Bagging jobs were often done by elderly people or children. But with a ban on plastic bags and most people preferring to pack their own cloth bags and paying with cards, the day's tips were very low.

The owners that listened frowned sceptically, then relaxed when she finished talking. Their limited eyes stuck stubbornly to her plaits, her brown skin, and aching feet. "No thanks, we don't have the space," they said, softening their rejection with an excuse. They cringed as they watched her step out into the street, worried she could fall.

At the end of the week, La Tortuga stopped trying the hardware stores. She was better off spending the time working and saving. She considered Harry's offer. She didn't like it, but it was income, and it would get her closer to her own bed. Maybe if she was in videos on the Internet, people would take her more seriously. She would think on it that night and tell him the next time she saw him.

She had 1,200 pesos in savings.

How to win

Harry had started his video channel off with one camera, little experience, lots of spare time, confidence, and the automatic respect of the public for a young, middle to upper-class white man from the US.

Then he bought a second camera, a shotgun microphone, and two tripods. He hired an editor who cut out Harry's mistakes and the duller moments and featured individual expressive faces from the audience.

He inserted b-roll of Mexico City, turned up the applause, and added in music, effects, and a title sequence.

The followers followed the followers, and Harry's 10,000 subscribers shot up to 15,000 within a week. The annual International Homemade Video awards were announced days later. Harry's aunt had a friend in the industry, who nominated him. A New York-based company had put together the judging panel of New York-based business people, who in turn chose people and topics they could relate to. Harry won the award for street performance. Most of the other winners in the international competition were also US citizens.

The prize helped Harry get even more followers and more corporate sponsors. A white male celebrity magician was among the followers, and he tweeted about Harry's channel, and that brought even more followers.

Within another week, Harry had 31,000 followers and 72,000 pesos from busking. He was nearing the busking record of 131,000 pesos in six months, but he only had a little over two months left.

Walking with bruises

The fungus parasite Ophiocordyceps unilateralis broke through ants' exoskeletons then spread throughout their bodies. It drained an ant of nutrients and took control of its mind. The ant's muscles spasmed and it walked around in circles until the parasite forced it to climb a plant near its ant town, and to lock its mandibles onto a leaf. Then it sent a stalk through the ant's head, which grew into a capsule full of spores. The spores rained down on to the ants living below and zombied them as well.

The Ophicordyceps beasts were over five hundred years old. They had started as colonial monarchs, viceroys, and officials, then morphed into the heads of state, cabinets, and executives of the US, Canada, Australia, and Europe. They had swollen foreheads, and their philtrum was on the bottom lip instead of the top because their upside-down mouths talked about helping poor countries, while their policies ensured poverty there was maintained so that their companies could benefit from the lower wages. Their ears were fake and had a plastic shine to them, and their faces and the fronts of their suits were tinged light yellow from all the photo ops during bilateral talks.

An Ophicordyceps beast watched Harry and La Tortuga and created impossible distances between them. It made it hard for them to understand each other and distributed undeserved superiority and inferiority among them so that real friendship with respect, care, and reciprocity was unfeasible. Harry felt the beasts' presence but refused to acknowledge it. La Tortuga found herself thinking about Harry and feeling intimidated, but also wanting to impress him.

The Ophicordyceps beasts sent their spores around Latin America. They controlled the region through tactful and guileful manipulation. They hoarded vaccines, then sent just a few to Mexico, and in exchange Mexico's national guard held back caravans of refugees and deported people with humanitarian visas. The beasts scripted inequality into unfair trade agreements and segregated the world into those entitled to live with some dignity and those who were not. They trained the sergeants and corporals of Latin American armies to torture and repress and they orchestrated coups against non-compliant presidents. They put a thick cloak of invisibility over the whole Global South so that only the biggest tragedies there made the news, and at the same time, they induced a trance of entitled sight over their own countries so that people there were unable to value the contributions and insights from other regions.

They created beggar countries and Premium People. It was an abusive relationship. Sometimes the lashings and beatings were disguised, sometimes they were decorated, other times they were direct and open, but justified by the beasts in curt memorandums, as necessary to democracy or freedom.

At the same time, the beasts eliminated self-determination and agency in the Global South. They blanched culture and repackaged it into sellable simplifications, discredited local knowledge, downgraded original languages to informal and unofficial. But with languages went people's thought systems. Their essences.

Social inequalities translated into individual relationships as one person using the other. And so La Tortuga and Harry were finding it hard to imagine ever being equals. And the beast watching La Tortuga nudged her thoughts towards the video offer. She tried hard to find a way to make it work. She devised proposals and strings of words to tell Harry and ensure he could understand what she needed if they were to collaborate. She knew that he didn't have any strings of words because he didn't need to. She went into maybe-list mode; maybe if they had a talk about the content before filming, maybe if he showed her the video after editing.

Mexicans too, assimilated the meaning of inequality. That it was a ranking of life value. That it wasn't just their homes and streets that were worth much less. They were also. They learnt traumatic lessons of unimportance. They absorbed their insignificance into their bones, which became brittle and breakable. And into their dreams, which became limited. Into their relationships, which became routine and artless, sometimes. Feeling undeserving, they put off health check-ups. They forgot the art of standing up for themselves, because their country was not modelling it for them. With centuries of beasts extinguishing the gist of who they were, and with long and low-paid work days taking up most of their lives, they became husks. Husk people in the deadzones, husks picking fruit, making shoes, working in the copper, gold, silver, lead, iron, and lithium mines.

Around Mexico, the trauma accumulated and coarsened into a hardened collective depression. Into a lack of ganas. Into a dog-eat-dog world of captured, undone peoples. Shrunken and slowed-down people in a state of fear, and alert to possible threats and attacks. People got used to tension and always being on guard and forgot about contemplation and creativity and care. On some days, anguish slit their tongues and inhibited them. And they crept about on their own land, trying to live even though their hearts and lungs had been stolen. They learned helplessness far too well. They made do. And that seemed like an okay thing to make, except when it was understood where it came from and that it meant not striving. That it meant taking on more abuse. Complacency thrived among people who were convinced that their actions were less consequential.

Scarlet macaws cried on the floor in the corner of the mall. Children wandered about Walmart with their ribcages stuffed with Coca-Cola and GM corn. A man made entirely of straws crept about Mexico City in a semi-permanent state of wreckage. And the wing pluckers bound people's feet in shoes that were too small and limited where they could go and who they could be.

People became accustomed to a body covered in bruises. But there was no time for hurting. They sewed up scars and wounds hastily with needle and thread, but there was always spillage oozing out. It consisted of unprocessed pain. Unnamed, uncleaned. The story of invaded countries a story of *aguantar*.

Aguantar: To put up with, bear, suppress, hang in there. Tolerate.

Often, people refused to be worthless. There were the twenty Puebla communities that took over a Danone water bottling plant and turned it into a community centre. And the Indigenous communities in Michoacan holding assemblies and resisting the incursion of organised crime into their lands. People in Mexquititlan setting up twenty-four-hour guards to stop companies from stealing their water. There were sparks. Brief flashes of luscious colours. A poetry night, a new and proud banner for all the vegetable growers of Atlixco, a corn fair, an exhibition of women's critical art, a Zoom conference of Indigenous scientists, a blockade of Los Filos gold mine in Guerrero, engravings denouncing the mega-projects hung from thin rope in main squares. Street art as a subtle party. A farmer who observed her oranges daily. She noticed their shyness, the way they stayed small in the drought. A Nahuatl teacher who told his class of adults, with a glint in his eye, "In spring, the sun's ray falls directly to earth, but the wind moves it around, and the shadow of that is the snake" and "spring is when the planet is hot and that pushes the flowers out." And an overworked and drained human rights observer doubted that their doing everything they physically could was enough.

Where hope gathered strength

It started out as an hijuelo; a tiny clone of its mother agave, growing out from her base. It stretched out and dropped down roots. Then it grew on its own, multiplying the fleshy leaves of its rosette and forming a thick stem in the centre. It grew so slowly and so steadily that tortoises sat and watched it, impressed. Sloths, garden snails, and banana slugs curled up near it to relax or sleep. Air all the way from the Andean Mountains, where life's pace was gentle and running was forbidden to all creatures bar the youngest ones, visited the little agave and found new wisdom.

And over the years, the little agave grew and became, eventually, a medium agave that was well-versed in the articulation between appreciation, respect, and patience. Then it learned about the close alignment of patience and strength. And eventually, it understood that the whispered insinuation of strength was persistence.

Drought struck, and each day was harsh because the agave missed the vibrancy of water, but it had stored some and it lived on. It wasn't alone; prickly pears, pineapples, and vanilla orchids also endured the drought. And when another drought came, they knew what to do, and they held out again.

One day, a mountain lion dislodged the agave and rolled it about, and it survived, upside down, until the wind rolled it over and it took root again. Floods came and soaked the agave's roots until they rotted, but it spouted more, and lived on. Smoggy air traumatised it. Careless beings lashed out at it and beat it, leaving deep brown bruises of broken cells on its fibrous leaves. But through years and years of severity, the agave stayed and survived and recovered and thrived.

Eventually, the agave was four metres wide, its earthly star of pointy penca leaves obscuring the short but thick heart stem in its centre. Its unseen sweetness. Mexican farmers often carved out wells in the stems of agaves, then used gourds to scoop out the *aguamiel*, or honeywater. For centuries, the Aztecs and Mayans had used the sap as medicine or allowed it to ferment into a lightly alcoholic pulque. Filtering and heating the sap, Mexicans made agave syrup, and by baking the stem, distilling and ageing it, they produced mezcal and Tequila.

But this agave wasn't farmed. It reached seventy-three years, and the stored sweetness had to come out. It shot up from the stem and in days, grew into a ten-metre-high stalk, craving the sun and warmth, reaching upwards as a gesture of the limitless ways of being. From the stalk came small branches and chartreuse yellow flowers, clumped together like sitting clouds.

That one day, the agave celebrated.

It had managed to convert desert and harshness

Into the briefest of joys

And then, like all monocarpic plants that can only flower once, it died.

Seeds leaped into the wind. Hummingbirds were the funeral celebrants who solemnly removed any remaining seeds and distributed them far away.

Storage

La Tortuga was between customers. Heavy chest. Distracted by worries. Whirlpool thoughts that wouldn't go away. That attracted bitterness. That brought What Ifs, and lined them up all in a row, as a display of all that was hard right now. She tried to count them in order to control them, but only felt more overwhelmed. So then she did the hardest thing and looked right at them. Faced their bared teeth. Asked them questions.

She dug out Miguelito's dentist's mirror from among her tools, to better examine her thoughts. She expected to see turmoil, rawness, weakness. She expected to observe the shrivelled ugliness of a being conquered by worry. Over-digested food and a bleak night. Haunted darkness, fear consuming street spaces. She thought she would see awkwardness and smallness. Hesitancy.

But she did not.

When she pointed the dentist's mirror at her own heart, she saw thick, rich, aguamiel.

What to count

La Tortuga had had a rough night's sleep. Box corners had jabbed her. So she had walked to her work spot near the market with bruised legs. The panda toy she slept with had deflated and she had ended up holding the shrivelled plastic to her, but parts of it had caught at her skin and twisted it, leaving rough red tracks about her chest.

And there was a new thing. A twitch in her thumb. It jerked every few minutes, particularly when she worried. Then, at 4 p.m, lightheadedness struck. It made it hard to think or focus. Cracks spread about her body, preparing it to break. Her shoes though, were quiet. It seemed to be sufficient that her shredded ankles were struggling to heal because of her lack of sleep and would soon be infected.

At lunchtime, Harry met her at her spot and took a bruised Tortuga in a taxi to the *Casa de los Azulejos* - the House of Tiles. Now mainly a restaurant, the baroque palace had been built in 1596, then 150 years later a count had covered the facade in blue and white tiles from Puebla. The repetition of the palm-sized blue tiles created a dazed, dreamy effect about the building. Its turquoise doors and ornate carved stone door frames on the outside along with high ceilings, decorative columns, and a fountain on the inside, combined to give it a calm grandeur. Its courtyard restaurant was part of the Sanborns chain, now owned by billionaire Carlos Slim. There was a mural depicting a golden-orange sky and peacocks and parrots in flight on the walls around the courtyard. Harry and La Tortuga sat near the fountain. La Tortuga's feet didn't reach the floor. Influenced, perhaps, by the happy birds flying about in the painting nearby, or the rhythmical cycling of the water in the fountain, she swung her legs back and forth.

Harry was paying, but La Tortuga flipped through the ten-page menu and felt intimidated. It didn't make sense to spend so much money on food. But she decided to order something that she could never get from a street stall, and with nutrients that she hadn't been getting lately. She asked for breaded fish with Russian salad. A waiter laid a paper placemat in front of her, then arranged her cutlery. La Tortuga didn't know whether it was worse to pretend the waiter wasn't there, or to watch him closely as he worked. She gave him a big smile, thanked him, and felt relieved when he was gone. Then her swinging legs accidentally kicked Harry's shin. He said nothing.

La Tortuga played with her cotton napkin, trying to turn it into a boat, but it wouldn't hold. The food arrived, and she cut up her fish fillet. It was warm and flaky. Her mouth became oily though, and she couldn't bring herself to wipe it on such nice fabric.

It was time to tell Harry what she had decided. She ripped a corner off the paper placemat and used that to wipe her face instead. She looked straight at Harry, and she spoke in Spanish, with his app translating, "I'd like to discuss the content of any videos we make together first. I don't want to be a sidekick or have a background type role in those videos. I want us to both contribute ideas and knowledge, to demonstrate what we do, and bounce off each other. I'd also want some transparency and to see income statements for any videos we do together and split any earnings between us."

Harry was taken aback. Stung. Bothered and rattled. She didn't seem to appreciate that he was giving her an opportunity. "You don't understand. I've built up this channel myself. I've grown the follower base, and I've invested in equipment and an editor."

The Eyes of the Earth

"You have used the money and time that you have, and that most people don't have. Still, I'm impressed at the way you try new things, Harry. You're adventurous and curious and creative. You said you've been working on this project a few months, but I have spent my long life learning how to fix things."

She didn't want to watch his face. She knew her words were fish bones and that his throat was distended, and his eyes were anxiously constricting. As she waited for him to respond, she observed other people instead. The people eating nearby had a different kind of presence. They had confidence, felt deserving. They didn't finish their food. They were taller, and polished. Like well-built, new cars.

Harry shook his head. This was his project. She knew nothing about videos. What made her think she could make decisions about content? And to ask to see his statements? To ask for more money? He didn't have to give her anything. Rattled and stung became irritation. "No, we can't do that. I have the whole image of my channel to consider. But definitely, if the videos with you ended up becoming really popular and making more than I thought, I would consider increasing your share."

La Tortuga's swinging feet became heavier. They seemed to pull downwards and bump against the floor. She imagined the extra income and sleeping in a bed again. Giving it a go to see how it went. Just for two weeks. Like the hostel had been just two weeks.

"Thank you for your offer then, but no," she said.

Harry just nodded and mouth shrugged, but La Tortuga saw his alebrije perched on his shoulder flop its head down against the top of his chest. Its tail too, pointed down, its eyelids half shut. La Tortuga laid her eyes on it gently to say, "I know how you feel, but you'll be okay." Harry looked over his shoulder, sensing she had recognised someone behind him.

Outside the restaurant, they looked at each other, knowing that they would not meet again. Harry's holes and perforations were loud. They itched like scraping gaping yawns. He felt dizzy, like there was little holding his spongy body upright and he could collapse, as a card tower, into his shoes. Then air from all his holes congregated in his digestive system and bloated him. He shifted his bag to his front to try and hide it. He said goodbye, and his voice came out wheezy. All air and no tone. He thought hate because it soothed him. He thought insults and aimed them at La Tortuga with his eyes. Pathetic, naive, useless. Being turned down shifted power dynamics. And he had believed that getting what he wanted was as simple as spending money, so it was a whole worldview that she had undermined by saying "no". He didn't realise that though. He thought he was angry because he had tried to be nice, and she hadn't appreciated it.

Harry now had 33,000 followers, 75,000 pesos from busking, and even more holes and perforations.

La Tortuga would have to make her own way back to her market spot, but she was near the city centre, so she could walk to Pino Suarez, then catch the train. She felt more clear-headed than she had in days, and she walked fast. Her feet hurt, but a little less. After swinging under the chair all that time, they wanted to skip now. A few of her bruises cleared. Like clouds dispersing. Her mind raced, planned, concocted. She smiled at a stranger she passed who had glanced at her curiously. She tried walking with the tallness of the people in the restaurant. She may have lost an opportunity for money, but she had gained a few counts, a few breaths of dignity. And she knew that, like all things, they could be converted. Dignity converted into determination.

How to fix the world

Gentle heat held bodies without burning them. It was a tender and bright afternoon, and for once, most people weren't in a rush. La Tortuga was working but hadn't had a client in a while. Near her, the pavement stopped abruptly and there was dog-sized triangle of unremarkable ground. Hard dirt coated in a layer of grey dust and microplastics, bordered by a curb and the road. It seemed to her like a piece of planet peeking through the concrete floor of the city. She took out Miguelito's dentist's mirror and touched it to the ground. She wanted to see the internal map of the world. To understand how it could be fixed so that things could be okay. People and planet just okay. Nightmare over.

She saw that all the necessary components were there. She saw that there was:

-Enough food. The world's farmers were producing food to feed eleven billion people. But, around forty percent of that was wasted, 821 million people were chronically hungry, and over two billion people couldn't afford a healthy diet that consisted of more than just a starch. Like a river bed without water, they carried a drought in their stomachs.

-Enough space. There were millions of empty homes and there were excessive numbers of shopping centres. But there were homeless people, refugee tent camps, and a lack of hospitals.

-Enough time. Time was the real wealth, and there was enough. There were millions of unemployed and underemployed people. But others were overworked, and of those, many were producing goods that no one needed, or that would be quickly thrown out. A majority of people suffered from time poverty, but the time was there. Like food and space, it just had to be redistributed.

-Capability. People had the organisational skills to get the food, space, and time to where they were needed. They had made postal systems that delivered 87 billion parcels around the world each year. They had built the Shanghai metro system and its 400 stations. They had imagined and perfected airports: symphonies of clockwork-coordinated parts, with planes landing every minute, intricate underground conveyor belt roadways transferring bags to the right plane, and plane fuel checks and cleaning within the hour. People were able to, but they weren't yet coordinating very many large-scale systems of justice, dignity, or care.

-Empathy. So many tender, giant hearts walking carefully among the ruins, trying to help.

-Determination. From athletes to inventors, La Tortuga saw that people were capable of the state that involved trying the almost impossible. They could try over and over, fight, and give everything. It was a Despite state: keep trying despite being out of breath, out of will, out of belief, out of support, out of hope, out of laughs, out of victories.

She also saw that there were blockages:

-Fear. Lots of people were afraid of failure, of uncertainty and losing any frail stability imbued in their vulnerable lives. Or they were afraid of prison, job loss, rejection, and repression. Fear took hold of the brain, stifled innate abilities, inhibited critical thought, action, and movement. It packed people into nervousness, silence writhing in their guts.

-Low levels of political literacy. People who didn't understand how power systems worked were crudely defenceless and easily malleable by lies and manipulation. La Tortuga saw large numbers of people whose eyes were scratched and irritated by sand and blocked by cataracts and glaucomas and macular degeneration and they could barely see economic and social forces, let alone name or analyse them. She saw capable people who had learnt quickly how to do their jobs and raise children or support friends, but who had never had the chance to learn how to make social change happen.

-Something else. There was another component there. It was menacing, it was the biggest obstacle of all. But when La Tortuga looked at it with the dentist's mirror, it fogged up.

The long line of impossible problems

La Tortuga's alebrije got up before she did and climbed into her shoes. It attacked the grates and blades when they were least expecting it. It pounded them until they were bent and blunt.

The tiny colourful alebrije woke La Tortuga and told her to go beyond. It drove its head into her heels and commanded that she walk.

The Eyes of the Earth

The wind came along and pushed La Tortuga forward also. Move. Life nudged and urged her. Fixing physical things had become routine for La Tortuga. The wind said, the news said, the victims of the arms industry said, the cracked mountains said, it was time to take things to the next level.

This time, the magic was happening to La Tortuga. Her experiences of recent events had come together and had combined, like chemicals, to create new possibilities. Refusing Harry's offer was a small act of bravery which had, in turn, activated new boldness in her. Looking inside the world opened up her mind and stirred her to think bigger. And Miguelito's death, apart from awakening her to a need to share her learnings, also insisted to her that life was too important for complacency. The synthesis process of possibilities plus awareness plus bravery was powerful magic, of the kind that formed superheroes. The kind that pushed her, urgently, towards the hardest thing she would ever do.

But for now, she put on her shoes, which were uncomfortable but not painful. It felt amazing. She grinned and clapped her hands. She wanted to start straight away. She made a sign using a small a-frame and yellow and lilac paint. It said; 'Fixer of all things / Free Fridays for what seems impossible.' On Fridays, people could bring her anything from broken contraptions to broken hearts, and she would give advice, with no charge. She hoped this would also get the word out and increase the number of clients she had on the other six days of the week.

She sat on a wooden crate with her sign in the middle of the Zócalo, with a crate placed opposite her. Unfamiliar sights like this provoked both curiosity and distrust. There were so many products and services promoted as life-altering that didn't work. So many false promises and disappointments. But this person was offering free advice, so there was little risk beyond wasted time. And so city beings titled their heads at La Tortuga and her sign, like parrots looking at rainbow balloons floating on past their branch, unsure what to make of them. And many of them were the kinds of people who were comforted by the same six quesadilla fillings available from stalls everywhere, and by the regularity of trains and the security of predictability, and they did not want to try talking to a stranger about the worst things that were happening to them. So after a pause, they shook their heads at boldness and walked on. But one teenager stepped forward and sat down opposite La Tortuga. The curious stayed nearby and watched what happened. After seven minutes, the boy stood up with a thoughtful smile, and walked off. He was okay, nothing had gone wrong. And so one of the watchers thought, why not, and sat down. She gave La Tortuga a personal problem as though it were a challenge or a riddle. A few more people circled past, and they saw that the people who had sat down with La Tortuga got up and left a little lighter. A little straighter in the back. They formed a short queue. And people saw a queue and thought that something worthwhile was available, and they joined it also. It grew longer and longer.

A few people brought broken items that they had given up on but kept around the house just in case. But most people just brought themselves. There was a woman who always felt unworthy because she had grown up with a father who was violent to her mother, and she learnt that women's feelings and needs didn't matter. There was a mechanic who missed his children because he had to migrate to Mexico in order to earn enough to support them, and there was a mother whose son was disappeared ten years ago and she still didn't know where, why, or if he was dead. There was a person with Parkinson's who couldn't work, and therefore couldn't afford the medication they needed, and a trans person who wasn't understood enough and faced constant discrimination and who had just lost their partner to suicide. There was a taxi driver who had been kidnapped and tortured and knew there was no point denouncing it, a middle-aged woman whose hands and back no longer worked properly after twenty years working in a beer factory, a Haitian teenager who lost his siblings, father, and home in an earthquake and was only given three bags of rice by a charity, and a man who was caught using drugs to block his pain and was imprisoned for eighteen years, then wandered the streets when he got out, trying to find ways to earn money that didn't involve selling drugs. By mid-afternoon, the queue was a Zócalo plus three blocks long.

La Tortuga looked out at it and saw the alebrijes accompanying their humans. She saw a queue of damaged and hurting souls. There were alebrijes missing mouths, a brolga that couldn't strut or twirl, an eight-legged turquoise and canary-yellow zebra with a blackhole consuming its heart, a sleuth-eyed frog that couldn't sleep, and a transparent cat carrying boulders. There was a macaw with a cat tail and a rubber beak that couldn't sing properly, a bat-owl missing a backbone, so it couldn't fly, and a manta ray that was spotted with black and brown bruises, like an old banana. A lizard, fearful of the sun, carried an umbrella for shade. A fish-beetle's feet pointed backwards so it couldn't ever walk forwards.

La Tortuga saw how many people hid their wounds and broken bits out of shame. Sorry, they said, for not working smoothly. She told them not to be sorry and asked them to name their wounds. She asked some people to speak those names to three others in the queue, while she asked other people to talk to the wound and to show anger or tenderness towards it. For those who could draw, she asked for a portrait of their problem. Others, she told them to close their eyes and zoom in on their ruptures, to look at the ways they were hiding and running. Either way, she explained to them that the first step to healing or solving any issue was looking right at it. She asked them how they could convert their pain into knowledge and empathy. She helped them distinguish between what parts of their problems were internal and what parts were external. And she gave them question lists. "Write this down, take this with you," she said. The questions were tools for unravelling, uncovering, mapping, and seeing boldly.

And so, each Friday near the market, people queued for questions. During the week, La Tortuga's client numbers increased a little, though not by as much as she had hoped. Perhaps, she thought, there were more broken people than broken things. Still, it was enough for her to save steadily and sleep better. The load of unshared thoughts in her shell was lightened as well, but also not as much as she had assumed. Talking to these people, she was learning even more. She was troubled by how long the queue was. She saw benevolent people trying to get by in a very anti-people world. The life nudging got even stronger. She was not doing the hardest thing, yet.

The harm of silence

There was no one though, for La Tortuga to describe her wounds to. If she stayed too quiet and too angry, she would get a migraine. And that would leave behind little rotting holes in her dreams. Over time, the sores in her dreams would fester, leak, and multiply.

Comfort stories

La Tortuga climbed three flights of bare concrete stairs to apartment 304. Weeds with leaves as big as adult gloves and thick, hairy stalks had claimed the cracks of the stairs, and broken tiles were stacked on the sides. On the first landing, there was a shopping trolley locked with chain and padlock to a rain pipe. The last flight of stairs that led to the roof top were made of metal slats and very steep. La Tortuga had to pull on the hand rail to make up for her lack of lower leg strength. Adjoined to a standalone rooftop apartment was a single room with its own entrance. It may have been a shed or washing room in the past. In the far corner of the room, La Tortuga saw that there was a toilet, a tap coming out of the wall at waist height, and a bucket below it. A plain, white shower curtain with mildew flecks was nailed to the two walls that formed the corner. She presumed there was a drain behind it. There was a wooden stool near the door and an electric outlet, and La Tortuga imagined she could plug in an electric coil hot plate there.

The rest of the room was empty, but there was enough space for a single bed. La Tortuga thought she could use one of the wooden crates found around the market as a side table, and that there was space for a table and chair for eating, preparing food, and reading or writing. The floor was concrete like the stairs, but it had been painted with one layer of waterproof burgundy paint. The roof was a glowing-green corrugated iron.

The space wasn't so different to where La Tortuga lived in Honduras. She knew the roof would heat the room during the day and it would magnify the sound of rain crashing against the metal. There were no windows. But it could be her own space, and it was only 1,500 pesos a month.

La Tortuga had almost 2,000 pesos in savings now. Normally, she would have been charged two months' deposit plus the first month's rent, but she had negotiated a 1,000 peso deposit, arguing there was little she could break or steal or ruin, and offering to fix up the room in exchange. She could install a proper sink, paint the walls, and extend the electricity connection around to the other wall.

She had a week to save up the final 500 pesos. After that she would also need money for a foam mat to start off with, then for a hotplate, paint, and a sink. But once she had moved in she figured that she would be saving more from not paying to use toilets or for lunch tamales.

She could imagine eating rice with tomatoes and onion, warm off the stove. And washing her whole body and being able to dry it before getting dressed again. She tinkered with images of the future. A mind game of hope. She saw her inflatable panda on the table, and she imagined cutting a skylight into the corrugated iron roof so that the place was less dark and she could grow flowers, basil, verdolaga, and grape tomatoes under it. She would get a book of poetry from the second-hand book market by Bellas Artes, and she would read one poem a night. But most of all, she pictured herself being able to close the door behind her and being safe from the world.

Then she packed away her postcards to the future, her soft comfort stories, and left the building. The owner was a regular client, and she would confirm details with her later. As she headed back to the metro, her heart took a break from years of running and panicking and sat down. Her cheeks warmed. Her hands itched to get started already. Her alebrije skipped ahead of her, glowing. At intervals, it touched parts of the street, and they lit up with intense colour. Hope was adding vividness and definition to La Tortuga's sight. She noticed doors and windows painted with the boldest turquoise and purple she had ever seen. The colours vibrated, shuddered, shouted. She resolved to work harder and longer and eat even less, so that she could get that 500 pesos.

But then came the counterdream. Worry was never far away when something was wanted. Experience had taught her that good things usually didn't happen, not to the poor. But also that it was wisest to anticipate any possible obstacles to getting what she wanted and prevent them before they happened. She tried to list all possibilities. The landlady hadn't mentioned identification or a reference. They were both normally required, but she hoped that the poor state of the place would be reason enough for the landlady to overlook them. Also, someone else could rent out the room before her. But that too had a solution; she could find another, eventually. The landlady could change the terms of their agreement last minute. People who owned more houses than they needed tended to be cunning like that, she had noticed. There could be problems with the water connection - she really should have been more thorough and tested it. But even that could be worked out. The worry that then began to weigh on her was the problems she couldn't anticipate. Her bitterness reared its head and told her to expect disappointment. Suddenly, the future postcards seemed to be printed on tissue paper. Held up to strong light, they became transparent. An angry gust of wind, and they were ruined. If only she could get this room, then she would have a place to store worries like this. That's what beds were for. They held the worries at night, pausing them, and making them smaller and more manageable by the next morning.

The last party

Sometime in one possible future, there was no more shade and no more relief, and it reached the point of pointlessness. Dust clouds hung low, patrolling deserted streets. Fried tree limbs were scattered about like expired and flavourless spices over the tissue remnants of towns. Mosquito colonies frothed out of the ceiling holes of museum halls. Vans, belly up and exposed, spun their helpless wheels in hamster shock. Rain rain rain, trash flowed along roads with a new name. Debris. Rubbish rivers wound their way past yellow hair wigs snagged on inoperative light poles, flung there by the last party there would ever be. Now they were the only flowers. Angry hummingbirds catapulted down the shaved mountain sides and no plants broke their fall. Kites dissolved. Along with happiness. No more gentle climate.

A lonely parade of one soggy man marching along an intrepid path of junk.

Not the last party

The time had come for the beasts of the System of Monsters to hold their exclusive meeting. The people squashers, wing pluckers, blood suckers, Ophicordyceps beasts, rubbish ranters, pain exploiters, and land rapists arrived at Davos in private jets. They were joined by the racketeer kings that ran the banks, the soul stealers who trafficked in humans, the producers of efficient death machines who induced wars in order to sell arms, and the slow poisoners who sold junk food and junk drinks. The fossil fuel and oil beasts were the second last ones to arrive. Their tyre bodies slushed about with petroleum, obscuring their suits, and noxious gases billowed from their mouths when they spoke.

The last to arrive were the bed stealers. The other monsters went quiet when they flew in. If they had been wearing hats, they would have taken them off as a salute. The bed stealers were giants dressed in impenetrable suits of armour, holding ceremonial swords. They had a special role within the System of Monsters, and the other beasts depended on them. As they disembarked, they hauled steel suitcases packed with book-length proposals, reports, and studies. When they entered the venue, dark grey clouds followed them like obedient pets.

The resort was a tower fashioned from the human bones of those who had died in the beasts' wars, on their work sites, and in their private prisons. The interlocking bones had been shaved down, so they had a uniform and smooth texture. Spiral stairs linked each floor of the tower, and adorning the walls of the staircases were taxidermy of endangered animals. The top floor had a round stage in its centre, which was draped in rugs by Iranian artists who weren't at the party and never would be. Twenty life-sized Barbie robots danced jerkily on the stage to a golden piano that was suspended with wires above them and played music automatically. In one corner, there was also a decorative fountain, where smart phones playing water ring tones moved along transparent belts and were trolleyed up a funnel, to then fly up and fall down into the depths of phones in the fountain pool. People in waiter uniforms stood, planted around the hall at five metre intervals from each other. The monsters walked about, and now and then took one of the white truffle or oyster canapes from a tray the waiters held, or just ripped off one of their ears and ate those.

Then, the brassy and blaring notes of a trumpet signalled the start of Seriousness. This was two hours of more formal and structured mingling and backroom deals, before the keynote talks and panels that the press were invited to. The kings of nightmares met in small and exclusive rooms and arranged deals and discounts, construction contracts, mergers, plans, and plots. They secured excessive accumulation, prolonged unaccountability, and went about further rigging the world for themselves. These meetings were Opportunities, with a capital O because they didn't see opportunities philosophically, but more as chess moves. Life was a game of who had the most money and power and they each wanted to win. At any cost. At the same time, they shared the same inconveniences: human rights and environmental regulations. In that regard, they formed strategic alliances, concocted joint ventures and fronts for specialised networks. Banker racketeer kings, including the heads of HSBC, worked with the biggest drug cartels to launder money. The beasts paid off their top political puppets to perform the barely believable dance of democracy. They traded in human bodies, human time, and nonrenewable resources. They chose death. They put wreckage and bullets on a pedestal. Bullets, not seeds, they intoned.

Then the panel sessions began. Loyal journalists were allowed into the tower and were provided with cucumber sandwiches and wine. They observed and documented the proceedings with the blank focus of shark's eyes. The beasts gave speeches that were barely careful rehearsals of how to market climate destruction and extreme greed. The elite monsters weren't very creative, and they used the same old slogans again and again. We all have to tighten our belts in these difficult times, they lamented. We provide jobs, drive the economy, innovate. You need us. They called things "green". Green pollution, green coal, green mines, green shopping centre colonies.

Jeff Bezos told them about his new rocket company, which would provide commercial space travel for individuals. He wanted to build streets into the skies, mark pathways up to the moon and scratch out more territory for his empire. His hands and feet were greasy with sweat and fossil fuel particulates. His eyes rolled about, and he adjusted his eyebrows back into place.

That night, the beasts gave each other trophies. They were made of gold because within the System of Monsters, expense designated winners. Gold came at a price of 100,000 litres of water per gram, at a price of mountain levelled into a death home, at a price of mercury and cyanide infecting landveins.

The day ended with perfunctory pats on backs and starchy handshakes. There was a buzz in the air that echoed around the resort. There was buttery excitement over the plan announced by the bed stealers during the formal mingling.

Finding the anti

At the end of the next Friday, after the second queue of things that seemed impossible, La Tortuga felt head heavy. Her alebrije wanted to be carried back to the sleeping spot because its legs ached as though it had walked uphill for days. La Tortuga shivered forcefully. Yet she wasn't cold. Perhaps it was the icy, salty water welling behind her eyes, building up in her shoulders, threatening to flood her lungs.

She was already starting to see patterns in the queue. Problems that were repeated in their essence but varied in their details. She was starting to diagnose more quickly because of that and had her question lists ready before people finished their stories. And she thought that if there were pain patterns, there must be something happening beyond the individuals living those traumas.

She had also noticed patterns in the kinds of people who couldn't join the queue. They didn't have the time. Or they weren't alive now. That's how impossible some problems were. There were the 43 student teachers who had been kidnapped and disappeared one night, likely tortured and murdered, and who now couldn't join the queue. And the seventeen million people in Mexico who were constantly hungry, weren't able to worry about the state of their soul. She had thought, what if a hungry person did join the queue, what questions would she give them. Who's fault is this? Why aren't you more angry? And as she thought that, she was asking the questions of herself. What had happened, that she could only eat once a day, while others filled their homes with items they didn't need? The people who drowned in the Mediterranean, fleeing conflict or drought, couldn't tell their stories to anyone. Nor would the Afghans who had had twenty years of war, ever join a long queue to fix their impossible problems. Most of them probably had more urgent things to attend to than being less broken.

La Tortuga gave herself another question. As she sat down in her sleeping spot
As her alebrije stretched its little turtle legs
and she rubbed her own ankles
as the moon screamed straw-yellow greetings at her
dropping them down from such a distance
that all she felt were rain drops prickling her arms. But there was no water.

The question was, where was the anti? If people were generally empathetic and well-organised and able to learn, as she had seen when she used the dentist's mirror to look at the internal map of the world, what factors were making the world so anti-people?

She needed to know. The shivering urged her. Her alebrije paced in circles and tugged at her pants.

The past week, she had worked four long days and saved 450 pesos. She could save the final 50 pesos on Sunday then pay the deposit that night. She would take tomorrow off, and search for the anti-people.

***

On Saturday, she held the dentist's mirror in her hand like a flag. Or a race baton. On a mission, she walked all about the city, pointing the mirror this way and that, looking beyond the bricks and concrete and tiles and walls. She passed by police stations, the National Palace, the Santa Martha prison, the hospital where Miguelito died, shopping centres, a Walmart, and a McDonald's. She pointed her baton-flag at the BMV building, where debt instruments, bonds, promissory notes, stocks, mutual fund shares, and warrants were traded. She went into jewellery stores, the archaeological museum, the museum of torture, and the museum of history. Through the mirror and plainly with her own eyes, she saw hints of the anti. Big hints, and smaller, subtle ones. She smelt petrol, witnessed insincerity, felt a lingering pain. She saw deliberate cruelty and detected impunity. She found callous indifference and a lack of remorse.

But she didn't find the anti itself.

Tired, and a little defeated, she went back to that piece of unremarkable land by the curb near her workplace - the place where she had seen what was possible. She looked at it again. And because she'd asked the right question, her eyes no longer fogged up. She saw the biggest obstacle. She saw anti-alebrijes. Un-art. Un-beauty. They turned away from the panel they were listening to at some sort of luxurious conference, and they looked directly at her. Concerned, they shot grimy gusts of annoyance towards her and hurled scorching pellets of disdain. They seethed acid, stinging her eyes, causing her to look away.

Two weeds by the unremarkable bit of land dried up, crumpled to the ground, and turned into rubbish. Two used Coca-Cola cans. La Tortuga was unhugged. A violent wind hurled her to the ground. Her tools became soft toys that didn't work. The wind split into mini winds that slashed at things, cutting people. The nearby market chatter and the dim of packing away stalls for the night, went quiet, like a radio battery dying. Clouds blackened into rough orbs of concentrated pollution. Women nearby lost their confidence and threw tins of white house paint over their brown skin. The metro train below the ground screeched to a halt, as though giving up.

Horrified and shocked, La Tortuga threw the dentist's mirror as far away as she could. It landed on the tarmac of the road nearby and a Bimbo bread van ran over it. The wind dropped down, the black clouds disintegrated, and the market noises resumed. She pat herself down. Her body was okay. The underground train restarted. But the two Coca-Cola cans still stood firm where weeds had been.

And now she could name the beasts. She knew that there were people squashers, wing pluckers, blood suckers, land rapists, racketeer kings, and pain exploiters.

She walked away from the unremarkable bit of land, rubbing her throat, holding her hands over her eyes because the sun was overly bright.

"So that was the other obstacle," she said out loud. It was too big, too outrageous, for her to carry on as normal. It was too much.

Last chance

Bolivian Indigenous writer Fausto Reinaga said humans were the earth that thinks. The land fed people, then took them back. So they were the earth's awareness, embodied and walking about.

It made me think of the time myself and another writer-activist were walking through his small town by the base of the La Malinche volcano. Plots of land had been burnt and emptied of all foliage so they could be sold and used for commercial residential complexes. In the surrounding area, where there used to be forest there were now spiky yellow grass clumps and gales of dust. The weeds appeared when that bit of the earth was sick, he said.

We walked about in earthwound, and the dogs ran ahead, managing to frolic among the ruins. Indigenous Nahua land. There used to be forest here, he said, again. It used to be green and lush. The fireflies have gone. And he, bit of the earth speaking out loud, talked about how people too had thrived and were well, and now they too were getting sick.

We crossed a dry river bed and looked at the construction leftovers someone had dumped into it.

We looked everywhere. Anxious, sad, concerned. The eyes of the earth.

La Tortuga came too, in a way. She was there, holding my hand. Picking up bits of rubbish that had stuck to the creases of farmland.

She massaged the plastic scraps and food packaging in her other hand. It was a habit now. She too thought humans were pieces of earth, lifethings trying to survive. And those that were most alive, understood they were caretakers. Felt the earth's grief and celebrations, then gave it voice.

Standard Fruit

When La Tortuga was twenty-five, she worked on a banana plantation run by Standard Fruit, a US company. It was one of a handful of US-owned banana companies in Central America. Earlier, the president of Guatemala had nationalised 80,000 hectares of unused land owned by United Fruit, so the CIA organised a coup against him. Banana companies were able to continue running the region, sending profits and bananas to the US, and leaving Central America with few resources for development.

La Tortuga was assigned to cultivating and washing the bananas. She cleared plant growth around the plants, propped them up, and removed the shoots or pups in order to replant them. Sometimes she harvested the fully grown bananas, but usually such heavy work was left to men. She got fungal infections on her hands because they spent too much time in water and the company didn't give her gloves. At the end of a 12-hour shift, her hands trembled, her shoulders burned, and she had no steps or smiles or thoughts left. The company supervisor looked at his watch, hurried her outside, and shut the gate behind her. The US$14 a day she was paid covered a bed in a dirt-floored home she shared with two others, and food for two meals.

It was after a few months at the plantation that she started making lists in order to cope with things. The lists revealed patterns and codes. She unravelled the patterns and within them, found that the negative or harmful experiences she was undergoing were in fact regular and secret classes in how not to be. The treatment by her bosses showed her how not to love or how not to relate to others.

She made separate header lists of learnings, written with careful handwriting in an olive-green notebook with rose-gold sticker stars on the cover. And she took to practising those lessons with the banana plants and with the other workers. She looked closely at each pup; the details of its leaves, the length of its roots. Despite the supervisors rushing her, she was always gentle with them. She accommodated their roots in their new spaces carefully. Love, she wrote on her list, was a relationship of deep listening and seeing. It was a celebration of the other, support for them, and a cultivation of respect. Employers, governments, or partners that didn't intimately see and respect their people, couldn't care for them well, and so they weren't safe.

La Tortuga was determined to love, despite how much her body hurt. And that's when her magic came, slowly, quietly, unannounced - as real magic and beauty tended to do. When she got so exhausted that her legs wanted to fold in half and lower her to the soft ground, she talked to the banana plants. She showered newly planted pups in water and talked to them gently. "You can grow on your own now," she told them. She checked on them over the following days and stroked their new leaves. "You're doing very well."

She was the same with her co-workers. They got carpel tunnel syndrome in their arms, and their stomachs bled from standing for so long each day. They buried the stress of not being able to send their children to school under jokes. The same jokes. So La Tortuga offered them hand words. Massages for their backs and shoulders and wrists. She told them it was an antidote to sadness because massage was an affectionate coaxing of sensation and of life. She asked them how they felt, and she watched their eyes as they responded. At night she cut out foam inserts for their shoes so their feet would have more support and hurt less, and in the morning before work, she led them in stretches to strengthen their backs and prevent lower back pain.

Her healing hands grew stronger, the tips of her fingers more sensitive and precise. As though they had their own eyes.

She took to massaging even her clothes, to make them softer and more durable, and the paws and ears of the street dog that shot hacking barks at them by the plantation entrance gate. Until one day, tired, absentmindedly, she massaged an empty rice packet. She was distracted, listening to the air. It was preparing for a storm by fretting about. It cooled suddenly, then the heavy grey rain clouds arrived. They dumped hail on the ground then were gone. Left behind them was a languid light, a moaning mist, a planet breathing more intensely from such catharsis.

In the hut, La Tortuga copied the weather, and sighed. She continued to stroke the rice packet like she stroked the pup leaves. And tiny flakes of it shed to the ground. But with the consistency of salt or a mineral, rather than plastic packaging. Months later, sitting on her bed, she stroked a straw, then propped it up on the ground. It became a single tiny plant shoot. Alfalfa. One, tiny, thin alfalfa grew from the dirt floor.

The slaughter behind the suits

Things that were too much couldn't be stored away for another day. Too Much was an emergency, a crisis.

After seeing the beasts and their damage, La Tortuga was overwhelmed by anger and grief. The feeling took the form of a blaring migraine. The worst that she'd ever had. It sucked at her eyes and gripped her neck. It was a piercing siren going off in her brain and in her blood. Too loud to ignore. Too loud to contemplate painting a bedroom or working. It will last for years or decades, her alebrije told her. Unless you do something.

So on Sunday, before paying the deposit, La Tortuga headed back to the stock exchange building; the BMV. She chose it because when she had seen the beasts at the conference, she had recognised a look, a blankness, certain features of face and attitude, that she had seen in some people when she had walked past the stock exchange.

The Eyes of the Earth

She walked there slowly because she was all filled up with fear, and it was making her skin dense and heavy. She didn't want to be hit by violent winds again, to feel her eyes stinging like that. And without her dentist's mirror, she felt unarmed and even more vulnerable. She also didn't enjoy confrontation, didn't trust her mouth to say the right things, and didn't have a plan. And yet she wasn't sure how she could be any more prepared than her whole life lived so far. "You could read," her alebrije nudged her. "You could talk to others, work with others."

"Yes, that is true. I will do that, but first, I will observe them and try to work out how to turn off cruelty," La Tortuga responded.

To visit the Mexican stock exchange, people had to fill out an online form at least a week beforehand, then turn up in formal attire. La Tortuga couldn't do that, so she went in through a back door. She took advantage of being generally overlooked, unseen, and too old to be perceived as any kind of danger. She walked through the back rooms and hallways and corridors, searching for the public area, and no one looked up at her. No one was concerned.

They assumed she was a cleaner or dishwasher.

She found beasts in the restaurant and in the boardroom, but there were a lot more of them on the trading floor. Among them, she saw at least six bed stealers. The most cunning of the beasts, they were huddled in groups and talking fast on their phones. They were starting to implement their plan. Their offensive, their comeback. She saw their armour, engraved with currency symbols, and their steel suitcases where they accumulated money instead of knowledge. She saw the codes and hints in their posture and the words they mouthed, and her spine quivered. Fumes of fever coiled into her limbs, shrinking her. These were the beasts that created and programmed and consolidated poverty and inequality.

They were discussing details, making phone calls, giving orders, sending off missives, adjusting the notches of power, tweaking exploitation levels. In Latin America, movements for all sorts of rights were getting bigger and bolder, profits were down, and weaknesses and cracks in the inequality system were showing, and so the bed stealers were scheming and contriving further privatisation of health, water, and utilities, more deregulation of labour, lower export tariffs, and parliamentary coups.

La Tortuga watched as they continued to organise with other beasts to shorten life and extinguish anticipation by increasing the number of informal workers with no retirement or health care. They spoiled food, stole people's clothes as they slept, then took their bed from under them, abolished any pretense of a weekend, then converted all that extra time into their power, into mansions and rockets.

La Tortuga saw how they smeared people into the pavement like flies, like a pestilence barely deserving of life, let alone moments of joy. There was copious black dust and persistent headaches and diarrhoea. It was a genocide by poverty, at a rate of 9 million deaths from starvation a year.

They encouraged deliberate dehumanisation through the thorough commercialisation of life and the dumbing down of news and entertainment. They simplified people. They hacked the colours and details from alebrijes and left them boring and similar, an army of compliance for their mission of self-enrichment. They cut at the alebrijes, slash slash slash, painted over their eyes, punched and beat them out of shape.

It was a massacre at the speed of years, the length of centuries. The Zócalo of Mexico City was strewn in shredded souls. The clothing shops and department stores stood tall and proud among the wreckage of beings. Dazed humans, hurting inside, lacking something important, wandered about the streets and spent money.

The artificial light of the trading floor quivered a little also. Maybe the sun and all of its light was in shock. The bed stealers filtered information and rigged Internet algorithms, and most of Africa disappeared. The figures and graph lines on the forty screens overlooking the trading floor in a circle around the walls, went up.

Some of the beasts looked up from their computers and nodded, coldly, but with approval. La Tortuga was standing behind one of the outer countertops, pretending to wipe it clean. But filled with horror, she stepped backwards, fell down, and bumped against a glass wall of one of the private rooms in the outer ring of the floor.

Three of the six bed stealers looked right at her. One stood up, and frowning, tried to get a better and closer view of her. "She's the one who interrupted the closed meeting yesterday," he said.

Her bag had fallen on the floor and rolled a metre away from her. He picked it up and felt around for the inside pocket to pull out her alebrije. With a squeak, it withdrew its head into its shell, but that was what the beast was after. La Tortuga's knowledge.

He dropped the alebrije to the floor and went to step on it, but La Tortuga was quicker and grabbed it back. Still on the floor, she curled around it, protecting her essence with her body, and willing to stay like that for the days or years necessary.

So the bed stealer beast issued a sanction. If she refused to give up her alebrije, she would go without food and medicine. They would tell the world that she was to blame for all the things that went wrong. And elsewhere, in other moments, a land rapist paid sicarios US$150 to drive by on motorbikes and shoot environmental and social activists and journalists such as Berta Caceres, Dumar Mestizo, Ronald Aceituno Romero, Samir Flores, Sonia Rosero, Abhimanyu Panda, Jeudy Charlot, and thousands more. In Brazil, people came out of the favelas to protest poverty and corruption. The police, behind their fence of shields, shot them down. In Oaxaca, activist leaders lasted an average of 10 years before they were murdered, often in car crashes so no one could be blamed.

"Banana plants," she said to the beasts. It seemed random. They didn't understand. But what she meant was, "You aren't letting us grow. You're cutting off our water, blocking out our sun, poisoning our soil. You hate us but expect our adoration."

And then out loud she said, "But we don't need the System of Monsters at all. We don't need you, you're just an obstacle."

The bed stealer put his hand over her mouth and nose. "Quiet," he said.

Her shoes cut cleanly through her ankles and removed her feet.

La Tortuga struggled. She couldn't breathe and she couldn't run away.

I can't fight him, he's too strong. I can't go on, she thought.

Repair

La Tortuga stopped breathing.

Somewhere, another snail shell stopped breathing.

From the alebrije's turtle shell held to her chest, she heard Miguelito's story that was stored there. She remembered his yearning to survive.

"What does his internal map look like?" Miguelito asked her.

She couldn't ply the beast's hands off her mouth. But she could still see.

She looked inside the bed stealer and saw his internal mechanisms. She no longer needed the dentist's mirror. She inspected the conduit wiring. Followed the different lines of his face to his neck. She observed copper and gold string ligaments but weakness at the joints and a risk of overload. To disassemble, she had to start at his neck. She sunk her thumbnail into the base of his neck, where a throat would normally be and using her nail as a screwdriver, undid the tiny screws holding the beast's mask-face down. With effort, and feeling dizzy because she still wasn't breathing, she pushed her thumb in further, until she could disengage, and the beast's face came off like a lid finally popping free of a jar. Then, to completely disable him, she inserted her thumbnail behind the tongue, and twisted it to off.

The beast lay in the middle of the trading floor. His underface was exposed and drying up. His suit though, was not dishevelled. His shoes were extra shiny, and his hair was also extra shiny and extra sleek and barely ruffled. But a yellow cream was trickling out both his ears and forming two slowly expanding pools.

A barely seen La Tortuga moved backwards into the crowd of people gathering around the fallen bed stealer. An invisible sulphur smell wafted up from the floor. People peered at the beast with hands over their noses, and La Tortuga hobbled quietly on her ankle stumps towards the back corridors. By the beast, her two shoes had retracted their blades and were trotting around the body, cleaning up the yellow cream, rearranging his legs and arms into a more dignified stance.

Away from everyone, La Tortuga had a feeling of finally. It was a satisfying feeling, but always ephemeral. Simultaneously, she had the persistent blue-grey feeling of not enough. She had briefly massaged the beasts' neck in an effort to transform and convert. But she'd only had a few seconds.

Still, that was enough that over the next few days, there was a short disruption in the bed stealer's business empire, glitches in his estate before handovers were made, drops in share prices. A few smaller companies failed. Policies he had been implementing through the IMF were paused and lost inches of legitimacy and believability. A few more people could see that the fund didn't ever rescue countries, that it was dedicated to debt production and privatisation. An oil field disappeared in the same strange way that hostel dormitories had disappeared as La Tortuga approached them. Where the oil field had been, there were now apple farms and a lake filled with trout and flamingos. A coal power station turned into a solar farm.

The people who had worked for the bed stealer's companies saw boldness in the way someone had resisted their boss' attacks. And that boldness disseminated on the winds of Mexico City and about the continent. The bold breezes brought news of possibilities. They sketched ways out, roads to something different. In a town with three giant shopping centres and no parks or cultural spaces, people took over one of the shopping centres and turned it into a community space.

They used sledgehammers to pound holes into the walls and make windows so the sunlight and more bold breezes could get in. And just one landfill mountain turned into a real mountain, with agave plants growing and ocelots crawling about.

For just one day, people marched to different points of the southern US border and let the fleeing and wrecked people from the other side in, welcomed them with lemonade and hot chocolate, band aids, new shoes, and a room for the night. That day, the land breathed a sigh of relief. Like removing an overly tight belt. Or a noose.

But within a few days, the System of Monsters declared a peril. They were concerned that more borders could be opened, and shopping centres occupied, and that people could imagine more things differently. They watched the stock exchange security footage, then circulated a photo of a barely visible person in the media. The rubbish ranters generated stories about a violent, illegal migrant being a danger. A reward was offered for her capture.

Breaking

Harry was wearing a navy suit and an earpiece and standing outside the BMV. He held the CNN microphone fifteen centimetres from his mouth and tested the volume, then he went over his key points. He looked directly at the camera and prepared to record the live broadcast.

The story about the dead business mogul and IMF executive had blown up, and after watching his videos, the station had approached him to be a temporary correspondent and commentator from Mexico City. The Washington Post had also contacted him for an interview as an expert on Mexico, asking him why he thought the country was so unsafe. "Why are people there so violent?" They asked. So far, Harry had done a few feeds for CNN, but this was his first live. He had told them he had a scoop, and they wanted to break it before other media outlets.

"And we're crossing over live to Mexico City, go ahead Harry Devin," said a voice in his ear.

"Well, you will hear it first with CNN," Harry said. He cleared his throat. He replayed the conversation he had had with the hostel about the bed he had paid for. He scratched his nose and the top of his head because his punctures and perforations were creaking suddenly, in a way that they hadn't in a while.

"The name of the person who allegedly killed the IMF executive is Clementina Cardoza Olmedo."

Alive 2

La Tortuga was 17 when she died for the first time. The death lasted twenty-two minutes, and then for a while longer after as well.

The tool shop man, hands greasy from spanners and coins, thinning hair greasy from gel, had taken her into the storage room behind his shop and locked her in there with him. He hung the keys on a hook out of her reach and La Tortuga was made passive.

Used

Like a template body without stories

Tool shop man took her name and extracted her alebrije as he rolled her over and discarded them in a paint can used as a rubbish bin.

Her decisions were

Overruled

He wouldn't hear her and so she became mute

Her eyes went blank, and her thoughts went blank and her colour trickled out of her and formed rainbow puddles huddled by the door.

A twenty-two-minute death gave her a working definition of what being alive wasn't, and therefore what being alive really was as well. She engraved a word on to the handle of her favourite screwdriver. Agency.

La Tortuga was much older when she considered that Honduras wasn't very alive.

Still, she saw how life fought. How hairy yellow flowers found footing in the cracks of concrete. How people in situations of war, drought, and great loss insisted on staying alive. Then, she hadn't expected to be one of the refugees that walked for months from one country to another in order to have a restful bed to sleep in and a day without death threats to wake up to.

Life was persistent. It shirked apathy and passiveness. Alebrijes misplaced their colours, but found them again, and glowing, they marched proudly through Mexico City. Life was a resilient swelling of being, an overproduction of dreams, the edges of things lit by trims of fire, radiant in clarity, a warm journey of layers.

Sunlight

La Tortuga got into her bed.

She lay straight on her back and pulled the stiff white sheet and the grey blanket all the way up to her ears. Her pillow was thin, so she folded it in half and inserted it under her head. The flatness and firmness of the mattress were comforting. Like a giant hand, holding and supporting her as she rested. She had tucked the sheet and blanket in tightly, so they pulled down against her. Secure. She could not drift up and away into the night. It was so silent here, by herself. She closed her eyes and rested them. She relaxed and rested her legs.

She rested her fixing brain, but didn't sleep just yet.

The walls of her cell were concrete, as were the floors, the bed base, the cylindrical stool, and the desk-shelf in front of it. The room was as long as her bed plus the desk, and as wide as the bed head and a toilet. The toilet tank was also a sink. The door was steel, with a flap for her food, and there was a security camera above her bed. Once a day she was taken down the corridor to a high-walled area so she could pace under the sun. The area was only a bit bigger than her room though, and she didn't know it yet, but come rainy season, these trips would cease.

Solitary was full of absence. Not just the absence of people, but of worldlife, of books, mosaic skies, sunbathing crickets, dawn shadows, hot bread and spices and millions of colours. An absence of places to be. Earlier that day, La Tortuga had swept up dust with her hands into a small pile, and she made herself one, tiny agave. The patient plant that held out through tough times. How would it cope with years of little sunlight though? Would it adapt, endure, or slowly wither? She couldn't know, yet.

There was a tiny window; six centimetres wide, twenty centimetres tall. Because the concrete was so thick, direct sun couldn't get in, but she could send her alebrije out with hints of hope, whispers and nudges, poems, fire sparks, breaths, and seeds. It brushed against people, and they caught fireheart. They looked around but saw nothing. Yet for a moment, they understood a new world was there, felt it as a warmth. The halo of unstated dreams.

Tamara Pearson is an Australian-Mexican journalist, world news editor, activist, and literary fiction author. Living in Puebla, Mexico, she campaigns for refugee rights and the environment. Her feature and investigative journalism focuses on global inequality and the Global South, the climate, and human rights.